erased faces

erased faces

A Novel

By

Graciela Limón

Arte Público Press
Houston, Texas

This volume is made possible through grants from the City of Houston through The Cultural Arts Council of Houston, Harris County.

Recovering the past, creating the future

University of Houston
Arte Público Press
452 Cullen Performance Hall
Houston, Texas 77204-2004

Cover design by James Brisson
Photo courtesy of Eduardo Vera, "Mayor insurgente Maribel, EZLN, October 1994"
http://evera.home.ige.org

Limón, Graciela.
    Erased Faces / by Graciela Limón.
        p.   cm.
    ISBN-10: 1-55885-342-1 (trade pbk. : alk. paper)
    ISBN-13: 978-1-55885-342-3
    1. Women photographers—Fiction.   2. Women revolutionaries—Fiction.   3. Americans—Mexico—Fiction.
    4. Indian women—Fiction.   5. Mexico—Fiction.   I. Title.
PS3562.I464 E7 2001
813'.54—dc21   2001035543
                                                                          CIP

♾ The paper used in this publication meets the requirements of the American National Standard for Information Sciences—Permanence of Paper for Printed Library Materials, ANSI Z39.48-1984.

6 7 8 9 0 1 2 3 4 5   10 9 8 7 6 5 4 3 2

In memory of those who perished in the
massacre of Acteal, Chiapas
22 December 1997

Although set against a background of conflict in Chiapas, this work is a novel. Places and people portrayed have been fictionalized.

G. L.

She meets with her face erased, and her name hidden. With her come thousands of women. More and more arrive. Dozens, hundreds, thousands, millions of women who remember all over the world that there is much to be done and remember that there is still much to fight for.

EZLN communiqué:
Twelve Women in the Twelfth Year
Subcomandante Insurgente Marcos
1996

Acknowledgments

I'm sincerely grateful to Letitia Soto, my dearest cousin, as well as to Andy Soto, who accompanied me to Chiapas during the month of June, 1999. Circumstances were intimidating to travelers at the time, especially since we had to travel through the mountains between Palenque and San Cristóbal de las Casas, a region filled with armed military check points. I know that I would not have had the courage to do it on my own. Letitia's and Andy's company, their courage, their *chistes* and *cariño* of what we saw and experienced, made that journey unforgettable and rich in information. Roberto Flores, valued colleague, shared remarkable photographs and documentation on the Zapatista War, and for that I'm indebted to him. I thank him most especially. I'm very grateful to Mary Wilbur, one of the first readers of *Erased Faces*. Her input, suggestions and research enhanced the work beyond my initial concept of it. Also, much gratitude to Toni Zepeda for her numerous readings of the manuscript and for her helpful input. Finally, but not least of all, is *Acción Zapatista* which has been so helpful to me in gathering information.

G. L.

Chapter 1

She didn't look like me.

The Lacandona Jungle, Chiapas, Mexico, 1993.

Her ankle-length dress caught in the thick undergrowth. Her legs and bare feet were bleeding from cuts inflicted by roots and branches matting the muddy ground. She ran, plunging headlong into a snare of decaying plants, oblivious to the pain that shot up her ankles, through the calves of her legs, lodging deep in her thighs. She ran because she knew the dogs were gaining on her; she could hear their baying, and in seconds she began to sense their clumsy paws pounding the darkened jungle floor. Terrified, she ran, lunging forward, panting, her body covered with sweat and her face smeared with tears of dread.

She could not be sure, but she thought that there were others running alongside her. In the thick gloom of the forest, she caught sight of women running, desperately clinging to babies, tugging at children trying not to lose their way in the darkness. Long cotton dresses pulled at them as they plunged through the growth; straight, tangled hair stuck to their shoulders. She saw that those women were also afraid that the snarling dogs would catch them and tear them to pieces. Men were running, and they, too, were terrified—their brown, sinewy bodies pressed through the dense foliage, their loincloths snagged and ripped by gigantic ferns that reached out with deadly tentacles.

The Lacandón women and men ran because they understood that soon they would be overcome and devoured by the ravenous pursuers. She ran with them, but suddenly she stopped; her feet dug deep into the jungle slime as she halted abruptly. She began to turn in circles, arms rigidly outstretched, but she could see nothing; she was blinded by fear, and she darted in different directions. She had lost something, but she could not remember what it was that had slipped through her fingers. She dropped to her knees, groveling in the mud, digging, trying to find what it was that she had lost. Her fingers began to bleed when her nails ripped from her flesh, and her desperation grew, looming larger than even her pain, greater even than the terror of being overcome by the dogs.

She was on her knees when she felt her long straight hair wrap itself around her neck. It got tighter and tighter. It began to strangle her. Frantically, her fingers dug into the taut coils that were cutting off her breath. Nearly drained of air, she felt that her lungs were about to collapse. With each second, the hungry dogs got closer, but she was paralyzed because the pain of having lost something that was precious to her nailed itself into her heart.

∽ ∽ ∽

Adriana Mora awoke startled, panting and covered with perspiration. She sat up choking, out of breath and in the grip of an asthma attack. In the darkness she fumbled, trying to reach the inhaler that she had placed on the rickety crate next to her cot, but her groping hand got tangled in the mosquito net. She struggled with the mesh, knocking her dark glasses to the ground, almost spilling a cup half-filled with water. When she finally reached the device, she pressed it into her mouth and plunged once, twice, relieved to feel air clearing her throat and reaching her lungs.

When Adriana's heart returned to its normal rhythm and her lungs readjusted, she sat with her back to the wall, still shaken and breathing heavily. Making out the palm ceiling as well as the earthen floor, she looked around the tiny hut, a *palapa*. Through the ridges between the cane stilts, moonlight seeped casting elongated shadows on the dirt. Trying to gain a hold on herself, she stared at the small table where she had propped her equipment: cameras, tripod, note pad, canvas jacket with its pockets stuffed with lenses she used to capture the faces and bodies of Lacandón women.

Adriana drew her legs up until her knees pressed against her breasts. Wrapping her arms around the calves of her legs, she leaned her head against her knees; she stayed that way, thinking of the nightmare from which she had awakened. She was listening to the jungle sounds that filled the night: the jumble of insect chirping that scraped against the heavy breathing of iguanas and other reptiles. Howling monkeys barked, chattering angrily as they swung from branch to branch. Screeching parrots complained because of the hooting of owls and other nocturnal birds. Adriana tried to decipher each sound. She wanted to identify what animal, which insect had made what noise, but it was impossible because it all melted into an indistinguishable cacophony of murmur, hissing, and howling. The night vibrations of the jungle fused with the sad groaning of the muddy waters of the river that coiled around the tiny village of Pichucalco.

She thought of the dream, trying to discern its meaning. She had experienced it before, but never had it been as vivid, as terrifying. The other times, the woman had been remote, someone else. This time, however, she had no doubt: It had been she who was being hunted, she who was running in the forest along with other natives. It had been she who had lost something precious, something loved and so riveted onto her heart that reliving the dream made her feel pain beneath the nipple of her left breast. With outstretched fingers, she rubbed the palm of her hand over her chest; she was thinking, concentrating, trying to recognize what she had lost. But it was useless, because she could not remember anything that had ever meant so much to her, not even the distant memory of her mother and father.

Unable to find the answer, Adriana straightened her head and cocked it to one side, this time listening to her dream. She stayed that way for a while until she realized that she heard only the sound of menacing dogs. Her searching mind then focused on the woman in the dream.

"She didn't look like me!"

Mumbling out loud, Adriana flung aside the net and slid off the cot. She went to the stand where she kept a basin and water jug that she used to wash her face and hands; above it, she had nailed a small mirror. She unhooked it and made her way past the gunny sack that covered the entrance of the *palapa*. Once outside, Adriana found herself in moonlight that was bright enough to see her reflection.

"It couldn't have been me."

She studied her face: brown angular features, high cheekbones. Adriana concentrated, turning her gaze on her mouth and head: thick lips; short, curled hair. Then she went back into the hut, stretched out on the cot and stared at the palm-frond ceiling. She reflected on her nightmare, the baying of dogs still echoed in her memory as did the sensation of pain. She brought her hands close to her eyes, turning them palms up, then down. There were no cuts, no bruises.

She touched her forearms, searching, but her fingertips found only the scar tissue inflicted on her left forearm by scalding water when she was a child; she had been seven years when that happened. Adriana's mind halted for a few seconds, remembering that day. Then she returned her attention to the dream, to any traces it might have left on her. She went on feeling her body, pausing, searching for signs of pain, or even a slight indication of having been hurt, but she discovered nothing.

A nagging sense of loss forced Adriana to shut her eyes because she felt the sting of tears burning behind her eyeballs. She flung her arm across her face and remembered her life, how ever since she could remember, she had felt lost, separated, alone, always filled with fear. She was twenty-four years old, but sometimes she still felt as she had when she was a child; nothing in her life seemed to change—not inside of her. She was now a woman, on her own, making a living as a photographer. Wanting to be accomplished in her profession, to publish her work, she had chosen to come to the jungle to create a photo history of the women of the Lacandona.

Adriana stared at the thatched ceiling, her eyes wide open and vacant. She was remembering that when she had finished college in Los Angeles, she had drifted to New Mexico, where she stayed a short while. After that she decided to go south to Chiapas, so she made her way to the border, and from that point down to Mexico City, and from there she traveled to Mérida, Yucatán, where she stayed only a few days. Then she pushed on to Palenque, attracted by the prospect of capturing on film what was left of Mayan civilization, but once there, she realized that it was for living faces that she searched. So she put her things on a dilapidated bus that had *Pueblos Indígenas* painted in large letters on its windshield. When she got off the vehicle, she was in Pichucalco, on the edge of the Lacandona Jungle.

Her thoughts drifted back to her childhood, probing incidents in her life, trying to explain why she had always felt such deep isolation. Then she relaxed her body, allowing her memory to return to the past.

Chapter 2

Adriana decided never to speak again.

Adriana was barely four years old the night she was awakened by loud voices. She sat up, hugging her raggedy stuffed rabbit, listening, turning her head toward the door, trying to make out who was screaming. Her eyes were beginning to adjust to the darkness of the room when a blast silenced the voices. The girl was struggling to make out the noise, when a second detonation shook the walls. Time passed but nothing happened. Then a smoky stench seeped into her room from beneath the closed door. There was no more yelling, no more explosions, so she slipped back onto her pillow.

Everything was quiet again; she could not hear or see anything, not even when she peeked out from under the covers. The girl listened for her mother's voice, or the sound of her father's heavy footsteps, but all she heard were cars driving by their apartment. She wanted her mother to come and wrap her arms around her, but there was only silence. Adriana drifted back to sleep.

She opened her eyes again, but this time it was the sun that had awakened her. With the frayed rabbit still in her arms and her legs cramped from being rolled in against her body, she stretched and looked around the room. In one corner were her toys and on the other side was the small closet. She could see her dresses hanging neatly, one next to the other.

"Mamá?"

Adriana called her mother just as she did every morning. She waited, hugging her toy to her chest, but nothing happened. Her mother did not open the door and peek around it to smile at her. Trying to see the sky, she looked out the window. There was nothing there except the bare branches of a tree.

"Mamá?"

This time Adriana's voice was edged with tears because she was remembering the noises she had heard the night before. She began to shiver, thinking that her mother and father had gone away, leaving her alone. She had never before heard the house that quiet. She decided to go out to the kitchen to find them.

Adriana, with her rabbit dangling from one hand, shuffled down the hallway to the bathroom, where she struggled onto the toilet. After that she went to the kitchen. When she walked in, she felt happy all of a sudden because she saw her father taking a nap at the table. She looked carefully, taking in how he was sitting in his favorite chair, leaning his head in his cradled arms. She was relieved to see him, although she had never seen him sleep that way.

She tiptoed across the kitchen to the stove, where she expected to find her breakfast. At that moment, she wondered why her mother was not there. She looked first in the service porch, thinking her mother might be putting laundry into the washer. When she did not find her there, Adriana searched the small front room, where she found the television set turned on. That was all. From there she made her way to her parent's bedroom.

"Mamá? Mamá?"

She found her mother lying on the bed; she was taking a nap, too. Adriana decided not to go near her; she might awaken her. Still clinging to the dingy stuffed rabbit, Adriana returned to the kitchen because she was hungry. Trying not to make noise, she opened the cupboard and looked for her favorite cookies, but when she saw that the package was on a shelf too high for her to reach, she put down the toy and struggled to edge a chair into position. She was able to do this quietly up until the last pull, when one of the legs stuck in a crack in the linoleum. She yanked, then flinched at the loud, grinding noise that filled the kitchen. She shut her eyes and hunched her shoulders, expecting her father to wake up and scold her, but nothing happened. When she opened her eyes to look at him, she saw that he was still asleep. Relieved, she climbed up and lowered the box. Then she went to the refrigerator, where she found a small carton of milk. Again she could not reach a glass, so she took the cookies and the container to the front room, where she munched as she watched cartoons until late into the afternoon.

When she needed to go to the bathroom again, she decided to awaken her mother. As she neared the bed, Adriana saw that the sheets and bedspread were stained red, and that her mother held her father's gun in one hand. She saw also that there was a big bump on one side of her mother's forehead, and that, too, was dripping with a red mess.

Adriana was so frightened that she felt pee dripping between her legs; she could not help it, and she did not know what to do. She reached out and grabbed one of her mother's shoulders and shook her, trying to awaken her, but she felt that her mother was stiff and cold. Crying, she ran to where her father was still sleeping, and she tugged at his shirt, hoping that he would wake up to help with her mother. Instead, her pulling pried loose one of his arms; it fell inertly and dangled from his shoulder.

She understood that something awful had happened to her mother and father. She ran to the front door. Doña Elvira would know what to do; she always did. When Adriana tried to open the door, however, she realized that the dead bolt was engaged and that it was too high up for her to reach, even if she stood on a chair. She screamed and pounded on the door, but no one heard her cries for help; no one heard her frail fists beating on the door.

Night was falling, and the gloom inside the apartment terrified Adriana so much that she ran to her room, where she hid under the bed, clutching her stuffed rabbit. She came out only to nibble on crackers or to drink water that was in a container by the sink. She banged on the front door several times during the days that followed, but gave up when no one heard her. Each time, she returned to the hideaway under her bed; its narrowness gave her comfort and lessened her fear. But the tiny space began to lose its protection for Adriana; its confines seemed to close in on her, taking away her breath, making her heart race and pound until she lost consciousness. She did not know how many times this happened to her.

Finally, it was the stench, not Adriana's weak pounding, that alerted Doña Elvira Luna. When that happened, the elderly neighbor stood outside the Mora apartment wearing an apron and still clutching a wooden cooking spoon in her hand. She twitched her nose, sniffing around the edges and hinges of the locked door, then banging on it as she stuck her nose up into the air, wiggling her nostrils and upper lip, her wide open mouth gasping because of the foulness that was polluting the air. When she realized what it was that she was smelling, she ran down to the manager's office.

"Don Luis, come with me! Now! Something is terribly wrong in the Mora apartment."

"What do you mean?"

"Don't talk! Come!"

The man and woman ran up the stairs and when they turned the corner going in the direction of Adriana's apartment, Don Luis came to a sudden halt. He, too, smelled the vile stench.

"¡Santo Dios!"

His hands were shaking so much that he could not insert the master key into its slot, so Doña Elvira snatched the ring, slid the key into place, disengaged the latch and opened the door. The manager flung himself backward as if he had been struck with a blunt weapon; he gagged and reached into his back pocket for a handkerchief, which he nearly stuffed into his mouth.

Doña Elvira was just as shaken, but she regained her balance after a few seconds. Taking off her apron, she tied it around her nostrils and mouth, and entered the gloomy pestilent place, going first to the kitchen. When she saw Mario Mora slouched over the table, one arm stiff and dangling, she knew he was dead.

"¡Marisa! ¡Adriana! ¿Dónde están?"

Shouting for the girl and her mother, Doña Elvira ran from the kitchen to the front room, where the television set was on but inaudible. Then she staggered to the larger bedroom; there she discovered Marisa Mora's decomposing body.

"¡Virgen Santísima!"

She spun around looking for the child's room, but when she finally found it, the door was closed. She flung it open and looked around;

it was empty. She was about to leave when something told her to search, so she went to the closet and began poking and pulling at hanging dresses and playsuits, but she found nothing. Then she glanced at the unmade bed. With difficulty, Doña Elvira got down on her hands and knees to peer under it; there she discovered Adriana, who at first also looked dead. Doña Elvira let out a wail so loud that even the cringing Don Luis forced himself into the apartment.

By that time, Doña Elvira had recuperated enough to drag Adriana out from under the bed. As she did this, she realized that the girl was not dead but unconscious. With the manager's assistance, the elderly woman got to her feet with Adriana in her arms, and with unexpected energy, she ran past Mario Mora's body, past the room where Marisa Mora lay; nothing stopped her until she reached her apartment. There, she put Adriana on the front room sofa. Adriana lay there for hours before she could be awakened from her trance, despite the ambulances, patrol cars, coroners, television reporters, investigators, and curious neighbors swarming through the apartment complex.

The girl finally sat up; she was groggy, hair disheveled, confused, but aware of two men speaking in hushed tones in the kitchen. She felt Doña Elvira hugging her at one moment, then gently nudging her out of sleep.

"Adriana, you have to wake up. Open your eyes!"

The girl struggled with confusion, trying to focus her blurred eyes on Doña Elvira. Suddenly, one of the men came and plucked her off the sofa and carried her to the kitchen, where the light bulb hanging from a cord made her blink even more. She thought she overheard Doña Elvira whispering to her husband, and she was almost sure she could make out the woman's words.

"No le digas ahorita."

"But we must tell her now. Later will be worse. You have to remember that the police want to talk to her. She has to know before then."

Doña Elvira's husband spoke loudly, clearly. He was opposing his wife's warning not to tell the girl what had happened.

"¡No!"

"¡Sí!"
Adriana was now fully awake and she knew something terrible
was happening. Whatever had occurred was so bad that Doña Elvira
and her husband were almost arguing over it. The man carrying Adriana intervened.
"Your husband is right, Doña Elvira. The child must be told. If
you wait until later, it will only hurt her more."
Adriana looked at Doña Elvira and at her husband, then at the
man who held her. They were neighbors, and although very old in her
eyes, they were kind. They often looked after her while her mother
and father were at work or out of the house.
"M'ijita . . . "
Doña Elvira's voice quivered, then broke off, leaving her unable
to speak. She turned away and put her hands on the side of the kitchen
sink. Her husband picked up where Doña Elvira had stopped.
"Adrianita. Listen to me very carefully. Something has happened to your mamá and papá. They were in a bad car accident. And
now . . . now . . . they are in heaven. Now you must stay with us."
Adriana knew. She had lost her mother and father. They were
dead, and she knew that it had not been in a car accident. Adriana was
only four years old, but she knew that her mother had killed her father.
She knew because she had been there when it had happened. What she
did not understand was the reason why her mother had done such a
thing, or why her mother had abandoned her. Knowing, in conflict
with understanding, collided in the girl's mind, causing her to lose her
breath, strangling the air out of her lungs, and it was there, in Doña
Elvira's kitchen, that Adriana experienced her first asthma attack.
After that, when Doña Elvira Luna took her in, Adriana decided
never to speak again, because she was afraid that if she opened her
mouth, the breathing attacks would recur. But despite her not speaking, the attacks did return to torture her. Years passed, and because she
was always silent, people became convinced that she was incapable of
speaking. Only Doña Elvira knew the truth; only she understood the
enormity of Adriana's anguish and confusion. That old woman was

the only one who realized that Adriana's soul had withered during the days in which she was a prisoner in her mother and father's tomb.

∾ ∾ ∾

In the *palapa,* surrounded by the murmur and hissing of the jungle, Adriana felt her recollections so vividly that her nose twitched because the memory of stench surrounded her, as did the isolation of self-imposed silence. Her heart beat wildly against her ribcage, just as it had done that night long ago, just as it did whenever she remembered.

Struggling to control her racing heart because she feared another breathing attack, Adriana conjured her mother's image in her mind: brown complexion, willowy body, black straight hair that hung to her waist. As a young woman, she had migrated with her family from Campeche in Mexico to Los Angeles. In that city she met Adriana's father, loved him, married him. Yet, she had shot him dead, taking her own life at the same time and leaving her daughter alone. Now Adriana's heart struggled with anger and longing to know what had compelled her mother to do such a terrible thing.

Then the image of Adriana's father rose from the rubble of her little-girl memory. She saw the skin of his African ancestors, the muscular body inherited from a mix of races, the nappy hair of his family. This picture blurred, giving way to the form of a man slumped over a kitchen table, one arm hanging inertly by his side. She was able to tolerate the image only a few seconds before her mind shut down, fatigued by the memory of hurt and abandonment. She drifted back to sleep until sunlight awoke her.

Chapter 3

We repeat ourselves.

"¿Qué soñaste anoche?"

The toothless Lacandón native Chan K'in asked Adriana this question every morning. In the beginning she found it strange that he never greeted her with a simple *buenos días* but always asked what she had dreamed the night before. After a few days in the village, however, she discovered that dreams were so important to the people that the question took the place of a greeting. At night, instead of *buenas noches,* she was told, *Be careful of what you dream tonight.*

"What did you dream last night, *niña?*"

Chan K'in repeated the question. Despite the humid, warm air of the jungle, Adriana felt a shiver as she recalled her dream. She had decided to put it behind her, to disregard it, not to try to find meaning in what she had experienced. It was too frightening because it brought back the pain of inexplicable loss. But now, as she stood looking at the old man, she felt compelled to tell him.

She was dressed in khaki pants and shirt, and she wore hiking boots. This was her usual way of dressing, and although it was different from the garments worn by the native women, no one seemed to mind. They knew why she dwelled among them, and they trusted her enough to allow her to take photographs of them as they toiled in the jungle or fished in the river.

"I dreamed many things, *viejo.* A dream that I've dreamed before, but never so vividly."

Adriana spoke to Chan K'in in Spanish because she did not know his native tongue. She liked conversing with him, asking questions

13

about the tribe's traditions, its history, its culture. It was Chan K'in who explained meanings to her when she did not understand. As she gazed at the old man, she studied his frail face, and body. She did not know his age, but as she scrutinized him she gauged that he was very old; the skin of his brown face was leathery and cracked. His nose was a beak, and his eyes were those of an Asian nomad, or an eagle, she thought. Chan K'in wore his hair in the tradition of the men of his tribe: shoulder-length with straight bangs that hung covering his eyebrows. But unlike the younger men of the village, his hair was completely white. Since he sat on the ground cross-legged, Adriana joined him, sitting down in the same fashion and facing him.

"It was very strange, *viejo*. At the end, I dreamed that I was being pursued by hungry dogs and that I ran because my heart was filled with terror. There were other people running along with me. I don't know who they were, but they were dressed like your people. The strangest part of the dream, what I really cannot understand, is that suddenly I stopped, even though I could hear the dogs, even though I knew that I would be torn apart by them. I stopped because I had lost something precious, more precious than my life. I began to choke and I awoke."

Chan K'in looked at Adriana. He seemed to be studying her face, and he was silent for a while as he gazed at her. Then he began to trace an image on the soft earth with his finger, seemingly lost in thought until he returned his eyes to Adriana.

"You know that the Lacandón people place meaning in dreams, don't you?"

"Yes."

"A dream, though imperfect, is a mirror in which we see our past lives. Centuries ago we were driven from our towns and villages into these jungles. We were hounded by white men who ran after us with fire weapons and dogs. We were forced to abandon what we had built and planted because the hunger of those men was without limit."

Adriana remained silent. She had lived with the tribe only a few months, but she knew already that there was much discontent. She was aware of voices that murmured, whispered, repeated stories passed down through generations. But she found little to connect her story with what resonated in those voices. Facing the old Lacandón, Adriana tilted her head, trying to understand, to find a similarity that would link her dream with what he was saying. Chan K'in closed his eyes as he spoke, his voice a hoarse whisper.

"It happened in Itza Canac, land of the Maya, in the Year of the Rabbit, as the Mexica people still tell. The woman had been wandering for days, perhaps longer, separated from her people by the soldiers. She was lost. She was not the only one. Most roads and pathways were clogged with roaming, uprooted people aimlessly searching. Some traveled alone, but others were in small bands; most of them were looking for someone they might recognize.

"The woman was thin, nearly emaciated, tired and thirsty, when she stumbled onto an army of Spaniards heading south. She discovered that their leader was a man by the name of Captain General Hernán Cortés. She saw that part of the entourage was made up of men and women like her, yet of a different tribe, people she did not recognize by their clothes or language. The woman noticed, also, that one of those natives must have been important, since he was always guarded by soldiers. That man, she observed, limped grotesquely, as if his feet had been mutilated.

"There was something about those people that alarmed her, but the woman was more afraid of being alone, so she attached herself to the group. No one asked her questions. She stayed with them as they hacked their way through the jungle, crossing rivers, making camp at nightfall. During those days she was fed by a woman who, by the signs of her body, was with child. The woman never spoke; she merely gave out food and then returned to her silence.

"Finally, the marchers came onto what had once been known as Itza Canac, now a bleak, deserted and pestilent place. They were all at the end of their strength; they could walk no farther. As they set up camp next to a mud-clogged stream, the Spaniards filled the air with cursing and loud words; the natives responded with morose silence.

"The woman thought that she was the most fatigued of them all. Her dress was torn and soiled. Her feet were bruised, as were her arms and hands. Her straight hair, matted with sweat, clung to her forehead and neck. She was so tired that she could not eat. She simply collapsed near the stream, and there she fell asleep under a *ceiba* tree.

"At dawn a clamor awakened her with a fright. Though her body ached with weariness and pain, the woman forced herself to rise and seek cover. From there she could see the soldiers standing by the native they had guarded so carefully. He shifted his weight from one foot to the other, as if to relieve pain. He had a rope tied around his neck.

"Soon a crowd formed around the captain general. He seemed enraged, uncertain of what to do next, and the woman saw that his gestures were followed closely by the others. To one side she made out the figure of a priest. She had not seen him before, but his rough brown garment distinguished him from the metal coverings and weapons of the others. Also, he held a cross in his hands. By now, most inhabitants of those lands knew the meaning of that symbol.

"In the throng, the woman was able to make out the woman who had given her food, but now her silence was filled with grief. There were many others, men and women of that same unknown tribe. Every one of them had their eyes riveted on the prisoner.

"'Cortés, you meant to do this from the beginning.'

"She heard these words but did not understand them; they were not in her tongue. She knew, however, that their tone was solemn, filled with meaning. She saw that the captain general ignored what the prisoner had uttered and instead made a sign with his hand. Suddenly, the prisoner's body was violently yanked into mid-air. The man struggled against the rope, but because his hands were tied behind his back, it was his body that contorted while his legs jerked grotesquely. He dangled from the rope, gasping and gurgling; his tongue wagged until after a short while it hung inertly between purple lips. Then there was stillness, and she saw that the prisoner was dead.

"The woman approached a man whom she had not noticed before, but whom she identified as someone of her land; his tunic and cut of hair told her that he was a Chiapaneca. Now she wanted to know who that dead man was and why he had been executed, so she crept close to the stranger and whispered her questions.

"'*Amigo,* who is it that just died?'

"The man was startled by her presence, so close to him all of a sudden. He looked at her, letting her know that he had understood her language but that the woman had frightened him. He turned his head from one side to the other before responding.

"'I've heard rumors that his name is Lord Cuauhtémoc, a noble, the last Speaker of the Mexicas, the masters of Anahuac.'

"'Where is that place?'

"'It is far to the north.'

"'But why are they here, so distant from their land?'

"'I heard that the captain general is in search of gold for himself and his master. He has already vanquished the Mexica empire and all its richness. When he was informed that these parts are rich in that metal, he felt compelled to come and see for himself. Tongues also tell that he distrusted the Mexica lord so much that he forced him to come along on the march. Our people wonder at the captain's foolishness, since Cuauhtémoc is barely able to walk. I hear he has been an invalid since having his feet burned by the captain for not revealing the secrets of the Mexica people. Now Lord Cuauhtémoc is dead.'

"'Why has this happened?'

"'It is said that Cuauhtémoc was a traitor.'

"'A traitor? To whom?'

"The man turned his gaze toward the woman. He seemed baffled by her question. He rolled his eyes, frowned and hunched his shoulders.

"'To them. Who else?'

"When the woman moved away from him, she saw that the other Mexicas were on their knees, weeping. She stretched her neck to see more and saw that the woman who had given her food was also crying. She returned her attention to the man.

"'Who is that woman?'

"'She is known as Huitzitzilín. She also is of the Mexica people, one of their noble families. She is famous among her people. I heard her tell that she was a witness to the assassination of Lord Moctezuma by the invaders, and that she even took part in expelling the captains from Tenochtitlán one terrible night.'

"'Why is she here? Is she related to the nobles?'

"'Ah! You ask so many questions! I do not know why she is here. No one knows why the others are here either. They are slaves now, no longer nobles, and perhaps that is why they are here. Perhaps they were commanded to come just as was Lord Cuauhtémoc.'

"The woman remained silent as she stared first at Huitzitzilín, then at the dangling body of Cuauhtémoc. She was inundated by deep sorrow and a sense that she had witnessed an event that would never be forgotten. Her thoughts were interrupted by the voice of the man.

"'But see how the woman is with child? It is said that the child is that of a white captain.'

"'One of the enemy is the father of her child? Did he force himself on her?'

"'I don't know. How can anyone know?'

"'That is a terrible thing! What will the child look like?'

"The man sucked his teeth and wagged his head, expressing confusion as well as irritation. When he began to move away, the woman reached out and held onto him. His eyes slipped down from her face, stopping at a large scar of burned skin covering her left forearm and elbow. His eyebrows lifted, questioning her.

"'I was burned when I was a child. Someone pushed me into boiling water.'

"'Ah! I'm sorry. Who would do such a thing?'

"'I have no recollection. When I try to remember, I can hear only my voice weeping.'

"The stranger looked at her steadily for a few minutes; he appeared to want to say something, but remained silent. After a while, he turned to look at the assembled Mexicas and then returned his gaze to her.

"'Forgive me, but I must leave now.'

"'Wait, *amigo!* What about the strange one? The man with the cross in his hands?'

"'He is a priest of the white religion. His name is Motolinía. It is a Mexica name, but I do not know what it means.'

"The man turned and walked away from her, and her eyes followed his movements until he disappeared into the forest. The woman felt saddened, because he was one of her kind and now he had vanished. She was alone once again. She returned her attention to the cluster of mourners who huddled around the body of their dead noble, still hanging from the *ceiba* tree.

"The woman felt compelled to help the Mexica bring down the corpse, and she assisted in disrobing the body, then rubbing it with ointments, and finally shrouding it. All the while, she joined the grievers as they burned *copal* and murmured incantations. These prayers she could only mouth, not knowing the words but understanding that they were petitions on behalf of the dead man for a safe journey to the other side. A litter was made, and on it the body was placed. She beheld all of these movements with curiosity, wondering where the Mexica would go to put their nobleman to rest.

"Finally, when it became clear that the mourners intended to begin their trek to the north, the woman felt an urge to follow them, but decided instead to return south, to the Valley of Ixtapa, where she might be reunited with her people. As the strangers departed, making their way through the dank forest, heading toward the place where she knew the gods dwelt, she turned in the direction of her land, leaving that sad place to the hooting of nocturnal birds and to sorcerers known to infest those parts.

"Months passed before the woman finally arrived at Chiapas, the land of her birth. Instead of family and home, however, she encountered grave misery caused by enslavement, whippings, persecutions, and dogs that ravenously mutilated bodies. No matter how much she searched, she found no one of her family. She crossed paths with men and women who wept, remembering the freedom into which they had been born but that had now been snatched away.

"But the day came when they could no longer tolerate that oppression. The Chiapanecas rose in rebellion against that injustice, and their resistance and battles were so fierce that the Spaniards fled in terror to barricade themselves in Comitán. It was from that small town that they regrouped, made contact with Captain General Cortés, and waited for assistance.

"When other Spaniards arrived, they brought cannons, rifles, horses, and more dogs. It was not easy for them, however, because the

Chiapanecas chose to resist, and she was one of them. Battle after battle took place; each time the Spaniards were the winners. Their strongest weapon was the cannon, which not only ripped holes into mountainsides and dismembered bodies, but caused terrible fear in the hearts of the Chiapaneca men and women. Slowly, her people were forced back, inch by inch, as they fought with arrows, sticks, and many times even with the nails of their fingers.

"The Chiapanecas backed away, heading for Tuzla, the cradle of their beginnings, where no one even remembered from where or when they had arrived. The woman knew the terrain; it was high in the mountains, split in two parts by an immense gorge that fell in ravines toward a river. Everyone knew it was their last stand; there was nowhere to escape to from there. That night, with the moon at its fullest, hundreds, thousands of the Chiapaneca men and women decided that neither they nor their children would live under the oppression of the invaders. The ritual began, and in clusters of families, they leaped over the ridge.

"The woman decided to join the others and take her life, but she was forced to wait for hours before reaching the ridge. The morning star was rising by the time she and the last wave of Chiapanecas were nearing the edge. They clustered one against the other, knowing that in a few moments they would be on the other side of the sierra, there to begin their new life of freedom. As they began to chant the prayer of those who are passing, she and the others heard the clatter of hooves. Pandemonium broke out. Understanding that the invaders would do anything to keep them alive for a lifetime of slavery, the Chiapanecas, desperate to cheat the enemy, pushed to reach the ridge before the soldiers arrived.

"The woman was close to the edge when she felt a pair of arms encircle her waist; at the same time, her feet were grabbed, and she was pulled to the ground. She resisted, freeing her feet, then kicking and thrashing her legs, landing blows on the bearded face that pressed against her, and finally on the man's groin. She heard the pain-filled howl just as she bit into his arm, her mouth filled with coarse hair, nearly making her vomit. Disregarding her disgust, she clawed and contorted her body, trying to reach the edge of the cliff, but it was useless. She was to be one of the many held back to live the life of a slave."

Chan K'in fell silent and returned to the pattern he had been drawing in the sand. He seemed to be waiting for Adriana to speak, but when she remained withdrawn, he spoke. He had no way of knowing that she was stunned into silence by what he had said about the nameless woman's scorched arm.

"You want to know what all of this has to do with your dream?"

"Yes."

"The people of this forest know that each one of us has lived not only once, but in other times. What is happening to us now is a repetition of what happened to us then. We also know that in each life we might have a different face or name, be a child or very old, or even be a man this time, and a woman the next. We repeat ourselves. You also have a repeated life."

Concentrating on Chan K'in's words, Adriana wrinkled her brow. She stared at him, listening, wondering if she had at last found the connection between the old man's words and her own story. She slipped her hand under the long sleeve of her blouse and ran her fingers over the thick scar that covered her forearm.

"*Viejo,* why do we not have a memory of those other lives?"

"We do have a memory. We remember in our dreams."

Adriana lowered her head and leaned it to one side. She was looking at the figure traced in the dirt by Chan K'in, trying to make it out, but it was abstract, geometrical, and it held little meaning for her. As she listened, she realized that his words were like that image: indecipherable, yet pointing the way to understanding.

"Could I be the woman of whom you've just spoken?"

"Yes."

Adriana, intrigued by the ancient man's ideas, thought for a while. She was moved by the possibility of being a native woman, living a repeated life.

"If dreams can mirror our past lives, do you think they can also tell our future?"

The old man's eyes narrowed to slits as he gazed at Adriana. Slowly, almost imperceptibly at first, he began to nod his head, which was then followed by a swaying of his back.

"What are you thinking, *niña?*"

"I'm trying to understand what it is that I lost in my dream, and I can't find the answer. I believe it could be the loss of my mother and father, but what I feel is different, so I'm thinking that perhaps it's something that I'll lose in the future."

"Perhaps it will be someone and not a thing at all."

Adriana tensed at the words coming from the old man because they seemed to begin to answer her question. Her mind leaped, lunging in different directions, searching, not for something but for someone whose loss might cause her such pain. She found only emptiness; there was no one. Her silence prompted Chan K'in to go on speaking.

"Did you find someone who is important to you?"

"No."

"Yet that loss has inhabited your dreams. Perhaps it is someone whose path has crossed yours in another time, another place, and who will again come to you."

With those words, the old man got to his feet, dusted off dry leaves that clung to his frayed tunic, and walked away from Adriana. She remained sitting a long while, still cross-legged, elbows on her knees as she reflected on what Chan K'in had said.

She braced her elbows on her knees to cup her chin in her hands. She closed her eyes. The sensations evoked by the nightmare were still with her, linking with other images she had recently dreamed. They blurred with the memories of her childhood, of her scarred arm, and those recollections stuck to the pit of her stomach, causing her much pain.

Chapter 4

She wondered if white things felt pain and sadness.

When Adriana was seven, Doña Elvira died. Her husband became ill shortly then after, and his children took him away. Adriana never saw him again.

"¿Qué vamos a hacer con esta niña? Es hija de negro, y su madre fue asesina."

Even then Adriana was aware that her African side made her unacceptable to many people in the barrio. Worst of all, no one had forgotten what her mother had done to her father. No one wanted her until a daughter of Doña Elvira, Ramona Esquivel, finally took her in as a foster child. It was not affection that moved the woman to do this; it was the money given to her by the county. Adriana knew this, and when she moved in with the Esquivel family, she did it filled with fear and sadness.

There were other children, and except for Raquel, who was her age, they were older than Adriana. All of them were resentful that she had intruded on their family, and her silence only provoked them. Sometimes they beat up on her, though she fought back, she was usually pounded to the point of welts, bruises and tears. She hid in closets and under beds, but she could not stay in those places for long because she imagined that a putrid smell wrapped itself around her, taking her breath away, forcing her to come out of hiding before her terror turned into an asthma attack. Ramona Esquivel did little to prevent her children from mistreating Adriana. At times she even joined them by making fun of her tight, curly hair and thick lips.

"Look at you! You're a real *negrita*, aren't you?"

The children laughed because of what their mother said, encouraging her to invent new ways to make them giggle. Adriana cried and tried to avoid those mocking eyes. She did this by retreating into herself, pretending that she was elsewhere, that she was someone else. It was at that time that she learned to be alone, and even to prefer to be by herself, although this only brought back the memory of her father asleep on the kitchen table and her mother lying on red sheets.

Adriana had been with the Esquivel family a few months when she and Raquel were sent to catechism school to prepare for their First Holy Communion. She still refused to speak, even to the nuns, who tried to coax her into responding to their questions.

"Who made us?"

"God made us."

"Raquel, I know you have the answers. I want Adriana to respond."

"Yes, Sister."

"Once again, Adriana. Who made us?"

Adriana looked at the nun, refusing to break her silence, despite her liking the nun. She thought that Sister Geraldine was beautiful; she even looked like the statue of the Virgin Mary that was on the altar in the church. Her eyes were as blue, her skin was the same color of milk, and the veil she wore was almost the same as that of Mary.

"Adriana, why won't you respond? You know the answer, I'm sure. Your eyes tell me you can speak. Let me try another question. Why did God make us?"

"God made us to love and serve him."

"Raquel! I know you know the answer. Please be quiet and give Adriana a chance to speak."

"She won't, Sister Geraldine. She never speaks, not even in school. She'll never get out of first grade."

In time, the nuns gave up on Adriana answering the questions on God and the Church. Nonetheless, they decided to put her forward with the group of boys and girls that would receive First Communion, hoping that it would help her to open up.

On that May day, Adriana was standing in line waiting for the procession to make its way into the church. Like the rest of the girls, she was dressed in a white dress, gloves and a long veil held at her temples by a band of flowers. Sister Geraldine went down the line handing each child a lit candle, which was to be held in the right hand, along with a rosary, as they marched up to the altar. Most of the boys and girls were talking to one another, or to a parent, or to a sponsor, but, as always, Adriana was silent. Her eyes were riveted on Raquel's head; she was looking at the veil that was so white that it sparkled in the sunlight. She wondered if white things felt pain and sadness, as she did.

Sister Geraldine gave the signal for the children to begin the procession, then took her place at the end of the line. Inside the church, the organ blasted out the hymn that signaled the children to begin the walk up the aisle. By the time Adriana stepped inside the high-vaulted vestibule, the choir was singing *O Sacrum Convivium,* moving most of the mothers to dab their eyes in a show of emotion.

As she walked, Adriana looked up at the paintings of saints and bishops; she was captivated by their faces and postures. Then she stared at the angels and the huge statue of the Virgin Mary. Once, when the procession had to pause, Adriana concentrated her eyes on the face of that statue, envying its porcelain-white skin, blue eyes, upturned nose, and powder blue veil. She looked down at her brown arms, made darker by the contrast with her white gloves and dress.

When no one moved, Adriana realized that someone must have made a mistake or taken the wrong seat, but she did not mind; she was not feeling impatient. Instead, she again stared at Raquel's veil, still wondering if it had feelings, and what would happen if she put the flame of her candle close to the fine mesh.

She looked around, trying to forget what had just come into her mind, but her curiosity grew until she decided to test it. At first nothing happened as she neared the flame to the edge of the veil. She put it closer and closer, until a puff of smoke suddenly enveloped her face. She recoiled in shock as she saw Raquel's head in flames. Adriana thought that she looked longer, taller, as the flames swirled upward and her arms flailed wildly, trying to rip the burning material from her head.

"*¡Ay! ¡La niña!*"

"*¡Raquel! ¡Raquel!*"

An uproar shattered the reverence of the congregation as people rushed toward Raquel in an attempt to help her. In a matter of seconds, a man took off his jacket and wrapped it around the girl's head and shoulders. The other children shrank back in terror, shrieking for a mother, a father, someone, anyone. The priest and two altar boys pressed their way through the milling, screaming crowd until they reached Raquel, whose whimpers became weaker with each second. By the time her mother reached her, the girl had lost consciousness. While all of this was happening, Adriana had fallen against a pew, watching, her eyes bulging.

"*¡Hija del diablo! ¡Hija de un diablo negro!*"

Raquel's mother, in a hysterical fit, lunged toward Adriana, intending to hurt her. The woman's words, telling her that she was the daughter of a black devil, shocked Adriana even more, transporting her to the apartment where her mother had murdered her father. Again, she smelled the stench that had invaded the place; she felt a tightness in her chest and her stomach turned until she vomited.

Ramona Esquivel disregarded the mess at Adriana's feet and she grabbed the girl by the neck, shaking her with all the strength of her arms. The crowd stood aghast as she thrashed Adriana from one side to the other. Everyone was shouting and babbling.

"*¡La policía!*"

"*¡Pronto!*"

"*¡Una ambulancia!*"

Suddenly, from out of the throng, a pair of hands took hold of Señora Esquivel. The strength of that grip forced the woman from Adriana's throat. The strong hands then took the girl through the crowd out of the church. Still gagging and breathing heavily, her face puffy and smeared with tears, Adriana looked up to see Sister Geraldine.

"Why did you do such a thing, Adriana?"

The nun muttered the question over and again, knowing that the girl would not respond. Nonetheless, she felt compelled to ask because she was baffled by what had happened. She had never before experienced such a tumult in church. Sister Geraldine stood staring down at Adriana; she, too, was breathing heavily.

"I wanted to see if it would hurt the veil."

The nun began to say something that had nothing to do with what Adriana had said, but cut off her own words abruptly. She blinked in disbelief at what she had heard: not Adriana's words but rather her voice. The girl had spoken, and she did so in clear, correct words. There was no slurring, no incoherent connections. It was a complete, understandable sentence.

"Adriana! You *can* speak!"

The nun, still shaken by the many unexpected happenings, took Adriana by the shoulders as she turned her face up to hers. She looked intently at her face and head.

"Little girl, you *can* speak!"

Repeating her words, Sister Geraldine expressed her joy to Adriana, who in turn was convinced that the nun was the Virgin Mary. If not, then she certainly was an angel, the only one in her short life who had ever shown Adriana that she cared enough for her to protect her from pain.

"She said that I'm the daughter of a black devil!"

"Yes, she did say those words."

"Is that true, Sister?"

"No! No one is the daughter of the devil. But you have to understand that Señora Esquivel was very upset, and people say strange things when they're frightened. God forbid it, but maybe Raquel will be scarred. You'll have to apologize most sincerely to her and to God, and you must promise never, never to do such a thing again."

As it turned out, Raquel Esquivel was not severely hurt; she lost most of her hair but that grew back, and there were no scars left on her face. Apparently, the blaze everyone saw was that of the veil only. After counseling and advice from the parish nuns, the family took

Adriana back, but Ramona Esquivel tucked the incident in her heart, and never forgave her.

Not long afterward, when she was nearly eight years old, Ramona told Adriana to heat water to wash the dinner dishes. Adriana did as she was told, even though she could barely reach; she had to prop a chair against the stove to put the pan on top. However, when the water boiled and was ready, she knew that she could not carry it over to the sink, so she called Señora Esquivel and asked her to do it for her. Adriana was standing by the sink when the woman, pot holders in hand, turned to her.

"You want the water, *m'ijita?*"

"*Sí, señora.*"

"Where do you want it, *mi chula?*"

Adriana turned to point her finger toward the kitchen sink when she felt the searing pain of boiling water crash against her left side. She felt heat invade her body, and it was so hot, so intense, that the light coming through the windows began to dim until she could barely see. The dimming soon became blackness, and then there was nothing.

When Adriana regained consciousness, her eyes opened slowly to see a nurse looking down at her. The face was a blur at first, then it began to take shape, until finally it became clear. As the woman scrutinized her, Adriana heard voices somewhere next to her bed.

"Doctor, I tell you this was an accident."

"Explain how such a thing could happen accidentally if the child was standing by the sink, and the water was boiling on the stove? Remember, I've gone to your place, I've seen the kitchen, and anyone can see that there is at least five feet of separation between the sink and stove."

"I'm telling you that she tried to pick up the pot and dropped the whole thing on herself."

"But you've already said that she was standing by the sink."

"Well, I made a mistake! I didn't mean it that way. Oh, shit! It's all her fault. Look at what her mother did to her own husband. And look at what the little brat did to my Raquel! She's a monster! I'm afraid of her."

"What does any child have to do with what her parents do, or don't do? And as far as I'm concerned, what happened at that ceremony was just a childish thing. She had no idea of what could have happened! But this was not a childish prank nor an accident! This, Mrs. Esquivel, is very serious. Adriana will be lucky if she comes out of this without her face being scarred. Her arm will be, that's for sure. This is a terrible thing that's happened to her. I can't prove what really happened, but I can assure you that she will not return to your place."

෴ ෴ ෴

"*¡Señorita Adriana! ¡Señorita Adriana!*"

The voices of several Lacandón girls yanked Adriana back to the present. It was time for her to join the women to begin the photo shoot. Adriana stood up, but the doctor's voice was still ringing in her ears, as was the memory of pain, which hardly ever left her. She smiled at the girls, grateful that they had retrieved her from her past life. She signaled to them that she would join them as soon as she got her equipment.

Chapter 5

The mountain spoke to us.

The whir of turning film filled the air as Adriana aimed the camera and snapped shot after shot. Surrounding her was a cluster of huts, each with its opening facing a center in which kneeling women ground maize. Others patted *tortillas* into shape, then baked them on a *comal* placed over an open fire. Some women were embroidering *huipiles*, shawls worn by the village women. Yet others were spinning cotton to be dyed and sewn into the full skirts that marked the women of the tribe. These products would be sold in the open markets of San Cristóbal de las Casas and Ocosingo.

Adriana had been part of the village for several months, and in that time the villagers, men as well as women, had come to feel at ease with her. It had been difficult in the beginning; no one would allow her to point a camera at them. Chan K'in explained that to reproduce a person's image on paper was the same as possessing the spirit of that man or woman. She had expected this, however, since many of the old women and men of her barrio in Los Angeles had similar ideas. She knew that trust had to happen before anything could be done, so she lived with them and waited until they understood that she was a friend.

"*¡Micaela! ¡Muévete más para acá, por favor!*"

Whenever she asked one of the women to move closer, Adriana's request was answered with a shy smile. She could overhear them twittering in their language. She knew they were gossiping about her, but she did not mind. She felt good about whatever they might say. She also liked the sound of their speaking because it echoed the sweet tones of bird songs filling the air.

As she took each picture, she concentrated on faces while trying to capture the dense jungle background. Sharp profiles with bird-like contours attracted her most of all. Next to side views, Adriana focused on the almond-shaped eyes outlined by long, straight lashes. She zoomed in on smiles curved around small, white teeth, knowing that the black-and-white film she used would capture the dark mahogany tones of the women's skin.

Adriana looked to her left just in time to catch sight of a young mother, and, hoping to capture that image, she rapidly pointed her lens at the girl's hand as it uncovered a full breast. Muttering under her breath, Adriana got closer; she wanted to catch the image of the child as it suckled its mother's milk.

"*¡Chispas!* The girl can't be more than thirteen."

She shot several frames of the mother and child before she lowered the camera. Adriana focused her eyes on the young woman, thinking that she was beautiful. She gazed at her face: an oval covered by brown, smooth skin. The girl's eyes were filled with light; although Adriana knew their color was black, she thought that they appeared to be cast in silver. The girl's hair was raven-colored, caught up in braids, with some escaped strands, clinging to her forehead and neck.

Adriana could not take her eyes off the girl's face. She found the contrast hypnotic: the sight of the mother, still a child, offering the breast of a grown woman to her baby. Adriana sat down by a tree, placed her camera next to her, and leaned against the trunk. She pulled a note pad from her pocket and began jotting down her impressions. As always, Adriana made careful notes, including not only the details of her subjects, but her own feelings as well. Suddenly, a mix of emotions crept over her as she scribbled: love for the young mother, envy because she was not the child sheltered in those arms, sadness at having been robbed of love, fierce desire to discover the reason for her mother having murdered her father. Without warning, the experience transported her thoughts to the beginning of her own adolescence in Los Angeles.

∽ ∽ ∽

She was eleven years old. She was standing with Mrs. Hazlett on the corner of Whittier and Kern; they were waiting for a bus. The social worker had been Adriana's case supervisor for a number of years, and the girl now felt at ease with her. In the beginning, when Adriana was recuperating from her scalded arm, she had been afraid of Mrs. Hazlett, mostly because she was different. She spoke only English, and she lived in a different part of the city. The woman was tall and lean. Her hair was a faded blond, her blue eyes were tiny, and she tended to squint them when she looked at people. Her looks intimidated the girl for a while, but soon Adriana learned that Mrs. Hazlett was kind, that she wanted to help her.

As they waited for the bus, Adriana, with her small suitcase propped against her leg, felt sad because she was being placed in yet another home. She had been moved from foster home to foster home, and now she would have to begin all over again. She would have to be with a new family, with different people, but by now Adriana knew that anything could happen. Those people might like her, or maybe dislike her. There was a bigger chance, she thought, that they would not care for her, and no matter how much she tried to tell herself it did not matter, she was still afraid of rejection.

The street was clogged with cars and people who bustled in and out of stores and small restaurants. Sidewalk vendors peddled fruit salad in paper cones, music on cassettes, handmade jewelry, even shoes and shirts. Adriana wiggled her nose, sniffing the odor of frying food as she stared at people eating off paper plates while they waited for the bus. She was familiar with the sounds and sights of that part of East Los Angeles because she had been living with a family around the corner on Arizona Street.

"My, my, that sure smells yummy!"

Adriana knew that Mrs. Hazlett was trying to make things easier for her by speaking that way. She doubted that the social worker really liked the smells. She even wondered if Mrs. Hazlett ever ate anything fried, or if she ate with her fingers the way those people were eating. She decided not to say anything; instead, she pretended to be looking out for the bus.

Mrs. Hazlett went on trying to cheer up Adriana. She made funny faces and quick remarks, hoping to lessen Adriana's latest displacement, to make it less depressing. The girl understood this, and she was grateful, yet she could not help feeling sad.

"Look, honey, it's better to have a change of scenery. Just think of all the rest of us who have to live day in and day out in the same old house. At least you move around. You'll never be bored, that's for sure."

Adriana pretended to giggle, but it was fake, unconvincing. She knew that the families with whom she had lived never wanted her in the first place, that not one had ever loved her. At times she blamed the scar on her arm, thinking that it must have made her repugnant to anyone who saw it. At other times she was certain that a smelly cloud hung over her, forcing people to back away from her. She wondered how it felt to be loved. Where did a person feel love? In the stomach? In the mouth? Where? The only thing she really knew was fear, which she felt all over her body, especially in her chest when her breathing became difficult and when her heart pounded against her ribs.

"I know, Mrs. Hazlett. I'm sure there are a lot of kids who would love to be like me. But I think that I would like to stay in one place for a long time, just for a change."

The bus finally came. It was packed, but Adriana and Mrs. Hazlett soon got a seat. Once they sat down, they were jostled back and forth, from side to side as the bus jerked, stopping, going, dodging traffic. Adriana looked around, convinced that people were staring at her, but then she remembered that Mrs. Hazlett was different from the rest of the passengers, and she decided that she was the reason people were looking at them.

Adriana was relieved when they got off the bus at the corner of Fourth Street and Soto. She knew they were in Boyle Heights, a part of Los Angeles not far from the east side. Adriana looked up and down the street and saw that it was just as crowded as where they had waited for the bus. Then she tugged at Mrs. Hazlett's sleeve to get her attention.

"Mrs. Hazlett, what's the name of the family that I'm going to live with?"

"Orvitz. No! Wait a minute, that's not right. Let me check." Mrs. Hazlett pulled papers out of a bulky satchel hanging from her left arm. She fumbled for a while, struggling because there was a breeze that whipped the pages from side to side. "Here it is. The family's name is Ortiz. The house is just around the corner. I've visited them, Adriana, and I know you'll like them. Señora Ortiz has fixed up a room for you of your very own."

She took Adriana's hand, and together they walked the short distance to the two-story frame house. As they moved, the older woman spoke to the girl, using encouraging and affectionate words. She said things that she had never before said to Adriana, so the girl listened carefully.

"Remember, Adriana, that even though you don't have parents, or brothers or sisters, or anyone else like that, still you'll find people who will care just as much for you."

"Like who, Mrs. Hazlett?"

"Well, like friends. Friends can love us just as much as family."

"No one has ever loved me."

"That's not true, Adriana. I care very much for you. I always will. Ah! Here we are. The Orvitz house."

"Ortiz, Mrs. Hazlett. Ortiz."

Adriana had no way of knowing at that time that the family in which Mrs. Hazlett placed her would be the last of her foster homes. Neither did she know that it was there, in the home of the Ortiz family, that she would witness her body change from that of a child into that of a woman.

〜 〜 〜

"Señorita Adriana."

Adriana was pulled away from her memories by a voice calling out her name. Caught by surprise, she could not make out where the voice was coming from, or who it was that was calling. She sat up, turning in different directions, but all she saw were the women at their tasks; no one seemed to be looking at her or wanting her attention.

"Señorita Adriana."

Soon a figure moved away from the dense shadows of the forest into a clearing, showing herself. The woman approached Adriana who, still sitting by the tree, squinted her eyes as she tried to identify the stranger. When she came near enough to Adriana, she extended her hand.

"Me llamo Juana Galván. Mujer de la gente Tzeltal."

Adriana stumbled to her feet to return the handshake and acknowledge her name. When she straightened up, she realized that she was much taller than the woman standing in front of her. She saw that Juana was diminutive, smaller yet than the other women of the tribe.

"Sí. Mucho gusto. Soy Adriana Mora."

The other woman nodded, letting Adriana know that she was aware of her name. Adriana looked at her intently, sensing that the woman was someone of importance in the tribe. For a moment, her eyes fixed on a crescent-shaped scar stamped over her left eyebrow. Adriana had never before seen her, but Juana Galván, Adriana saw, walked and held herself in a special manner. Both women looked at one another, taking in height, looks, ages.

"Why don't we sit down? Here where I was sitting."

They sat cross-legged, with elbows on knees. They were silent, still scrutinizing one another. The day was drawing to its end, and the jungle noises were escalating toward their night pitch.

"You were lost in thought. I had been watching you for a while, and you seemed to be far away."

"Yes. I was reliving my childhood."

"I do that often also. Where are you from, Adriana Mora?"

"I'm from Los Angeles in California. Have you heard of it?"

"Yes. Some of our young men have left us to go there to work and live. Most of them never return. They say it's too far to come back. Is that true?"

"Yes, it's true. Los Angeles is far away from here."

"How did you get here?"

"I first went to New Mexico. I went there to begin my work. I planned to take photographs of the women of the Hopi tribe."

"Are they people like us?"

"Yes. In many ways."

"Would you say that we're all related?"

"Yes."

Juana and Adriana fell silent, as if listening to the rise and fall of rhythms emerging from the jungle, but they were really considering one another. Beyond them, the howling monkeys, at times barking like dogs, then roaring like jaguars, made the loudest racket. Adriana returned to her story.

"I worked a few months with the tribe, but then I read a story about the people of these parts; it appeared in a magazine that had photographs included in it. Something in those pictures drew me. I wanted to come here and see this jungle with my own eyes, so I put my things together and came here."

"You did this by yourself?"

"There were other people. I wasn't the only one."

"What I mean is, do you have brothers or sisters? Do you have a husband?"

Adriana felt herself tightening with each of Juana's questions. She began to feel uncomfortable, edgy. Instead of responding, she turned the direction of the conversation.

"And you, Juana, are you from these parts?"

"Yes. I have lived in the Lacandona all of my life."

They again became silent, giving way to the inner threads that were connecting them one to the other. After a few moments, Juana spoke as she jutted her chin in the direction of the camera.

"You record images with that machine?"

"Yes. I'm a photographer."

"That's how you live?"

"I try."

"You were writing in that pad. Are you also a scribe?"

"Not exactly. I write down my impressions of a photograph, that's all."

"Why do you do that?"

"I might forget what I was thinking, what I was feeling, or there might be a color or a detail that I want to remember especially. Writing those things will help me remember later on when I examine the pictures I take."

Juana smiled as she pulled blades of grass from the ground, rubbing each one between her index finger and thumb. She looked at Adriana, who returned her gaze.

"When you take the images of our women, what is it that you're looking for?"

"I can't be certain, Juana, but I think that what I hope to find is the truth."

"The truth? About what?"

"About the women."

"You think you're looking at the truth when you take pictures of women toiling, breaking their backs, growing old before their time, buried in the mud of ignorance?"

"You find what I'm doing wrong?"

"No! Not wrong, but empty."

Adriana, feeling misunderstood, did not like the direction the conversation was taking. She did not want it to continue that way, so she decided to stop its momentum.

"Please tell me the meaning of your words, Juana. I recognize them but I don't understand their meaning."

"When you take the face of a woman with your camera, and her expression reflects misery, it is not enough to have that image on paper only. You must also capture her spirit, and the reasons for its anguish."

Adriana's mind jerked; she was astonished. The impact of Juana's words moved her profoundly because it was as if Juana had been able to reach into her heart, into her soul, and discover what she most desired to do with her work, with her life. She realized that Juana did understand her after all. She nodded, letting Juana know that she agreed with her.

Juana, her head tilted slightly to one side, did not take her eyes from Adriana's. Her gaze was intense; it lingered for moments on the other woman's face. She appeared to be deliberating, considering an idea, analyzing it, bringing it closer to her tongue.

"I know that you've seen the poverty in which we live. Our girls are sold for a few *pesos* without having the right to say if they desire to be married or if they want children."

Adriana, who had been shifting her weight from one haunch to the other, not because of fatigue but because of tension, nodded, acknowledging that she understood Juana's comments.

"Twelve years ago, when I was your age, I took refuge in the mountains. There I joined men and women of my tribe, and other people who had gathered to prepare to break the yoke that was imposed on us centuries ago. The mountain spoke to us; it told us to take up arms, and we listened. We have been training up there, gathering arms and information regarding our enemies."

"Why are you telling me this? I'm not one of your people."

"No, you're not, but soon you will be, and we're certain that you will not betray us. Besides, you, too, have suffered, haven't you?"

Adriana was astounded by Juana's question, which she heard more with her heart than with her ears. Her dream returned to her. Fragments of memory flashed in her mind: someone like her running, terrified and panting through dense jungle. Then Juana, contemplating Adriana, moved her lips as if to say something, but she kept quiet. A few moments passed, and when Adriana did not say anything, Juana again spoke. She repeated the question.

"You have suffered, haven't you?"

"Yes."

"Inside and outside?"

"Yes."

"That scar on your arm, is it part of the pain?"

"Yes. It happened when I was a girl. Someone wanted to hurt me."

"The hurt was much deeper than your skin?"

"Yes."

Juana looked away, thinking of Adriana's pain while she touched the scar that curved over her eyebrow. When she returned her gaze, it was to again look into Adriana's eyes.

"Some anguish is never forgotten."

It was Adriana who now opened her mouth to speak, but no sound came out. The words froze in her mouth, suddenly blocked by an intense surge of affection for Juana. This unexpected emotion startled and confused her, causing her to recoil and to want to end the conversation. Sensing the turmoil that was accosting Adriana, Juana pursued.

"Join us, Adriana."

"What good could I be to you? I'm not a native, much less do I have training in what you're planning."

Juana straightened her back and she crossed her arms over her breasts. It was only then that Adriana focused on that part of her body; until that moment she had concentrated only on Juana's face. She took in the embroidered, faded cotton blouse. The sash around her waist showed off the small woman's plumpness.

"We are about to embark on a plan for which we've been preparing for many years, one that will return to us what was snatched away long ago. It will be painful, and it will cause anguish, but it must take place. All of our actions should be chronicled in writing as well as in images for the world to see. You can do that for us."

Adriana's body drooped, accosted by a mix of fear and excitement. A swirl of unrecognizable emotions caused by the woman facing her filled her, shaking her, forcing her to confront the vulnerability and loneliness that had stalked her since her childhood. She felt a compelling attraction, a pull towards Juana she had never before experienced for anyone. She looked away from her because she feared that what she was feeling would leak out through her eyes.

"Will the people accept me?"

"They already have. That is why I'm here speaking to you."

"Where will I get my supplies?"

"We will see that you have what you need."

"Is there going to be bloodshed?"

"Yes."

The thought of violence shocked Adriana, forcing her to wonder if she had the courage. On the one hand, she found it easy to identify with the suffering of the natives; she had recognized it each time she focused her lens on a woman; she saw it stamped on her face. She was convinced that she understood their misery because it reminded her of something inside of her. Yet the shedding of blood was another consideration. She looked at Juana.

"I don't know if I have the courage."

"None of us knows that until the time comes."

Adriana nodded, remembering that she had yearned to understand the reality behind the images she captured on film. How else could she do that, she asked herself, except to get as close as possible to her subjects. To join Juana would be dangerous, yet the idea of being in the heart of the conflict enticed her, making her forget whatever peril might come her way. However, without knowing it, much less admitting it, Adriana was above all seduced by Juana's image, by her voice, by her ideas. In her mind Adriana had already said *yes*.

She returned to the *palapa* to pack her personal belongings; the cameras and attachments she would carry separately. As she sorted lenses, film and notes on the cot, she felt apprehensive about what she was about to do, and the haste with which she had agreed to join the rebels. She was more fearful, however, of the storm of emotions that had been unleashed in her soul by her meeting with Juana. She tried to stop thinking of her and to concentrate on what she was about to do, but the indigenous woman's face and her figure would not be erased from Adriana's thoughts.

She forced herself to think of practical things. She had been able to mail part of her work to an editor in Los Angeles, but she had a collection of recent shots, along with numerous notes, still to be organized. She had to decide what to do with those photos and descriptions. After a while, she placed the material in a canvas bag, left the *palapa* in search of Chan K'in. She found him at the edge of a clearing, working with a boy; they were mending a broken farming tool. At first, neither of them saw Adriana standing by their side, and she had to clear her voice to get their attention.

"Buenas tardes, Chan K'in."

Her words startled him out of his concentration. The boy, too, was surprised. When they realized that she was standing by their side, they got to their feet.

The old man smiled a toothless greeting. *"Buenas tardes, niña."*

With an eye signal, he told the boy to leave. When they were alone, Adriana sat down on the ground and crossed her knees. Chan K'in did the same; he was still smiling.

"I hear you are leaving. Voices say you are going up to the mountains."

Adriana was unable to mask her surprise upon discovering that the old man knew her plans, since she had told no one of her conversation with Juana Galván. She looked at her watch and realized that less than an hour had passed since she agreed to leave the village.

"What do you think, *viejo?*"

"I think it is good for you to do that. Your work will be important; the world will see what is happening here."

"But I don't even know who I'll be living with, or in what way I'll be able to help. Perhaps I'll be nothing more than an intruder, a foreigner."

"That is not the case, *niña*. You are part of us. We used to be like stones, like plants along the road. We had no word, no face, no name, no tomorrow. We did not exist. But now we have vision; we know the road on which we are to embark, and we invite you to come and seek, to find yourself, and to find us. We are you, and you are us, and through you the world will come to know the truth."

Adriana narrowed her eyes, concentrating her gaze on Chan K'in's craggy face. She was touched, even surprised by his words and the intensity of their meaning. His voice, too, sounded youthful, vigorous; it filled her with the courage that she had been missing only minutes before. She slowly rocked back and forth on her haunches, thinking of what the old man had just said, especially about his invitation for her to find herself. Juana's image flashed in her mind, and behind it came a memory she had long before forgotten. She had made love with a man, but she had not felt then what she was feeling now for the small, indigenous woman.

∽ ∽ ∽

"I love you, Adriana."

Kenny's mouth clung to hers as he rolled off of her. They had just finished making love, but they were still locked in an embrace of legs and arms, hoping that the pleasure they had just experienced would not go away. It was a dark night on Point Fermin, the place where she and Kenny often met to talk and to be with one another.

They were quiet for a long while, listening to the sound of waves crashing against cliffs and rocks, but the breeze skimming off the Pacific was cool, forcing them to put on their clothes. After that they sat side by side looking out toward Santa Catalina Island; scattered lights glimmered from that shore.

"Let's get married, Adriana."

She listened to him but did not respond. Instead, she drew her knees toward her chest and wrapped her arms around them, resting her chin there. Adriana seemed to be concentrating on the island's far-off lights.

"Why won't you marry me?"

"I don't know."

"I don't understand. We go through this every time we make love. I know you love me; I can feel it. Yet when it comes down to marrying me, nothing!"

Adriana could not deny what Kenny was saying. When she was locked in his embrace, her body did not hold back its pleasure. But, whenever he spoke of marriage, something inside of her shut down. She was afraid, and she did not know what it was that frightened her. All she understood was that he offered something she could not return because her soul would not let her do it. She felt that something inside of her was locked up, closed in on itself.

"Kenny, I'm about to finish my courses. After that I'll be able to begin work as a photographer. I need to see how that goes. I need time, that's all."

He got to his feet, frustrated with her response. Without a word, he turned from her and made his way toward the car. Adriana followed him, but once in the car, he refused to speak to her as they drove toward East Los Angeles. That was the last time she and Kenny Wallis saw each other.

↜ ↜ ↜

Adriana and Chan K'in remained silent for a long time facing one another, listening to the heightening of the jungle's nocturnal voices and murmuring. She felt the clamor intensifying their silence, creating an energy that coursed its way through her arteries, her bones, muscles, brain, her entire being. Adriana smiled at Chan K'in, nodded, and then turned to the satchel she still clutched in her hands.

"*Viejo,* will you take care of this bag for me? It contains photographs and writings about the village. I think it's good material, and when I return, I want to send them back home."

"I'll watch over your things. In the meantime, let me give you my blessing."

Adriana bowed her head when she felt the weight of Chan K'in's gnarled hands on it. She had little memory of her father and mother, but she imagined them to be inhabiting the old man's body at that moment. It was their blessing that was coursing through her body and soul, and it came to her through the bony fingers of the old Lacandón man.

Chapter 6

You have already been among us.

Their trek to the mountain began at nightfall. Juana explained that it was safer that way; the moon was full, and there would be enough light. As they began to make their way through the jungle, Juana said that they would be alone, but soon after this, Adriana felt that other people were walking along with them, heading in the same direction they were taking. Sometimes Adriana slowed down, focusing her eyes on the gloom that surrounded her and Juana, but she saw nothing; she could only sense forms of people somewhere nearby.

Juana, with only a rolled-up *petate* lashed to her back, silently led the way, picking her way through the matted undergrowth. Adriana, toting a full backpack, followed the diminutive figure closely and concentrated on her black hair twisted into a braid reaching to her waist, the embroidered blouse covering her narrow rounded back, the wide sash girding her hips, the dark woolen skirt hanging limply to her ankles.

As Adriana struggled with her load, she noticed that Juana moved steadily, confidently, each step placed carefully on the right spot. Her *huaraches* appeared to be part of the earth, curving around stones, molding themselves into the soft soil as she moved. Adriana's boots, on the other hand, became heavier, more cumbersome with each step, and she wished that she had exchanged them for sandals.

The women moved through the jungle for several hours, pausing only to relieve themselves or to drink water. Finally, Juana stopped and gave a signal with her hand; it was time to interrupt their march. Adriana was grateful because she felt fatigued, thirsty and sleepy. She was soaked in sweat, and her hands and face were scratched and stung by mosquitoes. Adriana eagerly looked around, searching for a place to unroll her sleeping bag. As she did this, she again sensed that others were with them, but she still could not make them out. She saw nothing as she squinted. There were only shadows. She remembered the dream she had experienced the previous night. In it she had felt the same thing: others beside herself, in the jungle, lost and frightened. She decided that it was her imagination, prompted by her dreams and the ghostly shadows of the jungle.

"We'll rest here for a few hours. We can begin our march before dawn. We'll be in camp by sunrise."

Juana spoke in clipped sentences, putting her lips close to Adriana's ear; it was almost a whisper. Without thinking, Adriana eased her head closer to Juana's mouth, and her nostrils picked up the other woman's scent, a smoky fragrance mixed with the aroma of damp earth. She nodded and watched her as she laid out her *petate*, on which she sat back on her heels. From a sack she took out *yuca* and, after a moment, she handed half of it to Adriana. They ate in silence until Juana spoke.

"You will make a good *compañera*."

"Why do you say that?"

"Because I feel it here."

Juana tapped her chest and smiled at Adriana, who wrestled with a flood of emotion. She stared at Juana, both hoping and fearing that she would say more, but Juana kept quiet, and after a while she rolled off her heels, reclined on her side and appeared to fall asleep.

Adriana tried to sleep, but she was so tired that she could not. Every time she began to drift off, a jerking muscle violently yanked her back. Not even the lilting sound of murmuring cicadas and chirping crickets that filled the jungle's darkness could put her to sleep. Finally, she decided to concentrate on the shadows cast by moonlight, hoping that this would help her relax.

She stared at a large spot, a lagoon of light, not far from where she lay. It shimmered like a mirror, reflecting different patterns against a tree trunk. As fronds and vines moved in the breeze, Adriana thought she made out strange forms: a serpent wrapping itself around a tree; an enormous insect swooping over her, spreading its wings, fluttering and opening them, then closing in on itself; a creature with a pointed snout, sniffing, rummaging in the gloom.

Despite the heat Adriana shuddered. So she clamped her eyes shut and drew the top of the bag over her head, but the images persisted behind her eyelids. That bright jungle mirror seemed to reach out to her. She concentrated, trying to dispel its lure. After a while she was relieved when the reflections began to fade. Her mind calmed, drifted.

෩ ෩ ෩

She remembered another mirror; she was eighteen years old. She was in the bathroom of the Ortiz home, naked and contemplating her body. Someone was knocking at the door, telling her to hurry. She continued staring at her reflection, ignoring the pleading. She looked at herself. No longer a child, she had grown tall, thin but shapely. Her skin was the color of coffee with cream, lighter in some places, darker in others, especially along the inner part of her thighs and the cleavage between her breasts. She stared at the nipples, which stood out taut, nearly black.

Her eyes shifted to the side and focused on the scar on her arm; she touched it carefully, softly, nearly expecting to feel the old pain. It was difficult for her to forget the anguish, and often she imagined that the scar was hurting her all over again. She closed her eyes to get rid of the sensation. When she opened them again, she looked below her waist, stopping to examine the mound of thick hair between her legs, and from there down to her knees, calves and feet.

With her eyes riveted on the mirror, Adriana gazed upward to her neck and face. There she saw a broad forehead, a straight, short nose, slightly bulbous at its tip. Beneath it were her full, wide lips, outlined by a dark brown hue tinged with purple. She lifted her hands to her hair, feeling its tight curls, its thickness. She then looked into her eyes, which peered back at her. They were almond-shaped with short, curled lashes; their pupils were dark brown, flecked with green.

The knocking became pounding, but Adriana refused to move. She was spellbound by the sensations welling up inside and outside of her body. Her skin and hair felt connected to desires she sensed in her mind, in her stomach, on her breasts, in the intimacy between her thighs. Soon the fists were hammering on the door with such force that she felt the vibrations on her shoulders. Suddenly, the door broke down, and something came at her, forcing her to run, to sprint through the jungle, naked and vulnerable. Her breath caught in her throat; she began to choke because her lungs had run out of air. Something was behind her, gaining on her, lunging at her. She cried out.

୭ ୭ ୭

"Adriana. ¡*Despierta!*"

She awoke to find Juana holding her. Drenched in perspiration and with her face smeared with tears, Adriana felt her heart pounding wildly; she could not breathe. She struggled against suffocation while she stretched and grabbed at the backpack, fumbling, tugging. She finally found the inhaler. She shoved it into her mouth and pumped, then she inhaled deeply and waited for her lungs to stabilize.

Juana held her in her arms until Adriana was able to calm down. She wiped the sweat off her face, all the time reminding her that it had been a nightmare, that she was safe, that nothing would harm her. Juana's soft words reassured Adriana, calming her, allowing her to again fall into a deep and this time peaceful sleep. She was unaware of how long she had slept until she became aware of Juana's voice.

"It's time."

Juana was nudging her shoulders, whispering, trying to awaken her, but Adriana's sleep was sound, and it took her seconds to realize where she was and who was calling her. She shook her head, trying to clear her mind, but she was still half asleep, unable to distinguish where and how her dream had ended. Suddenly, she felt a rushing urge to relieve herself. She eased herself away from Juana's arms and crawled out of the sleeping bag stood up and walked to the ferns, where she unzipped her pants, squatted, and allowed her body to drain. Then she returned to where Juana waited for her.

Without saying a word, Juana turned and began to make her way
through the jungle. Adriana looked around expecting to see someone,
whoever it was that had pursued her in her dream, in her mind. She
saw only trees and thick undergrowth. She walked slowly, following
Juana, at the same time reminding herself that it had been only a
dream, her imagination that had evoked those shadows. Nothing
more. The words uttered by Chan K'in floated back to her, and she
wondered if it really could be possible that perhaps in more than a
dream she had been chased through this jungle in another era. She
shrugged her shoulders, balanced her backpack, and picked up her
pace behind Juana.

By the time the sun was rising, Juana and Adriana filed into camp.
The fragrance of tortillas hissing on *comales* wrapped itself around
Adriana's nose, making her mouth water. Despite being exhausted,
she felt a burst of new energy as she took in her surroundings. She saw
at a glance that the camp took up a large clearing in the jungle, where
palapas and other structures served as shelters. In most of those huts,
she noticed that there were weapons of different types.

To the side she saw a sturdier house with windows. It was raised
on a foundation, with stairs leading to a deck, then to the front
entrance. Juana made her way to that structure, and as she and Juana
approached, men and women came out to greet them with smiles and
embraces. There was much noise and jabbering.

After a few minutes, however, Adriana perceived a marked change
in mood. Serious expressions replaced smiles; joyful eyes became
somber. Astounded, she looked around, taking in faces as she tried to
discern the cause of the sudden change. Juana signaled her to stay
where she was while she moved aside to speak with two members of
the group. Adriana kept her eyes on the three, all the while knowing
from Juana's body movements that something important was being discussed. In a few moments, Juana nodded and walked toward Adriana.

Meanwhile, Adriana's attention returned to the men and women
milling around her. She saw that they were all indigenous. She was
surprised by the number of women, most of them young, who had
made themselves part of that army. She concentrated on their faces, on
the strength reflected in their eyes. Those were the faces that the world

beyond the jungle would soon be seeing through the camera lens. There were a few older people, but most of that army of men and women, she noticed, appeared to be in their twenties and thirties. Adriana could not understand what they were saying in their language. She did realize, however, that no one spoke Juana's name. Instead, she heard the word "capitán" as it was repeated over and again in Spanish.

When they reached the stairs leading up to the house, the throng dispersed and Juana gestured to Adriana to put down her gear.

"Here I am known as Capitán Insurgente Isabel."

"You're an officer?"

"Yes. We're an army."

Adriana, not knowing what to say, kept silent. She inwardly reproached herself for being naïve, for not having prepared herself for what she was encountering.

"Why are you surprised? All armies have officers."

"But you're a woman."

"We're all equal in this army."

"You even have a different name."

"We give up our original names as we give up the old ways."

Embarrassed, but not knowing exactly why, Adriana was at a loss as to what to say; she only nodded. Again, she admired Juana's way, the manner in which she transformed what could be complicated into something simple and natural.

When they reached the top of the stairs, Adriana looked through the entrance and caught glimpses of men and women in discussion. As she and Juana entered, everyone turned in their direction, momentarily surprised, but then obviously relieved to see them. Adriana sensed that they had been worried about their well-being. Along with this impression, she felt a heavy mood in the room; tension seemed to hang in the air like a pall.

Her eyes scanned those faces, moving from one to the other—seeing that some of the men were mestizos, and that they, as well as the women, were all armed. These men and women were the leaders—of this she was certain—and as she had done minutes before, she concentrated on expressions, observing the jutting jaw of the man turning toward her, the prominent forehead of the woman looking intently at her, the nose of the woman standing next to her. Later on, when these same people would put on masks to erase their faces, Adriana would be able to recognize each one by the characteristics she first observed as she met them.

Again, Juana moved away from Adriana to approach one of the men. With him she engaged in a long, whispered conversation that betrayed surprise, then what Adriana interpreted as exasperation. As they spoke, the others kept silent, apparently knowing what Juana was hearing. When they were finished, she nodded to the man and returned to the group. Juana spoke in a low voice, her eyes shrouded as if she were thinking of something else. "*Compañeros,* this is Adriana Mora. She has agreed to become part of our cause and to chronicle the enterprise on film. From here, the images she records will go out to the world."

Juana's voice was steady and clear as she spoke in Spanish. Adriana was moved by Juana's words because she had never been made to feel so welcome. The apprehensions she had experienced melted away, leaving her certain that what she was about to do was important and necessary.

Juana took Adriana to each of the officers, women and men, indigenous and mestizo. Even though they did not speak to her, she saw that they accepted her. Most of them shook her hand, others patted her on the shoulder.

"This is El Subcomandante, our spokesman."

"This is Major Ana María."

"This is Comandante Ramona."

Juana paused when they neared a man who wore the long cotton tunic of the Lacandones over which he had strapped a cartridge belt and revolver at his waist. Adriana looked down at his feet, taking in the worn *huaraches* that did not cover heavily callused heels and toes. She noticed also that his feet were oversized, too big, for his medium-sized body, and that one toe was missing from each foot.

"This is Coronel Insurgente Orlando Flores."

Juana paused as she looked at the officer, and her face took on a serious expression showing respect as she introduced the Lacandón rebel. She then went on to name the other insurgents.

After that she helped Adriana with her gear and showed her where she would stay. It was a *palapa*, like the one she had in Pichucalco. Here, too, was a cot with a net covering as well as a basin and water jug placed on top of a small table. Adriana understood that she was being shown privilege because she had already noted that the rest, males and females, inhabited the long, open huts along the fringe of the camp, and that they slept in hammocks.

From there Juana took her to the stream that skirted the living area and pointed to a bend where a waterfall churned up foam and spray. Then she showed her to the outhouses and to the communal kitchen. Everyone, she explained, helped with the cooking, cleaning and laundry. After the tour of the grounds, they returned to the *palapa*.

"For now, rest and get used to your new base. Tell me what you need, and I'll see that you get it. I'll show you what we do tomorrow."

Adriana gazed at Juana. She again felt a strong pull toward her, compounded now by a sense that something dangerous was about to unleash itself on the camp. She hesitated, not knowing if she had the right to ask, fearing that her question might sound like prying. After a few moments of wavering, she spoke up.

"Juana, what's happening?"

"Why do you ask?"

"I felt that something was wrong from the first moments with the group. The *compañeros* appear apprehensive."

Juana, with her usual directions, did not delay her answer. She looked at Adriana, head tilted to one side, allowing her face to show her thoughts. "Two policemen were killed. It was a brutal murder. They were mutilated and cut into pieces. Now the *catxul* blame our people; thirteen men from the canyons have been arrested. We have no doubt that they will be tortured and killed."

Juana's terse words had a deep effect on Adriana. She understood that the violence she had feared was already staring at her with unblinking eyes. Despite the little knowledge she had of the insurgents and her lack of awareness of their plans, she knew that they were at a crossroad.

"The Bishop has called for a rally. It's to take place up there, in the canyons," said Juana, jutting her jaw, pointing in an upward direction.

Then Juana tapped Adriana's shoulder to let her know that she had nothing more to say. She turned and walked away, heading for the center of the compound.

Adriana stood looking at her until she disappeared into a hut. She wondered if Juana was experiencing a similar inner turmoil. In her mind, Adriana examined every detail, every gesture of Juana's, trying to discover a hint of what the woman thought of her, felt for her, but only the sensation of Juana's arms around her as she fell asleep prevailed.

Intense heat and humidity had now taken hold of the jungle. Adriana felt sweat seeping through her clothes and socks. She tried to put aside her discomfort as she rummaged through her backpack looking for her note pad. When she found it, she went to the small table and began to record her thoughts, observations and feelings.

She noted the impact Juana was having on her and the confusion that was gripping her, as well as the unaccountable joy she was experiencing. With equal detail, she noted her fears and her admiration for the fierce determination she had detected in the insurgents. When she finished, Adriana reread her notes and absentmindedly mouthed a faint *yes*.

She sat at the rickety table for a while, allowing her thoughts to focus on the insurgents. Like vivid photographs, each face was etched in her mind, and she again felt apprehensive, understanding the magnitude of their mission. Again, Adriana wondered if she had the courage to be a part of it.

With that weighing heavily on her mind, she moved to the cot, bent over and untied the laces of her boots. Putting one foot on her knee, she grunted and struggled to pull off her drenched socks and heavy shoes. Adriana sighed with relief as she wiggled her toes in the air.

She got to her feet and began peeling off clothing: canvas vest, khaki shirt and pants, bra, panties. She stood naked for minutes, letting the sweat evaporate off her body. Then she reached into the backpack and pulled out a long shirt, put it on and went out, making her way up the stream to the waterfall. There she took off her shirt, slid down the grassy bank and waded in toward a small pool of clear, swirling water. Heavy mist covered her, drenching her hair and skin, relieving her of the extreme heat her body had been experiencing. Adriana dove down to discover that the bottom was several feet below. Resurfacing, she surrendered to the swirling emerald-colored water, face uplifted, arms and legs outstretched as she floated listlessly, allowing the current to swivel her in repeated circles. She clenched and unclenched her fingers, enjoying the pleasure of weightlessness, feeling the watery caress on her breasts and thighs. She looked up at the mahogany and *ceiba* trees, their branches and leaves meshed into a plush, green-black canopy above her. She narrowed her eyes taking in the colors: deep green, amber, black, emerald, yellow, orange. She was dazzled by the jungle that teemed with butterflies, birds and flowers. Everywhere she looked there was dampness, richness, beauty. She closed her eyes and listened to the roar of the cascade and the incessant cacophony of the forest. Her body and soul floated. Adriana remained there for a long while as her mind filled with Juana's image, her own struggle with feelings of abandonment, and her new life among the insurgents.

Chapter 7

Our people built that church.

Juana's body was limp as it surrendered to the curve of the hammock where she had lain awake during the long hours of night. The storm had passed; only the echo of thunder rumbled as it crashed against the distant mountains. The camp was silent except for the repeated whistles of sentries, signaling that the compound was secure.

She felt a breeze whip under the hammock, lifting moisture sucked from the dampened jungle floor. There were gaps in the *palapa's* thatched roof, and through them, Juana's eyes gazed high above at the blackened canopy of entangled *ceiba* and mahogany trees. Her vision was riveted on the treetops, but her mind was concentrated on the impending crisis facing the insurgents. She closed her eyes, trying to capture some moments of rest, but from deep behind her lids Adriana's face emerged.

Juana shivered, making her think that rain had dripped onto her through the thatching, wetting her shoulders, or perhaps her hips. She ran her hands up and down her body, examining, touching, but found that she was dry. She sighed, realizing that it had been Adriana's image that had made her shudder.

Easing herself back into the hammock, Juana wrapped her arms around her head. With her eyes closed, she contemplated the sentiment she had never before experienced. She turned on her side, curling in on herself, unable as yet to understand what she was feeling, yet clinging and yielding to its allure because it brought her solace and serenity.

Juana sighed deeply and closed her eyes; she forced herself to think back on her life, hoping to discover in her past a similar sentiment, one that would explain what she was now feeling. Memories quickly wrapped themselves around her thoughts, transporting her back to her childhood.

∽ ∽ ∽

Juana Galván labored under the burden of woven shawls, *huipiles* and sashes piled high on her back. The bundle was secured by a band strapped around her forehead, and except for her bare feet, her diminutive figure was nearly obscured by the huge pile. Dawn had just broken. Streaks of sunlight were cutting their way through the narrow stone passages of San Cristóbal de las Casas, past colonial façades, wrapping church spires and bell towers in a golden shroud.

She had just turned fourteen, but Juana had been doing this work since before she could remember. Every Wednesday, she and her mother made their way from the outskirts of the city towards the open market, where they would set their wares on blankets stretched out on cobblestones. There they would spend most of the day, selling what the women of the tribe had fabricated.

The city and the surrounding valleys had been lashed by a storm the night before, transforming the streets and plazas into muddy streams. The heat, churned up by the tropical rain, was already rising, and Juana felt sweat sliding its way down her back, dripping to her ankles. The temperature intensified as the women trudged past the Zócalo, a vast square dominated by the cathedral. As she walked, Juana turned to the left to catch a glimpse of the distant sierra, almost always shrouded in thick clouds. She then turned to the right, trying to see the top of the huge crucifix planted in the center of the square, but the weight on her back kept her from raising her head and eyes. It was easier for her to trace its shadow, which covered nearly all of the plaza. She felt a slight shudder because, just as everyone else did, she knew it to be the place where people had been flogged by the *patrones* up to just a few years before.

She followed her mother as she made her way around corners and past alleyways. After a while, she stopped to catch her breath. When she looked up, Juana saw that her mother had also stopped and was leaning against her goods. The girl didn't have to wait to be told to put down her load. Together mother and daughter rested on top of their colorful mounds, each breathing deeply, knowing that they still had a way to go before reaching the stalls of the *mercado*.

After a few minutes of rest, a smile spread across Juana's face. She felt a sudden surge of playfulness overcome her when she saw that the fringe of her mother's rebozo, which encircled her waist, dangled behind her almost dragging to the ground. Juana giggled softly to herself, remembering the many times her mother had scolded her in disapproval of the pranks she often played on her sisters and the other village girls.

In spite of the threat of a reprimand, Juana found that she could not resist giving into temptation, so she crept over behind her mother's back and softly, silently, took the fringe of the shawl and wrapped it tightly around the cord that bound the bundle on which her mother sat. Then, even more stealthily, while struggling to smother her laughter, Juana moved back to her own things and waited.

Soon enough her mother tried to get to her feet, only to be yanked back onto her haunches. She struggled again only to have a repeated force pull her back down. She jerked and squirmed, jiggling her legs, until she finally understood. She smiled to herself and relaxed, but not before snapping her head in Juana's direction, shattering the girl's self-control as she burst out in a fit of laughter that doubled her over in cramps. Juana's laughter was so filled with girlish mischief and mirth that it infected her mother, who joined her, laughing first softly with a closed mouth, then in a loud, wide-open belly laugh.

Mother and daughter laughed without restraint, so much that other people stopped whatever they were doing, and they, too, chuckled without knowing exactly why they were laughing. All this was happening in front of the Church of Santo Domingo, where people were rushing up the steps to make it in time for early mass. Even those men and women stopped in their tracks and joined in the fun.

As Juana wiped tears from her cheeks, she gazed silently at her mother, wishing that they could be that happy always. But when she saw her face return to its usual sad expression, Juana realized that it had been only a brief moment that would soon disappear. Trying to dispel that thought, Juana looked upward at the imposing façade. She could not remember the number of times she had stood in that place, looking up in that way, always feeling the same astonishment. Each time she was drawn by the ornate stonework, the niches, the statues of saints. She looked at it not because she found it beautiful, but because of intense curiosity and because it helped her forget her mother's unhappy face.

She wondered how it was that an artisan could carve a piece of stone until it looked like a *patrón*, the owners and bosses of the haciendas. Even the winged figures looked like the women of the haciendas and city mansions. How could it be, she asked, that a stone nose could be chiseled to look like one of a mestizo? The same happened with eyes, chins, mouths, hands. As always, she wondered what those statues and stone robes concealed. Was the body of a man or a woman under that rock? Since Juana had never seen the body of a white person, woman or man, she could not know how they might look; so she wondered.

Suddenly, the bells of the church began to ring, calling people to mass. The metallic clanging was so loud that Juana felt its vibrations tug at her hair and pound on her chest. She looked over to her mother, who had freed her rebozo, and saw that she was already on her way to the stalls lined up behind the church. She got to her feet and struggled with her load until she balanced it on her back. In a few moments she caught up to her mother, shuffling briskly as she watched her point repeatedly toward the church.

Our people built that church with the sweat of their bodies.

Juana silently mouthed what she knew her mother was saying as she pointed at the church with a short, skinny finger. The thought of women toting stones instead of shawls made Juana grateful that priests no longer ordered such places to be constructed. The image of stooped women abruptly halted her, and she envisioned the people who had been forced to build that church. Without thinking, Juana let the bundle slip off her shoulders as she recalled a story her mother often told.

∽ ∽ ∽

At that time their city was named Ciudad Real. That had been so many generations before Juana that all she knew was that it had been during the first reign of the white masters. It was a time when women who had been her ancestors trudged up and down the mountain to mine stones for the church. Her mother told her that there was among them a special woman, singled out by her resistance to the bosses, as well as by the scar that marred the skin above her left eyebrow. Every day, that woman staggered down the steep, narrow path, bent low under the burden of a stone-filled basket. Its handles were strapped around her forehead; its weight pressed against her curved spine.

On a certain day, the woman's hands reached backward, clinging to the load so that it would not shift from one side to the other. She moved slowly, deliberately, knowing that a false step would send her headlong down into a ravine. She turned and looked upward to the pinnacle of the mountain, toward the long line of women: brown, bent, sweating, intense on accomplishing the same task. In the rarefied air of the high altitude, the human snake gingerly coiled its way down, stooped and breathing slowly through its opened mouth.

After a few moments, she swiveled her head forward, concentrating on her next step. When she reached the bottom of the trail, she dumped the rocks onto the growing mound, then she turned around and began a fresh ascent to the mouth of the stone quarry.

She and other women of her tribe had been doing this for years. Each day, they wearily climbed the mountain, then returned down the slopes, ridding the cavern of the stones loosened by men who dug with picks as well as fingernails. Here stones were produced for the new city named Ciudad Real.

"¡Más rápido, indios perezosos!"

The foreman barked out his offensive demand for more speed, more efficiency. The woman, however, did not heed his words; she had heard them for too many years. They had been uttered in different forms, by different lips, at different times, but the meaning never changed. She instead focused her thoughts on the load under which she struggled.

It was dark by the time the shift was halted. Wordlessly, the men and women took knapsacks and other possessions, and headed for town. There they were forced to attend evening mass. She walked slowly, her back still bent because it had forgotten how to become straight even without a load. As she made her way to the Church of Santo Domingo, she chewed on a piece of *yuca*. She held each pulpy bite in her mouth to soften it because her teeth were decaying and loose.

Soon she and the others entered the high vaulted church, where the heavy odor of incense and burning candles curled itself into her nostrils. She felt nauseous, but she ignored her churning stomach as she joined the women and men of her tribe, squatting on the stone floor, backs bent, eyes drooping under the weight of fatigue.

She nailed her vision to the floor as she rubbed her fingers first on the scar over her eyebrow, then on the floor's surface, wondering if that stone was one of many she had carted down the mountain. She remained that way, hunched over her crossed legs, not looking toward the high altar. She was too tired to lift her eyes.

෴ ෴ ෴

The woman's stooped, haggard silhouette suddenly melted into the vaporous air, vanishing from Juana's eyes, which had become bright with tears of pity and admiration for that woman. Although she desired to be with that distant ancestor, she realized that she had fallen behind, so she snapped out of her trance and picked up her pace in an attempt to reach her mother.

As she neared the marketplace, the charred maize aroma of *elotes asados* was the first to coil itself through Juana's nostrils, and soon this blended with the smell of *panuchos* being served to a merchant who made his way to his store. Fragrant scents collided with the pungent, acrid odors of spoiled vegetables, moldy corncobs, rancid fruit, muddy corners. Everywhere there was noise, a clamor made up of vendors hawking wares, buyers driving a bargain, babies crying, dogs barking, bells clanging, dirty-faced children playing and shouting at one another.

When Juana finally caught up with her mother, she found her already sitting on her heels, unfolding shawls and placing them on mats. Juana's father, who had gone ahead of them, was securing a corner of the canvas that hung overhead, protecting them from the glare of the sun. She got down on her knees where she, too, sat on her heels as she began to put out the garments she had carted. They were silent.

Hours passed. People came to examine certain pieces, to ask prices, then tried to lower them. Some women bought blouses, or belts; others merely looked and walked away. Juana felt drowsy and hungry, but she knew that her mother would soon bring out the bag that held their tortillas and beans. The thought of food made the girl's mouth water.

Juana looked at her mother, letting her know that she was hungry, but her mother ignored her. Juana was about to ask if something was wrong, when a man stepped under the canvas and stood in silence holding a straw hat in his hands. Juana stared at him; she had seen him before in the village. She remembered that at times he would follow her and would not take his eyes off of her.

"*Juana, ven acá.*"

Her face snapped toward the side of the stall from where her father was calling her. He was sitting cross-legged, with his back rigid, and he held his hands, palms down, on his knees. Her mother sat behind him, as usual, on her heels. Juana obeyed and moved toward him. She, too, got down on her knees and sat on her heels. He spoke in the Tzeltal tongue, as they always did when they were alone.

"Do you know this man?"

"No, Tata."

"His name is Cruz Ochoa. You may greet him."

Juana knew that this was not a permission that her father was granting; it was a command. Juana felt her stomach begin to ache, knowing that something terrible was about to happen. She nevertheless turned to the man and nodded. He returned her gesture.

She continued to look at Cruz Ochoa, taking in his face and his body. He was not old, yet older than she. He was not handsome, yet not ugly. She saw by his dress that he was not a Tzeltal man but a Lacandón. He wore the white cotton tunic of those people, and he wore his hair in their fashion: straight, covering the forehead down to the eyebrows, and long enough to reach the shoulders.

Juana stretched her neck and looked behind her father to where her mother crouched. She saw that her eyes were cast down, but she could see by the frown pasted on her face that she was feeling sadness for her daughter. Juana returned her gaze to her father's face, but his eyes were riveted on a point somewhere above her head. She could hear people coming and going by their stall, but she knew that they were stragglers, because it was not the time of day to market; that hour had passed. She turned her head toward the man, who stood without saying anything.

"*Buenas tardes.*" Juana spoke in Spanish, since she did not know the Lacandón tongue.

"*Buenas tardes, niña.*"

The brief greeting was followed by more silence because no one could speak until Juana's father gave permission. Finally, he spoke.

"This man will be your husband. He is willing to take you as his wife, to live in the Lacandona, where you will have his children. He is a man of influence. He even owns a mule, which he has offered to sell in exchange for you. I have accepted his offer."

Juana felt as if a hand had gripped her throat, cutting off the air that her lungs needed to breathe. Vivid pictures of her three older sisters flashed in her brain. One by one, they, too, had been married by her father and at an age even younger than hers. She saw them as they grew thin and sickly with each pregnancy. She saw them losing their teeth after being battered by drunken husbands. She saw them become sullen women, worn out before their time.

She looked at her mother, and for the first time in her life, Juana realized that she, too, had undergone the same brutal treatment as had her sisters, as well as the other women of the tribe. Juana saw that although her mother was not more than thirty-five years old, she was toothless, her breasts sagged, her hair was ragged and gray, and her skin was blotched. This realization made her shiver because she knew now that this would also be her fate, and she did not want this for herself. She did not want to marry Cruz Ochoa, or anyone else.

At that instant, the image of the woman stooped under an intolerable burden of stones again came to Juana. The picture was vivid, stark, haunting, and she was so shaken by the turmoil she was experiencing that she sprang to her feet in an attempt to run away. Her father, however, moved faster than she, and he was able to grab one of her ankles as she lunged toward the street. She tripped, lost her balance and fell on her face, splitting her upper lip on the cobblestones. When she rolled over, her face was covered with blood.

෴ ෴ ෴

The hammock swayed slowly, responding to the motion of Juana's hands. She moved her arms upward to her face, where her fingers touched her lips, her nose, her cheeks. She massaged the scar over her eye, reminding herself that it had not been caused by her fall in the marketplace, but by something that happened later on. This thought moved her mind to take flight again, back towards the years that had launched her on the path that led her to this encampment, to the struggle for which she was now a leader, and to the mystery of what she was feeling for Adriana Mora.

Chapter 8

The soil was gray; it had no color.

Two weeks after meeting him, Juana stood by Cruz Ochoa on a side altar at the rear of the Church of Santo Domingo. The mass and marriage ritual were over and the altar boy was snuffing out the candles. The family members and friends who had attended began to leave without saying anything; they only patted the couple on the shoulders or on the arms. Juana's mother was the only one to approach the couple to offer a blessing. After that, everyone dispersed, and Juana followed Cruz Ochoa as he led the way to the second-class bus station. She carried her belongings in a small cardboard box.

Juana was glad that Cruz was silent because she did not want to speak. She felt dejected and would not have known what to say to him if he did attempt a conversation. She knew, however, that sooner or later he would approach her. In the meantime, she distracted herself by looking around at the crowds of people waiting their turn to board buses. She looked in one direction and saw people elbowing and shoving one another to get to the front of the line. She turned her gaze in the opposite direction and saw a woman, a little older than she, with a child hanging on to her skirt, another one wrapped in her rebozo, and another in her womb. A man, who Juana was certain was the husband, stood apart with his straw hat pulled low over his brow. Everywhere Juana looked she saw people from different tribes, each wearing their native garments. She saw some like her, the Tzeltales, but there were Chol, Tzotzil, Zoque, Lacandón; there were even poor mestizos in the crowd.

Juana shut her eyes and mopped her forehead with the back of her hand. It had not rained in several days and the air was sweltering, oppressive. Most of the passengers were irritable and impatient to leave the city, hoping to find relief from the heat once in the countryside.

"Ruta número cinco dirección Huixtán, Oxchue, Chol, Ocosingo. ¡Pasajeros abordo!"

The shrill voice over the loudspeaker bleated out the route that would take Juana and Cruz Ochoa to the point of their first transfer. From Ocosingo, they would take another bus to their final destination, El Caribal. As soon as people were able to make out the muffled announcement they had just heard, the shoving became intense. Juana was barely able to hang on to her box as the flood of travelers pressed toward the front entrance of the vehicle. Since the men pushed the hardest, they were the first to find seats, leaving most of the women and children standing in the middle aisle, or sitting there on their bundles and boxes.

Seeing that Cruz had secured a place for himself at the front, Juana was glad that she had been shoved all the way to the rear. She edged back as far as possible, placed her box on the floor, sat on it and leaned her body back. When she looked down the aisle, she saw that most of the women would have to stand in uncomfortable postures until they got off the bus, making her even more grateful for her place. From where she sat, she could see Cruz's square head and flinty eyes as he turned to stare at her from time to time.

The driver got on the bus and sat at his seat, turned the key in the ignition and cranked the engine. Loud backfires erupted from the rusty muffler, and everyone instinctively held onto whatever they could, knowing that the trip would not be smooth. Juana braced herself for the trip from San Cristóbal to El Caribal, the village where she would now live. The village was distant, on the fringes of the Lacandona Jungle, and because the bus would stop at most of the towns and settlements along the way, the journey would take between seven and eight hours.

The bus rumbled onto Highway 190 southbound, then on to 186 eastbound, but just as the driver picked up speed and Juana felt that some distance would be covered, the vehicle pulled over. Its first stop was Los Llanos, then after a short while they halted again at Huixtán, and onward, stopping almost every fifteen minutes. In the beginning, Juana was relieved when she saw that several passengers stepped down, but her mood changed when she realized that more people got on than got off. This happened at each stop, until she thought that the bus would explode if more passengers were taken on board.

Three hours later, the bus rolled into Oxchue. At the time, Juana was drowsing, almost asleep, but the bumpy stop awakened her with a jerk. She looked up to see that Cruz was once again looking back at her. She decided to ignore him, thinking that each time he craned his neck and face toward her, his eyes became smaller. His eyes frightened her; they were tiny slits, like those of a wooden mask that glinted at her, boring into her, cutting like a knife.

"*¡Media hora, más o menos! ¡Todos abajo!*"

The driver was grumpy as he shouted that everyone was to get off the bus; they would have at least a half-hour wait. Juana was grateful for the chance to stand; her legs were cramped and her buttocks ached from crouching. She gathered her box in her arms and followed the press of bodies off the bus. It was near dusk, the heat was diminishing and the passengers didn't mind walking down the dirt path that took them to food stalls and roaming vendors.

As Juana strolled, happy to exercise her legs, she passed butcher stalls where chunks of raw beef and pork were hung out on giant hooks. She looked at the pieces of meat, blackened with flies and dirt. The smell disgusted her, making her nauseous, forcing her to cross the highway to the other side, where grocers had erected their stands. In contrast to the putrid stench of rancid flesh, this side of the road brought the aroma of tortillas cooking on *comales,* blending with the fragrance of fresh popcorn.

"*¿Quiere palomitas?*"

Juana whirled around, startled by the outstretched hand offering her a bag of popcorn. She had forgotten about Cruz, but now his face, so close to hers that she felt his breath on her cheeks, reminded her of his presence in her life. Dejection again flooded over her. Yet his offering struck her as thoughtful, unexpected, and she smiled stiffly as she put down her box so that she could take the small bag. He intercepted her move, taking hold of the parcel. She responded in Spanish, *"Gracias."*

She nibbled the fluffy corn without saying anymore while walking, aware that Cruz was by her side. They continued until the structures ended; beyond that point only tiny *palapas* could be seen in the thick of palm fronds and banana trees. Juana, with nowhere to go, turned around, intending to head back where the bus was parked, but she felt Cruz take her by the arm and edge her toward the rear of the last stand. There the grass grew taller than she and almost as tall as Cruz.

Juana resisted, but his grip on her arm only tightened. She knew what he was going to do. She knew that she did not want it to happen, but she also knew that there was nothing she could do to avoid it. It was inevitable, she had already told herself. It would come sooner or later. Cruz nudged Juana toward the thickest part of the growth, forced her down to the ground, onto her knees, out of sight.

"¡Quítese los calzones!"

Repugnance and nausea flooded Juana when Cruz ordered her to take off her pants, but she knew that if she did not do as he ordered, he would beat her until she obeyed him. It would be no use shouting for help; no one interfered when a husband demanded what was considered to be his due from a wife. Juana removed her pants as Cruz stood looking down at her. She saw that with one hand he was lifting the tunic that reached his knees. He shoved her onto her back with the other one.

"¡Abra las piernas!"

She let herself roll back on the grass and opened her legs as he had commanded. She clamped shut her eyes, not wanting to see him come down on her because she knew what he was going to do. She had seen it happen many times to girls and women of the tribe. She had seen a man take a girl as she planted maize, or as she wove a *huipil,* or as she put tortillas on the pan. She had seen her father do it to her mother. She had seen her sisters pinned down to earthen floors, straddled by men they called their husbands.

Pain coursed up from her vagina to her brain. She felt that she was suffocating. The weight of Cruz's body pressed the air out of her lungs, forcing her to gasp over and again. She clawed at the damp earth, hoping to diminish the pain that intensified each time he plunged in and out of her for what seemed an interminable time. Finally, he gasped, shuddered and sighed. Then he rolled off her, coiled and pressed in on himself.

Juana lay motionless, unable to move. It took time for the pain to diminish, allowing her to control her racing heart. She ran her hands up and down between her inner thighs, trying to wipe away the thick discharge that coated them. After a few minutes, she thought she heard Cruz snore softly, but when he sprang to his feet, she knew that she had been wrong. He looked at her with blank, squinty eyes.

"¡*Vámonos!*"

Juana stumbled to her feet as she struggled with her clothes and fumbled in the grass for her box. She followed Cruz to the bus, where she found that most of the passengers were already seated. She realized that they were staring at her because they knew what had happened. She realized that Cruz had asked the man seated next to him to watch his belongings while he was with his wife.

She made her way back to her place and sat staring through a dirty, cracked window, wondering, for the first time, why her father had given her to Cruz Ochoa for the price of a mule. She stretched out her hands on her lap, palms up, as she examined them, seeing that they were smeared with mud and blood. The thought crossed Juana's mind that although she might look the same, she was different because she had crossed over a bridge that took her to an unknown land, which she neither loved nor hated. Her feet were now planted on soil that was gray; it had no color.

◁ ◁ ◁

In the darkness of her *palapa*, Juana brought her hands close to her face, fingers outstretched, palms in front of her eyes as she remembered how resentment and disgust for her father replaced her first childlike questionings. It happened during the grayness of the first years of her life with Cruz Ochoa. She squinted her eyes in the gloom, then she closed them, trying to remember another color, but it was of no use the murkiness of those months that had passed into years washed over her memories. She turned her head to one side as her thoughts once again leaped over the *ceiba* trees, scurried through palm fronds, hovered over rivers and ravines, until reaching those past years of her life in El Caribal.

Chapter 9

She felt that floating would turn to flying.

El Caribal, a village on the fringe of the Lacandona Jungle, 1978.
Torrential rain had deluged El Caribal for three days and nights
without letup. The narrow river that fringed the cluster of huts had
swollen and flooded, dragging trees and chunks of mud downstream.
Animals howled in protest as thunder and lightning caused the earth
to shake disturbing their hideaways. At night, when the jungle was at
its blackest, streaks of light flashed on and off, sending terror through
the dense growth of ferns and giant trees.

In her *palapa,* Juana was lying on a *petate* on the earthen floor.
Except for a small fire, the place was dark. She was covered with
sweat, slowly regaining consciousness, blinking her eyes as she tried
to dislodge the coating that blurred them. In a few minutes, forms
began to take shape as she looked over to the corner of the hut where
she was able to make out the silhouettes of three women. They were
the village midwives: toothless old women with wrinkled, parched
skin, shoulders stooped from years spent toting loads to the marketplace, hands gnarled from a lifetime of toiling in the fields.

Juana concentrated on their heads and faces, trying to clear her
brain. She took in more of the women's appearance, seeing how their
hair was braided but disheveled and streaked with gray. After a few
moments, she realized that from her place near the side of the hut she
could make out only profiles: beaked noses, flabby jowls, hollow
mouths, furrowed necks. For a time, Juana was vaguely aware that
they were speaking in hushed tones. She concentrated. In a few min-

69

utes her hearing became attuned, and she could make out their whispering. It sounded like dry fronds scraping on bark.

"*El niño se murió.*"

"*Nomás no puede. Pobrecita mujer.*"

Juana's hands moved to feel her abdomen. It was empty. The child had slipped out between her legs, and it had done so soundlessly because it was dead. She felt her heart shiver. She dragged her hands to her breast and rubbed, trying to stop the trembling. Then she clasped her hands on her ears because she did not want to hear the hags pitying her, repeating over and again how she could not keep a child in her womb long enough to deliver it alive.

More lightning flashed, filling the *palapa* with a light charged with violence, made more threatening by the explosion of thunder that followed almost immediately. Juana felt the earth under her shift; it too was filled with fear. Four years had passed since her father had sent her away with Cruz, and this was the third child she had lost. Remembering this pushed her into a pit of sadness, made intolerable to her because her grief was coated with dread.

"*Pobre hombre.*"

"*Buen hombre.*"

"*Desafortunado hombre.*"

Poor man. Good man. Unfortunate man. The toothless mutterings of the midwives reached her again, this time sympathizing with Cruz Ochoa, pitying him for having a useless woman as his wife. Juana filled with desperation, wondering why they pitied him and not her. Inside of her a voice asked why did they not understand that each child had been conceived in fear and repugnance, robbing it of a reason to live. She turned her head away from the silhouettes, hoping that she would again lose consciousness, making them disappear, wishing that a bolt of lightning would strike her, erase her from that hut, erase her existence.

In the village, Cruz Ochoa was considered a good man. He neither drank alcohol nor did he beat his wife. For these two reasons alone, the women of the tribe envied Juana, because in most *palapas,* drunkenness and battering were common. What no one knew, however, was that Cruz was a man filled with anger, with a rage that washed over Juana every time he glanced at her, every time he commanded her to open her legs. No one knew that the intoxication that possessed him was caused not by alcohol, but by fathomless bitterness. No one knew that although he did not beat her with his fists, he attacked her with eyes filled with ire.

Days after the last miscarriage, Juana emerged to return to her tasks, grateful that Cruz had, at least for a while, disappeared into the jungle. In her heart she wished that he might be devoured by jaguars, poisoned by serpents, swallowed by a river, but her mind yanked her from these thoughts, reminding her that he would, in time, return. She braced herself, not knowing how he would vent his rage on her this time. During his absence, her mind filled with questions: *Why was Cruz so embittered? Why did he hate her, yet bury himself in her body with such abandonment? Why did he not speak to her as other men did to their wives?* The answers to these questions never came to her. She resigned herself to living with a man filled with shadows.

One day, Juana knelt by the river, washing clothes. She was lost in thought, oblivious to the other women who chattered, exchanging gossip. The rain had stopped, but the river was still swollen, dragging tree trunks and dead animals down its course. Some of the women had tied their skirts around their hips, wanting to keep dry, but Juana had not bothered; she was wet up to her waist. Her motions were listless, mechanical, as she rubbed soap onto a shirt, then scrubbed it against the flat rock at which she worked, then rinsed the garment in the rushing current. All the time, she was thinking about how much she wanted to vanish.

Suddenly, a fist from behind struck her neck, plunging her headlong into the muddy water. The force of the blow knocked her unconscious. She did not feel the pain of her face scraping against a rough surface, nor was she aware that Cruz had leaped into the current, grabbed her by the neck, and dragged her limp body from the river. Had she not been unconscious, Juana would have resisted him, hoping that her wish to be erased might have come true by drowning.

When she regained consciousness, she was on her back, where Cruz had thrown her. Her face and nose were bleeding, making it hard for her to see, but after a while, when she was able to make out his features, she saw that this time he would go beyond just spilling his disdain for her through his eyes. She realized that his fists would pound her with a strength that matched the bitterness that was devouring him.

Juana and Cruz glared at one another for moments before she leaped to her feet and ran, slipping over the muddy banks of the river, regaining her balance by clawing into the soil with her fingers. She did not have a direction or place to go. Her legs simply obeyed the compelling impulse to escape Cruz, who sprinted behind, narrowing the distance between them, until she could feel his fingertips grazing her back.

He latched on to her blouse, ripping it off, leaving her naked except for her skirt. He grabbed her shoulder with one hand, and with the other he spun her around to face him. Juana tried to defend herself by pushing against him, by trying to wiggle loose from his clutch, but it was useless; his grip was as strong as a vise. Then she saw one of his arms rise above his head, fist clenched. When it struck her face above the left eye, intense pain froze her brain, and the day lost its light as blackness again enveloped her.

Juana awakened to find that she was lying in mud. She put her hands to her face. It was puffed, bruised. She realized that she could see with only one eye because the other one, the one that had received the blow, was swollen shut; the gash above it was deep and still bleeding. Then she put her hands to her breasts and felt the nipples hardening under her touch. She shivered, relieved that Cruz had not mutilated her body.

She stayed there until her thoughts cleared, until she could think of what to do next. One thought dominated the others: She had to leave Cruz Ochoa. She had to separate her life from his. She had to escape, even if it meant being devoured by the jungle. When this thought came more clearly into focus, she struggled to her feet, stumbling and tripping again as she made her way toward the river's edge. There she began, with difficulty, to remove the clothing still on her body. Her hands were bloody and her fingers were so bruised that taking off her clothes was painful, but finally she was completely stripped.

Naked, Juana stepped into the water and waded towards its center, where it was deepest and where the current was the strongest. It crossed her mind that surrendering to the rage of the river would be better than submitting to Cruz. When she was at the point where her feet no longer touched the ground, she allowed her body to submerge, covering her breasts, neck and head. Slack and inert, she floated downstream as the force of the current carried her with growing speed. Instead of resisting, she surrendered to its pull, not knowing where it would lead her, but satisfied that it was taking her away from Cruz Ochoa.

Wanting, intending to die, Juana floated with the current of the river, grateful for its energy and speed, thankful for its embrace, which would carry her to oblivion. But as she yielded to its flow, she began to feel an emotion that contradicted her desire to vanish. It was a small sentiment at first, but one that grew with each second, intensifying, possessing her entirely, and in a while she recognized the feeling: it was the desire to live. Eyes closed, arms extended away from her sides, she felt that floating would turn to flying, and that once airborne, she would find liberation. She opened her good eye and saw that day had turned to night. She flipped her body over and began to swim across the current toward land.

Juana walked for hours through the darkened jungle, oblivious of its dangers, never once thinking of the coiled snake or the hiding *jabalí*. She walked, her nakedness and her bruised face forgotten. She moved, not caring in what direction she was going, knowing that sooner or later she would come to a village, where she would be given shelter. She stumbled upon such a place at dawn, when the women were busy preparing breakfast.

"*Me llamo Juana Galván. Necesito quedarme aquí.*"

"*Está bien. Quédate aquí.*"

No one seemed surprised. Her nakedness and battered face told them she was escaping, and they took Juana in as one of them. She remained in that village, working with its women, earning the food she ate and the hut where she slept. She did not allow herself to think of Cruz Ochoa, nor of his village. Whenever she was assaulted by those thoughts, she forced herself to erase them from her mind. In that

way, Juana passed several months, aware that although her body had
healed, her spirit was shattered.

One evening, three women came to her. They sat down cross-
legged on the earthen floor to face each other over the small fire that
Juana continually fed with twigs.

"Tu hombre te busca."

"Vino a la aldea mientras sembrabas maíz."

"Dice que te llevará con él."

These words stunned Juana, making her stomach ache. Each
woman took her turn uttering what sounded like evil incantations.

"Your man is looking for you."

"He came to the village while you were planting maize."

"He says that he will take you with him."

Cruz Ochoa had stalked her, hunted her, and found her. She put
her fingers to the scar over her eye; the skin was still tender, and she
winced, feeling pain under the pressure of her finger. Juana's mind, its
thoughts scattered and disrupted by what she had been told, soon
focused. Cruz had found her, and he had spoken to the villagers. That
meant that he had been watching her, waiting to ensnare her. Her back
stiffened as she understood that he had been secretly spying on her for
a time, perhaps days, or even weeks. While she was unaware of his
presence, his disdainful eyes had been riveted on her as she walked,
planted, ate, and even as she slept. Her head snapped toward the *palapa's* entrance, expecting to find him standing there.

"¿Dónde está?"

"Afuera."

Juana had not been wrong. Cruz was waiting outside the hut.
Knowing this cast her into a pit of sadness. She could not help or control the tears that welled first in her heart, moved up to lodge behind
her eyelids, and finally spilled over her cheeks. She understood that
her liberation had been a false one, that it had been a trap that had just
slammed shut, catching her inside.

In silence, Juana got to her feet to gather her things, which she
then rolled into the *petate.* She lashed it over her shoulder and stepped
out of the hut without saying a word to the women. Cruz was standing under a gnarled, stunted *ceiba* tree with his hat pulled down low

over his brow. Juana could not make out his eyes, but she knew the fire that was burning there. Without saying anything, he turned to make his way into the jungle, and with a silence that matched his, Juana followed Cruz Ochoa back to his village.

Not noticing if it was day or night, she lost track of time as they trekked through the jungle. She lost a connection with her body, not caring whether it was tired, or hungry, or needing to relieve itself. She followed Cruz, watching his back and the rear of his sandaled feet, watching as he hacked a way through the dense jungle with a machete.

It was morning when Juana and Cruz made their way though the center of the village, he in front and she several paces behind him. She was aware of the villagers' stares; she felt the impact as those harsh looks pasted themselves onto her body. She could hear the secret thoughts crossing the minds of those women and men.

"Mala mujer."

"Bad woman."

"She deserves to be punished."

"Buen hombre."

"Good man."

"He does not deserve such a woman."

Juana stiffened her back and straightened her shoulders, rejecting the villagers' scornful thoughts. She felt bewildered by the pitiless looks cast on her by the women as she passed by them, so close that she could almost feel the fringes of their *huipiles*. She knew that they suffered similar cruelties from the men in their families, and yet they apparently chose to deny it, refusing to recognize what she was feeling. As Juana walked behind Cruz Ochoa, she wondered if those women secretly felt sympathy for her, if they privately wished that she had escaped, and whether, out of fear, they were hiding it instead.

෨ ෨ ෨

In the *palapa,* Juana snorted through her nose, remembering. She now knew that the women had indeed wished that she might have escaped. Now she knew that they, too, were waiting for someone like her to show them the way, that their gossiping and words against her had been a pretense. She now knew this because when she finally left Cruz Ochoa, dozens of women had come to join the army of *compañeras* and *compañeros*. They were women who would never again return to those huts in which misery had encased them.

Chapter 10

The gods made men and women of maize.

El Caribal, 1980.

"The gods made men of gold, but those men were hard, arrogant, unbending and ungrateful to their makers."

Juana Galván sat on her heels, bent over a *metate*. She was grinding corn for *masa,* which she would then pat into tortillas. Most of the women of the village were busy at the same chore; they worked in the clearing around which the *palapas* and other living areas were clustered. The scraping of stone on stone floated in the air. Despite the din a man's voice was clear. He spoke in Spanish, but Juana and the rest of the women could understand every word.

"Seeing this, the gods were dissatisfied with what they had done, and so they made new men. This time they were made of wood. But they, too, were unbending and stupid, so once again the gods repented."

Juana stopped what she was doing to listen more intently. What the man was saying was not new; it was a common belief among the people of the region. What did capture her attention, however, was the sentiment behind the voice. It seemed to be promising something more.

"Then the gods came upon a new inspiration: They made men and women of maize. Those people were flexible, grateful, diligent and just. Soon, the gods saw that their labor had been good, that those made of maize were the true men and women of this world. So they showered those people with land, fruit, and children, making them rich. After this, the gods were satisfied with their work, and they rested."

Juana listened, absentmindedly rubbing bits of *masa* from her fingers. She was thinking of the men of gold and wood. She, like all others of those tribes, had been taught that her people were made of maize.

"Then the men of gold and wood rose in anger against the gods because they had been replaced. They conspired and plotted, envious of the men and women of *maíz* who had inherited the richness of the land. Then, four hundred years ago, they transformed themselves into the *Catxul,* false men, taking back what was given to the people of maize. The *Catxul* now govern our lives because they possess war machines to protect their brutal conquest. The servants of the *Catxul* are the *Aluxob*, the liars who make up the false government that rules us, the ones who deceive us and oblige us to forget our past. Together, these evil men have spread death and pain among us."

Juana by this time was intrigued by the man's words. She looked around and saw that other women were listening as well. She saw that not only women were interested, but also men.

"Do you not long for another life? Would you not like to be educated like the men and women of gold? What about you, the women—would you not want to feed your children better food? Don't you want to give them medicine when they are sick?"

She sat back on her haunches, thinking. Six years had passed since she had been married to Cruz Ochoa, two since she had attempted to escape from her life with him. He had stalked her and found her, and she had followed him to his village, unresisting, knowing that any struggle would be futile. At the time, she had realized that to refuse to return to his hut would mean death. Although she had desired death rather than life with him, something inside of her had compelled her to cling to life.

Juana put her fingers to the scar over her left eye; she stroked it over and over again. The skin layered on the gash was slightly discolored, so that it stood out on her forehead like a reflection of the eyebrow beneath it.

Cruz had shown his disdain for her with more intensity since her attempted escape. He was always sullen, angry with her. This, however, had not kept him from accosting her sexually. He often came to her unexpectedly, as she was preparing a meal, or when she was on the hillsides planting seeds, or even when it was the time of month when she bled. At those times he penetrated her with a heat that seemed to pour out of his skin, but never again did Juana get pregnant.

"Are you not tired of being told whom to marry and when to do it? Would you not want to choose your own partner? Would you not want to say when you are to have children, and how many?"

Juana was impressed by the stranger's words because he had uttered them just as she was thinking of Cruz. She wanted to believe that there was hope for a different life, but she mistrusted what he was saying because she thought that the choices he proposed were impossible; they went against everything she and others had been taught.

"Look, everybody! I want you to know that we're gathering, up there in the mountain. Men and women just like you, who are tired, fed up! We need you. We need the strength of your arms and legs, we need your intelligence, but above all, we need your courage. We are the people of maize who are faceless right now, but soon we will regain the face that was erased by the *Catxul* so long ago. We will fight until that face is returned to us. When that happens, you must be with us."

Juana got to her feet, forgetting about the dough and about the tortillas that she should already have made. Her hands and forearms were crusted with the yellow paste; even her hair and nose were smeared with it. She stood because she wanted to speak to the stranger; she needed to know more about what he had said.

"I want to hear more of what you're saying."

"*Compañera,* that's why I'm here. What's your name?"

"Juana Galván."

"Juana, my name is Orlando Flores. I'm a Lacandón."

Juana was at a loss as to where to begin. She fidgeted, scraping *masa* off her fingers and arms while she thought of what to say to Orlando Flores. She finally blurted out what first came to her mind.

"Are there others like you?"

"Do you mean others who think and hope for the same thing as I do? Yes. There are many others. They're just beginning to gather—up there. Why don't you come and see?"

Orlando pointed with his chin in the direction of the mountains and the heart of the Lacandón Jungle. He smiled and Juana saw uneven teeth poking through a thin, drooping mustache. She examined his face and body, seeing that he was dressed in the white cotton tunic typical of his people. When she looked at his feet, she saw that they were too large for his body and that, despite the heavy *huaraches* he wore, his feet were covered with calluses. Then she noticed that a toe from each foot was missing.

"*Amigo*, are there females up there?"

"Yes. There are many of them."

"Are there only girls?"

"No. There are also women who are married. Some come in couples; others have chosen to leave their husbands."

Juana's eyes widened as she wondered if she had heard Orlando's words correctly. She wrinkled her forehead and narrowed her eyes while she reflected on what he had just said.

"There are married women who have left their husbands?"

"Yes."

"Who feeds those women?"

"We do. We work together and share our food and other supplies."

"What about children?"

"No. There are no children. They are left behind with someone else."

"What about husbands? Do they come by themselves?"

"As with the women, some come in couples, some by themselves."

"Why do they come?"

"To prepare for the day when we will rise against the government that is taking away our lives and our spirits."

"Do you accept only Lacandones?"

"We accept everyone."

Juana stared at Orlando for a few moments, trying to put order to the clash of ideas and thoughts racing through her head. There was much to decipher, but most important of all was her strong attraction to what Orlando was describing. His words seemed to be aimed at her, only her, but when she looked around, she saw that other women were looking in their direction, evidently interested in what was being said.

"*Amigo,* I think you will be destroyed by the *Catxul,* and if we join you, we will be destroyed, too."

"You're wrong, *hermana!* We will *not* be shattered."

"When have our people ever been able to overcome our oppressors? If you can tell me that it's happened before, I'll believe you."

Orlando's face drooped, and Juana moved one step away from him without taking her eyes off of him. As she did this, however, he followed her, coming even closer to her than he was before she had moved. When he spoke, his voice was husky.

"Look, *compañera*, there have been many times when our people have overcome the *Catxul*, but each time they have recuperated because help has come to them in time. That will not happen again. Why? Because we can no longer endure the burden placed on us by them. It's very simple. When there is no more blood in a body, there is no more blood. That's the way it is. The *Catxul* cannot drain us anymore because they have already sucked us dry, and now that we are without blood, we will rise against them, because not to fight is to die."

"What is the name of the group?"

"We don't have one yet, but we will have one very soon."

That evening, Juana and Cruz ate in silence as usual. The distance separating them, she was convinced, was widening with each moment. Her thoughts were in turmoil as she contemplated what Orlando Flores had said about the people who were gathering in the mountains. She wanted to speak to anyone who would listen. She wanted someone to hear that a fire had been ignited inside of her. She needed someone to know that the stranger's words, as she ran them over and again in her mind, added fuel to that fire.

It was early evening, and the jungle had begun its night song. She and Cruz were squatting on the earthen floor of the *palapa* they shared, she on her haunches and he cross-legged, hunched over as he ate. The glowing embers in the small fire pit that separated them crackled as they died out, filling the air with smoke. She knew it was growing cold, and although she was expected to keep it going, she did not try to stoke it.

Juana stopped chewing, her mouth still filled with a half-eaten tortilla. She stared at Cruz, hoping that he would look up and catch the expression in her eyes, but since he did not even glance at her, she took her time examining him. His nose, she thought, had grown longer over the past six years, and his mouth was an inverted half-moon that pulled down his jowls, and the reflections cast by the fading embers cut strange patterns on his face. She put a cupped hand over her mouth and spit its contents out into her palm. She was still hungry, but could no longer eat. The sight of Cruz had churned her stomach into nausea.

Suddenly, his eyes snapped up in her direction. His gesture was so unexpected that she nearly lost her balance, almost toppling over on her side. His eyes were on fire, she thought; they glowed more than did the embers in the fire pit. She braced herself. She knew what was coming.

"*¡Quítese los calzones!*"

His command for her to take off her underpants was the signal for what he intended to do. But when he began to squirm closer to her, crawling on his hands and knees, Juana knew that she was not going to obey Cruz this time. She hunkered in a hostile position, glaring at him as she snatched a charred branch out of the fire. She gripped it with one hand, and with the other she threatened him, thrusting her clenched fist in his direction as she jabbed the burning stick closer and closer to his face, nearly scorching the whiskers under his nose. At the same time, she heard her voice hissing words with unexpected defiance.

"*¡Esta vez, no! ¡Nunca más!*"

Cruz fell back on his rump, gawking at her with disbelief stamped on his face. Juana saw that he was overcome with surprise, that he did not know what to do, and that he was shaken. After a few seconds, however, he lunged at her, pouncing on top of her, momentarily overcoming her with his body weight. But as they rolled over and again in the dirt, she managed to pull up his tunic, exposing his naked rear end. She still gripped the burning stick in her hand, and with a strength prompted by the indignity of six years of obeying his command to take off her underpants, to open her legs, to remain inert while he emptied himself into her—with that energy, she pressed the point of the burning branch against his buttocks with one hand while she held his body with the other one.

"Ahhhgggg!"

Cruz groaned as he rolled over, jiggling his legs, twisting and thrashing in the dirt, trying to yank the stick away, but his contortions kept him from getting a grip on the fiery prong that stuck to his flesh. Juana, her chest heaving with anger and exertion, watched him but did nothing. Finally, he got on his hands and knees and crawled out of the *palapa*, the stick firmly seared onto his rump. He disappeared into the blackened jungle.

Breathing through her mouth because her racing heart blocked her from taking in air through her nose, she waited on the alert, widening her eyes, turning her ears in all directions, hoping they would absorb any hostile sound. She knew that Cruz would return as soon as he regained his composure and understood what had happened. She had defied him, even hurt him. Soon the entire village would know the truth, and Cruz could not sustain the humiliation. She knew also that because of this, he would come to kill her, and no one would prevent him from taking her life. Juana strained her ears, expecting to hear him, but there was only the racket of howling monkeys and the shrill scraping of cicadas and crickets.

Juana was frightened at what she had done because she never imagined that it was in her to do it, to defy Cruz. She was afraid, not knowing what to do next. She crouched, pressing her back against one of the supporting poles of the *palapa*. She brought her knees tight up against her breasts, wrapped her arms around them, and there leaned her head. Her eyes were closed, but her ears were alert. It had grown dark in the hut. Only a few of the embers still glowed, but their light was dying.

She lost track of time. She knew that hours had passed when she noticed that the moon had risen, its rays cutting long shadows on the earthen floor. Then a light flickered in her mind, and Juana knew what she must do. She crawled to the *petate* on which she slept. She unrolled it, put a blouse, underpants, and *huipil* on it, and rolled everything into a bundle, which she put on her back. Last of all, she filled a gourd with water. She walked out of the *palapa* that had served as her cell for six years, knowing in which direction she would go.

Chapter 11

Why don't you come and see?

Juana Galván left the *palapa* in El Caribal and headed west toward the sierra, where she knew she would find Orlando Flores. She knew also that she was going in the direction where the Lacandón Jungle became the thickest, where the trees and growth grew so dense that in some places not even sunlight could penetrate its cover. Her people called it the place of eternal night.

She walked steadily, stopping from time to time only to rest. In places, the undergrowth was so thick that she was forced to retrace her steps to find a more penetrable path. As Juana traveled, flashbacks of her life in El Caribal ran through her mind. Her thoughts filled with images of women her age who toiled on mountainsides, doing the work of mules and oxen. She thought of beatings inflicted by demoralized, drunken husbands. Then her mind focused on the image of Cruz Ochoa, and she felt a surge of energy, because she knew that returning to the village was now impossible for her. She trekked on without hesitation, disregarding danger.

As she walked through the darkness, Juana remembered her father, certain that if he were with her, he would force her to return to Cruz to beg his forgiveness. Her father's face, as he accepted the price of a mule for his daughter, burned behind Juana's eyes, filling her with rage. To erase that anger, Juana looked back on her childhood in an attempt to find something that might bring her joy.

No matter how hard she tried, she could not remember when she had begun to help her mother with the heavy work done by the tribal women. If she and her mother were not going into San Cristóbal de las Casas to sell their wares, it was Juana's task to cart water to the village. When she was not doing that, she and the other girls prepared the soil for planting. Because the land the owners allowed the villagers was usually nothing more than meager hillside patches scattered here and there, it was thought that children could best manage the task of pulling out roots, small rocks and other growth. So she spent her days on her hands and knees, clinging precariously to steep inclines, gathering rocks in her apron and lugging them down to where they were dumped.

Juana also remembered days when she and her mother went into the city. Often they would pass the street on which scribes sat at their desks, some with writing machines, others with only paper and pens. Juana recalled the wonderment she felt seeing the lines of people who waited their turn to sit by the scribes, who would listen and write for them. She had envied those men because they could capture on paper what a person uttered with his lips. Even more intriguing for her were the times she saw the scribe look at a letter or a document handed to him by a Tzeltal, or a Lacandón, or a Tzotzil, and she witnessed the wise man decipher what was written on it. It was a mystery to her how signs and symbols scribbled on paper could be transformed into words that could be spoken and understood.

Overcome by fatigue, Juana finally allowed herself to stop her trek and try to sleep. She fumbled in the darkness until she discovered a sheltered cove between trees. There, she squatted, holding her legs and leaning her head on her knees. After a while, she gave up trying to sleep; she was filled with too many thoughts. Most of all, it was impossible for her to forget the threat of Cruz Ochoa, who would come after her, as he had the last time. So she got on her feet and moved on steadily until daylight began to filter through the thick mesh of mahogany branches and palm fronds. Soon after daybreak, she reached a river where she discovered a bank of water cress. There she ate and drank from the river.

Juana wandered through the jungle, most of the time lost. She followed the course of the sun by day, but at night, when blackness and animal sounds filled the wilderness, she hid in nooks and under trees, until once again daylight crept through the green density. It was not until the third day that she came upon two women and a man walking single file in the direction in which she was going. She saw by their dress that they, like she, were Tzeltales. She spoke to them in her tongue.

"*Amigos,* I'm lost. I'm looking for a man named Orlando Flores. He's a Lacandón, and I know he lives in this region. Can you help me?"

They looked at her and then at one another. Juana saw that they distrusted her, not sure who she was, nor why she was searching for Orlando Flores. She was certain, however, that they recognized the name.

One of the women spoke up, "Why are you looking for him?"

Juana looked directly at her, taking in her size, her age, her garments. She saw that the woman was of medium height, near her in age, and that she had a broad face with a short nose and small, bright eyes.

"He's asked me to come to join him and the others who are here preparing."

"Preparing for what?"

This time it was the man who spoke, and Juana turned to examine him. He was barely taller than the women and, she calculated, younger than any of them. He appeared to be just beyond boyhood.

"I don't know exactly what it is that they're preparing for, but I want to be part of it."

Juana was disconcerted when the three people burst out in loud laughter, and her confusion heightened when she saw that they continued to laugh. The man hunched over, hugging his stomach while he howled in merriment. One of the women covered her face with her hands, trying to disguise her amusement, but her belly, which heaved in and out with suppressed guffaws, betrayed her. The other woman was laughing so hard that she pressed her knees one against the other as she stuffed her hand into her crotch.

Juana's bewilderment turned into irritation as she understood that they were laughing at what she had said. It apparently had been a stupid thing, but she remained calm despite the rising heat inside her. She crossed her arms on her chest, planted her feet wide apart on the soft earth, and quietly waited until the chuckling ceased. Soon, the three of them wiped tears from their cheeks and paid attention to her.

"I know that I'm ignorant. I know you're laughing because I know nothing. Still, I am one of you, and I want to join Orlando Flores and the other people like him. Please take me to him."

Juana's words appeared to erase their distrust, and they looked at one another, showing that they regretted having mocked her. Confirming their trust in her, one by one they gave her their names.

"My name is Porfiria."

"Mine is Torcuato."

"*Amiga,* my name is Tirza. Forgive us for laughing. We're very foolish. We're close to the camp, and I'm certain that Orlando will be glad to see you. He's always happy to welcome new recruits."

"My name is Juana Galván."

With Juana trailing, they formed a single line as they made their way towards the campsite, which turned out to be less than an hour away. As they approached, she began to hear sounds of life: echoes of voices, clanking of metal, neighing of horses. Smells reached her; she caught the fragrance of wood burning and of food cooking. Noises and aromas grew louder and more pungent with each step, and something inside of her told her that she was crossing over into a new part of her life. She felt a mix of joy, excitement, apprehension, doubt, and curiosity, all at once. She knew this would be her home, perhaps forever.

Soon Juana saw that she had allowed her imagination to run wild with unchecked images, and her stomach churned with disappointment when she stood at the edge of the clearing and saw the stark reality. Having listened to Orlando's words about the community, she had thought she would encounter a large organized station, with living areas, a school, a center for communal gatherings, fields for planting, weaving areas, sheds for tools, animals and equipment. But as her eyes scanned the site, she saw only a few dilapidated *palapas,* one or two leaning roofs, two scrawny horses, and a solitary campfire in the center. She looked at her companions, and they discerned her feelings. Torcuato took the lead by nudging Juana towards the center as he pointed with his chin.

"Hermana, don't be disappointed. We're just beginning. What is important are our ideas, the rest will follow. There's Orlando Flores. I'll take you to him."

When Orlando saw them approach, he nearly ran to greet them. Juana saw happiness stamped on his face, convincing her that she had made the right decision, after all. He took her hands in his and shook them with enthusiasm. Then he patted her on the back, all the time grinning his toothy smile. When he spoke, he did so in Spanish.

"You came to see, after all!"

"Yes."

"Are you thirsty? Hungry?"

"Yes. I'm very thirsty."

"Come with me."

He led her to the largest of the huts, which served as a kitchen. He found a gourd, which he filled with water. After rummaging in a basket, he handed her a stack of cold tortillas. Juana did not mind. The water and tortillas tasted delicious.

"I hope you can stay."

"I know that I will stay."

"Why do you say that?"

"Because I will be killed if I return to the village."

"Ah!"

Without another question, Orlando gave Juana time to eat and drink. Then he showed her the grounds, explaining the purpose for each hut and place. The settlement was small, so it was only a short while before he showed her where she would live.

"We'll eat again at sunset. Come at that time so we can all speak."

As soon as Orlando left her, Juana took the pack off her back and unrolled the *petate.* She hardly had time to put aside the clothes she had rolled up in it, when she could no longer resist her fatigue. She flopped onto the mat, where she fell into a deep sleep for several hours. When she awoke, it was nearly dark and the jungle was already teeming with sound. Just as she sat up, wondering how long she had slept, Tirza came into the hut. As Juana was to discover, she would share the place with her and Porfiria.

"Juana, come with me. We're going to eat before the meeting."

"We're going to have a meeting?"

"Yes. Decisions have to be made."

"The women, too?"

"Yes."

Juana was baffled and did not know what to say, so she did as she was asked. She followed silently to the center of the cluster, where she saw a group of men and women gathered around a campfire. She took time to examine faces, but besides Tirza, she recognized only Torcuato, Porfiria and Orlando, who stood to one side listening. Her eyes focused on his big feet, wondering why he had not grown taller to match their size.

Food began to be circulated from hand to hand. A basket filled with fresh tortillas was the first thing to reach Juana. After this came a bowl filled with beans, seasoned with chopped onion and salsa. She was so hungry that she squatted on the ground, placed her food between her crossed legs, and ate with her fingers, dipping a tortilla into the beans, then stuffing it all into her mouth. She closed her eyes, savoring the spicy flavors with pleasure.

When she finished eating, Juana noticed that people chatted quietly. No one spoke to her directly, but she did not feel uncomfortable because she sensed that she had already been accepted as one of the them. Eventually, silence came over the group, although some of them were still licking fingers or drinking from a gourd. Juana realized that everyone looked in the direction where Orlando now sat cross-legged. She took her time as she studied his face in the reflection of the fire. She focused on how his mustache drooped over his thick upper lip and saw that his eyes, which were small, became slits as he spoke.

"Two people have joined us today. There, standing next to Saúl is our new *compañero* Roque. And over there sitting next to Tirza is our *compañera* Juana. We welcome you both."

"Orlando, why are we wasting time with names, welcomes and introductions when it is important for us to know what our next step will be?"

Faces snapped in the direction of the audacious voice. Juana heard its challenging tone. Curious, she stretched her neck, trying to catch a glimpse of the speaker. Before she was able to identify the man, however, she saw some people nodding their heads in agreement with him. Others mumbled, some loudly, others under their breath. She returned her attention to Orlando and saw that he sat with his back rigidly straight, his lips clamped so tight that they appeared to be a straight, hard line.

"Our next step is to have patience because we must wait until we gather more members. Then we must train until we are ready to defy the *patrones.*"

These words unleashed a torrent of remarks and questions that pelted Orlando from different directions. Juana had never witnessed such outspoken men. Her experiences had taught her that silence was usually her people's response. She saw, however, that Orlando answered every inquiry and comment looking each speaker in the eye.

"Who will train us?"

"We will train ourselves."

"To defy the *patrones* we need weapons, vehicles, clothing, boots, food, ways to communicate. Above all, we need money. Where will that come from?"

"All of that will be provided."

"Provided? Who will provide that, Orlando?"

"*El Norte.* People know about us up there, and they are collecting everything we need. They will provide us with materials. For now, it is for us to get more people: men and women willing to fight a war, and even to die."

When Orlando kept tight-lipped and silent after these comments, everyone else followed his example. A hush fell over the group as if a veil had been torn from a forbidden topic, and no one spoke until the same bold voice again rang out.

"Women? That's crazy! *¡Estás loco!* Women are useless in war! In fact, why are women here? War is not for women! This is none of their business!"

As if they had been seared with burning prongs, all at once the women howled in rage. Loud muttering and hissing combined as clenched fists slashed the night air. Women's voices rang out, and hostile gestures were aimed at the man who had uttered those words.

"*¡Cabrón!*"

"*¡Qué chinga!*"

"We have toiled as much as you for centuries. Why shouldn't we have the right to fight?"

"We have endured not only the fist of *el patrón* but that of our fathers, our brothers, our husbands. We have earned the right to be in the war!"

The uproar coming from the women was such a clamor that it silenced the man who had voiced his opposition. He said no more. Instead he slunk back where the reflection cast by the fire could not reach him. Juana stared in disbelief because she had never before seen women force a man away in fear. Just then, the image of Cruz crawling away from her flashed in her memory, and she realized that she had already made a man slink away in pain, and maybe even in fear. She breathed, forcing air into her lungs, then exhaled slowly, coming to terms with the truth that she had already fought a war when she defied her husband.

She returned her attention to the questions that had picked up once again, and to Orlando, who answered them, intentionally disregarding the issue of women and war.

"Orlando, it will take time to gather such an army. It cannot be done overnight."

"We've got time. We've waited centuries."

"What will keep the *patrones* from wiping us out?"

"The jungle will protect us as it has for so long. Secrecy will protect us, as it has for long years."

"If we make war on the mestizos, we will be destroyed."

"You and I might be destroyed, but others of our people will follow."

The onslaught of questions, doubts and demands for answers pounded Orlando, coming at him from men who had no experience in defying the authority of the mestizos, and women who were for the first time believing they had rights. Juana observed that the women with their silence demonstrated confidence in what Orlando was saying. Then the barrage of questions stopped as suddenly as it had begun. It had been a rapid exchange of words followed by a silence so complete that Juana thought that the sounds of the jungle had grown louder.

Juana looked around, taking in the expressions of those around the campfire. She stared at the men: disheveled, overworked, aged beyond their years. Juana then concentrated her eyes on the women, who were like her, mostly young, with determined faces that nonetheless reflected weariness and impatience. After that, she looked into her own heart and saw that she was in turmoil and confusion because she understood so little of what she had just witnessed and heard. She knew, however, that what Orlando was proposing was rebellion.

After the group dispersed, Orlando came to where Juana remained sitting. He sat by her side for a while before speaking. Behind them, in the *palapas,* the murmuring of men and women mingled with the soft strumming of guitar strings, accompanied by humming voices. The crisp sound of crickets and the faraway cascading rumble of water filled the air in the distance.

Chapter 12

In the end, los patrones *are severe and unforgiving.*

Juana gazed at Orlando's face, knowing that he had fallen into thought and that his spirit was engaged in secret worlds. She contemplated him freely, without shyness or reserve, taking in his profile, its long beaked nose, the straight lashes and the tiny wrinkles that wrapped around his slanted eyes. She had already taken in the brilliance of those eyes and saw how they shone with a mixture of hope and apprehension. Left on her own, Juana scrutinized the man who was proposing resistance, even war, against the mestizos. She focused her gaze on his chest. It was shrouded by the coarse Lacandón tunic, but its bony frame betrayed an underfed and overworked lifetime. She looked at his rough hands, thinking that their veins and knuckles appeared to be carved from hardwood. Juana's eyes returned to Orlando's face to concentrate on the long, limp hair that covered his forehead and dangled down to his shoulders..

"What are you thinking, *compañero?* Do you believe that the man who cried out a while ago was right about women and war?"

"No. Women will have much to do with our struggle."

"Why do you say that when you know that in the *palapas,* in the *mercados,* in the *llanos,* we are less valued than burros?"

"It's because you do more than half the work, because you suffer twice as much as men, because you have the children, that you have earned and should have an equal amount of authority."

Juana leaned her head to one side as she studied Orlando's face. She had never heard a man acknowledge what in her heart she had felt, especially since her life had been joined to Cruz Ochoa.

"*Compañero,* if that ever happens, it will be the first time. Don't you think that more than one man thinks like the one who spoke out? I can't imagine we would be allowed to participate in your plans as men do."

"He was wrong. Didn't you hear how the women responded? Women have fought with men before, and it will happen again, because we will not overcome the *Catxul* and the *Aluxob* if we don't allow women to be our partners."

"The thieves and the liars . . . yes, you've spoken of those people before, *compañero.* But tell me, how can women help overcome those who have grown used to being *patrones?*"

"By not being afraid, and by fighting with weapons as well as words. By masking our faces in order to give a face to our people. By changing our names, and returning lost identities to our ancestors. By forgetting our own pasts so that we can give a future to our children."

Juana liked Orlando's words, but she cared more for the way he spoke to her, because it was intense yet calm. She looked into his eyes despite her having been taught that a woman should not do so when speaking to a man.

"Look, *amiga,* I will tell you of a woman who lived among us many generations ago and who led the first insurrection against the bosses. She belonged to the Tzeltal people. I first heard about her when I was a boy working on an hacienda in Lacanjá. That history was told to me by a man, a Lacandón who was educated and who became a teacher to the children of *el patrón.* Whenever that *maestro* came into the kitchen to eat, I would ask him to repeat the story, and it became so important to me that I memorized it until it became a part of me. Now I'll tell it to you completely, but please don't interrupt me because, if I stop speaking, I'll lose the thread of the story and be forced to begin it again."

Juana sat with her eyes riveted to Orlando's face, which soon appeared transfigured as he began the story. She now stared at him without inhibition, because she saw that his eyes were closed and that he was no longer aware of her presence, much less her gaze. He sat cross-legged, with his hands resting on his knees, palms cupped upward, as if he were lost in prayer.

～ ～ ～

"This story begins in Cancuc, Chiapas, in 1712, when the woman I speak of was sentenced to a lashing for having claimed to have heard the voice of the Virgin Mary commanding her to lead our people to freedom. She did not resist when she was strapped to the pillory by the soldier's rough hands. She remained calm, her frail back naked and exposed to the lashes of the whip. Her body shuddered with the first blow, but when the next strokes descended, her limbs refused to feel pain. What she did feel was the blood trickling down her back onto her buttocks, coursing past the rear of her thighs until it saturated her ankles, finally seeping into the dirt, drenching it until its brown tones turned black. The whipping went on, biting into the woman's back. Only the lashing sounds broke the silence.

"And still she stood, enduring the searing pain of the whip, her forehead pressed against the pillory in such a way that the scar over her left eyebrow began to ache almost as much as the lashings. She tried to forget the misery by concentrating her eyes on the people witnessing her punishment. She saw that she was surrounded by men and women of the commune whose faces reflected rage and frustration at seeing one of their own people endure such meaningless and undeserved suffering.

"As she swiveled her head from one side to the other, stretching her neck to get a better look, she saw that there was a multitude of people on every side, and that their presence extended even beyond the range of her vision. They had come to witness the ordeal, and they did it respectfully, because the woman was now to them a special person. They had walked from as far away as Chilón and Ocosingo to pay homage to her because she had received and told of visions of freedom for our people.

"The hissing of the lash was the only sound to shatter the silence while the whip ate at her flesh. Despite the pain, she focused her mind on whatever she could see. She looked at the people, concentrating on those emaciated, dark faces, masks carved in wood, slits in the place of eyes, veiling pent-up rage. She suddenly realized that oppression and hatred had transformed the faces of our people; they no longer resembled our ancestors.

"'*¡Infiel diabólica! ¡Que Dios Santísimo te perdone este pecado mortal!*'

"She turned around to see who had shouted those condemning words. Behind the soldier who was whipping her stood Brother Simón de Lara, a Dominican priest, the only white man in the village of Cancuc. It was he who had ordered the whipping with the intention of cleansing her of her dangerous ideas, and it was he who spoke. It was a lesson, he had told everyone, for those villagers who would not abandon their bent towards their ancient ways.

"Brother Simón, spitting accusations of sin and devilish deeds at her, stood erect. His big jaw pointed toward the pillory while he held his arms crossed under the long black cloth that covered his white gown. He nodded as each lash bit into the woman's skin, but to his angry dismay, she did not cry out.

"Unexpectedly, a shrill voice rang out from the crowd. Startled, she and everyone, even the soldier, looked at each other and in every direction trying to identify who had screamed, trying to make out what the voice had yelled. But they heard only silence. And so the soldier returned to his task, and his grunting, along with the whirring sound of the whip, again broke the silence. Then the faceless voice rang out again.

"'*¡Cabrones! ¡Asesinos! ¡No tienen derecho! ¡Mátenlos!*'

"This time the woman heard the words clearly and she saw that everyone else had also understood. It was a signal to take vengeance. Our people murmured and shifted, moving one foot, then the other. Brother Simón looked into the crowd and saw its growing agitation. Then he raised his arms high over his head as if defending himself against an invisible enemy.

"'*¡En nombre de Dios . . . !*'

"His words were cut off by howling. She did not hear what he was about to say because our people lifted their arms and screamed out the pain of generations of bondage. The wail was loud, anguished, and she heard her own cracked voice as it joined the clamor. Years of paying tribute to faceless masters became intolerable. It was as if famine, scourgings, uprootings had become a gigantic knot that was strangling them. They were Lacondones, Tzeltales, Tzotziles, who would not tolerate that burden any longer.

"The woman was cut down from the pillory in time to catch a glimpse of the soldier as he dropped his whip and ran towards the forest. She also saw the expression of horror stamped on the priest's face as he realized what was happening. He stumbled over his long garment, trying to escape behind the soldier, but Brother Simón was not fast enough. Rough hands took hold of him, knocking him to the ground. Hardened feet stomped on him until blood spurted from his nose and cheeks while he rolled in the mud screaming for pity.

"The woman, bloodied and weakened by the flogging, was one of the first to accost him, tugging at his hair until she felt a handful rip away from his scalp. The others pushed, tearing at the priest's garments, leaving him stripped. Men and women struggled, trying to at least dig their nails into the white skin that had caused them so much misery, but the priest wiggled and thrashed his legs against our people until he was able to free himself. Naked and bloody, he disappeared into the jungle.

"From that place the news spread throughout the province of Zendales, reaching disbelieving ears and filling hearts with hope. The woman was one of the messengers who traveled from village to village, telling of how the people had lifted their voices in outrage and forced the soldier and the priest to flee in fear. She, along with the other messengers, stirred the hearts of the people to courage, calling them to Cancuc.

"It was in that village, in August of that same year, 1712, amidst the crowd, that the woman who had been flogged gave the signal to begin the struggle against the Spanish rulers. The women and men of the villages of Los Zendales, Las Coronas, Chinampas and Huitiupán rose up in anger. They rebelled, overcoming the Spaniards and mestizos with the weight of their numbers and causing them to flee in terror to take a last stand in Ciudad Real.

"Later that month, our people marched on Ocosingo and Chilón and prevailed over their former masters. They fought with machetes and sticks, beating, hacking, screaming and terrifying the enemy. Emboldened by their victories, our ancestors pressed forward with one thought in mind: to cast out the Spaniards once and for all.

"After these encounters, the *patrones* tried to engage our people but were besieged in Huixtán, and from there they retreated back to Ciudad Real, where for three months they languished, imploring help from their brothers in Tabasco and Guatemala. During that time, our people formed a new country, one free of menace, one joined by Tzotzil, Tzeltal and Chol. It was at that time that messengers again went out to the multitudes with the woman's counsel. Everyone listened attentively because her words were filled with truth.

"'Believe me and follow me, because there is no more tribute, or king, or bishop. The prophecy of throwing off the yoke and restoring our lands and liberty has been fulfilled.'

"But the end came in November, when the Spaniards were re-enforced by soldiers from Guatemala who were armed with stone mortars and other more advanced weapons. The first defeat of our people happened at Oxchue, then another at Cancuc. After that, one village after the other surrendered, despite our people knowing that what awaited them was worse than death. The rebellion weakened, faltered, and ultimately was squashed by the soldiers. Not long after that, a report reached the Bishop of Ciudad Real assuring the *patrones* that order would soon be restored.

"'Your Excellency,' the message said, 'the natives have been overcome; we are once again in control. But it must be noted that this has been the most extensive and most serious challenge to the presence of His Majesty's authority since our arrival in these lands. We must do all in our power to guarantee that the natives never again raise a hand against our sovereign rule. May Almighty God preserve us from another such rebellion.'

"The woman and the rebels fled into the Lacandón Jungle and sought shelter in the vastness and thickness of its growth. Soldiers and hounds pursued them relentlessly, not caring that their swords slashed and slayed women and children, as well as men. The woman ran, exhausted by hunger, but kept on the move only out of fear of falling and being torn apart by those dogs. That is where the story of the woman ends."

∾ ∾ ∾

When Orlando ended the narrative, his eyelids fluttered as if he were coming out of a deep sleep. After a while, he put his hands to his eyes, rubbed them and opened them as he focused on Juana. He licked his upper lip while staring at her, evidently waiting for words that might tell him what she was thinking. All he saw, however, was that she sat cross-legged and hunched over her hands, which she held clasped in her lap. He reached out, hesitated, then lifted her chin with his forefinger. He was surprised at the brilliance of her eyes, but more by her words.

"Why are we persecuted? What have we done to be so hated? Why do their dogs want to destroy us?"

Orlando shifted his weight while he pondered Juana's questions. When he began speaking, his words baffled her because they appeared not to be answering what she had asked. Nonetheless, she listened.

"*Compañera,* when I was a boy still working on Finca Las Estrellas, Don Absolón Mayorga, *el patrón,* had a sister. She was so young that everyone thought she was his daughter. One day, all the workers were assembled out in the field where a post had been planted. All of us, servants, maids, laundry women, everyone that served inside and outside of the main house, were ordered to that pillory. We didn't know what was going on, but I remember hearing the older people say that something terrible was about to happen.

"Then, the sister of *el patrón* was brought out from the big house. We could all see that it was by force, because it was Don Absolón himself who was pushing her forward. I remember that she was crying, that her face was swollen and smeared, as if she had been struck many times. When they reached the pillar, *el patrón* tore off her clothes until she was naked. Ashamed for her, we turned away, but he scolded us and ordered us to look at his sister. We obeyed. Then he tied her to the pillory and whipped her until she fainted. After that he cast her into the jungle."

Orlando fell silent, leaving Juana more baffled than before. She tried to tie his words to her questions, but could not find the connection. What she did see, however, was a repetition of the scourging of the woman in Orlando's story, only this time it was a mestiza, the sister of *el patrón.*

"*Compañero,* what does this sad story have to do with the hatred the *patrones* have for us?"

"You see, Juana, Don Absolón's sister was discovered to have been in love with another woman. She was a *manflora,* a woman who loved one of her own kind. I remember that he shouted for everyone to hear that what she did, what she was, and what she called love was a sin, that it was repugnant, that she was an animal with no reason to live."

Juana sucked in a deep breath, feeling frightened without fully understanding why. She, herself, had never experienced love, much less had she ever imagined that a woman could have such feelings for another woman. Hearing and knowing this made her heart pound. She thought of her mother, of her sisters, of all the women of her village, and she was unable to grasp what it would be like to love one of them.

Orlando narrowed his eyes as he concentrated on Juana's face, discerning her astonishment at hearing the story. Without waiting for her to say anything, he continued.

"Juana, after many years spent in cities and villages in search of the answer to questions like yours, I now see why Don Absolón was so enraged. His sister had gone against his and all the other *patrones'* rules and religion. She was different and had dared to do what was forbidden, so he punished her even though she was of his own flesh."

Juana's silence was deep. She had withdrawn so much into herself that Orlando thought she was no longer listening to him. He waited for her to return to him and his words, but when she remained silent, he went on.

"I also see that to the men who want to be our masters, being *una india* or *un indio,* being poor and forced to scratch a life out of a piece of dry dirt, being a *manflora* or a man who loves men, being anyone contrary, is all the same. In their eyes, we share a common destiny in which we are hated, persecuted, tortured and condemned because we threaten their way of life. In the end, *los patrones* are severe and unforgiving."

Orlando moved closer to Juana and raised his hand to touch the scar on her forehead. It was a fleeting, tender touch. After a few moments, he cleared his throat.

"Will you stay?"

"Yes."

Chapter 13

He even owns a mule.

Juana, under the guidance of Orlando Flores, became Teniente Insurgente Isabel, and embraced the life of a guerrilla without reservation. Along with men and other women, she rose daily before sunrise, ate tortillas and drank black coffee—the usual breakfast fare—and put in a full day of training. Getting used to wearing pants and a man's shirt posed a difficult obstacle for her; she found those garments tight, restraining, hot. But she soon realized that dressing like a man also gave her more mobility and protection than did her long dress. Another hardship for her was wearing boots in place of the *huaraches* she had worn all of her life. Her feet blistered, they became swollen, almost hobbling her, but in time she adapted, and she enjoyed being able to step on sharp or prickly rocks and plants without worrying about her soles or ankles.

Soon she learned to slither on her belly, almost silently, and crawl on her hands and knees as she approached mock targets, or enemies. Her elbows bled, and her hands and arms ached from the pressure of carrying the unaccustomed weapon until her skin became coarse, scabbing over with new bleedings on top of those wounds.

Juana had never held a rifle and felt awkward when she was first ordered to take hold of one, but she soon became acquainted with its weight and feel. She practiced shooting long hours, beyond what was expected, until she was able to place the bullet on the exact mark on the designated tree or branch. This was also the case with running, ducking and leaping, all of which she did with more success than any of the other new recruits, the same *compañeras* and *compañeros* who in the beginning had laughed at her because she was short. That scoffing soon turned into admiration when it could not be denied that no one could match Juana's accuracy and speed during maneuvers. Through the years, she changed. Not only was she transformed from the girl who had sustained the blows of a morose husband into a woman now trained as a guerrilla, but during that time she had also developed her mind, concentrating on learning to read, write and expand her skills in speaking Spanish. It was Orlando Flores who provided her first lessons, guiding her until she was capable of reading newspapers, written notices and other articles.

Her face had also undergone a change; once round, it became elongated and angular. Her nose had also thinned to a point, and her eyes were nearly always veiled by caution. Only her mouth remained the same. It was still as full as when she had been a girl, and appeared always on the verge of a smile. This characteristic caused confusion in those who did not know her because her lips contradicted the seriousness of her other features.

After a few years, when Orlando Flores and other members of the leadership noticed her dedication, and even more important, her successful transformation into a guerrilla, Juana was included in the small group of leaders. Shortly after that, supplies were purchased, brokered and even donated for *la lucha;* they came from different parts of Mexico, and even from other countries. Food, clothing, medicines, stockpiles of firearms and explosives grew steadily. They were warehoused at strategically hidden points, where they were held to be transported to Lacandona. This was done by train, boat, and even on the backs of mules.

It was determined that Juana would be the best of the group to bring in those materials because of the self-assurance with which she walked and talked, and because she was a woman, a Tzeltal, who would hardly draw attention. Teniente Isabel accepted the mission, but not until she trained herself, learning the terrain, the cities, the rivers, the lakes, the borders that might present potential obstacles. When this had been accomplished, she chose to travel by herself, accepting the company of others only when necessary to return with supplies.

It was at those times that she mingled, dressed in a native skirt, blouse and *huipil.* Unnoticed, she traveled to hidden caches in Tabasco, Veracruz, Oaxaca, north to Monterrey and south across the border to El Petén and Frontera Echeverría in Guatemala. She forged rivers: Río Negro, Río Santa Cruz and others that flowed in various directions, but that always yielded fresh supplies. Strangers often saw her leap on barges or rafts, ride into a village on the bare back of a burro, unsuspecting that she was no ordinary Tzeltal woman but someone on a mission.

Juana outwardly threw herself into the life of an insurgent, but inwardly she found herself trapped in loneliness, which grew as time passed, and her isolation deepened as she became obsessed by the memory of her father bartering her. She tried to understand why this feeling gnawed at her. After all, it was tradition; she was not the only girl to be exchanged. It had happened to her mother, to her sisters, to all the women she knew.

He even owns a mule, which he has offered to sell in exchange for you. Juana was tormented by those words; they were engraved on her spirit, they tortured her, and no matter how much she tried, she was incapable of forgetting those lisping sounds as they dripped from her father's lips. After several years, she understood that unless she confronted that memory, she would never be free. That was when she went out in search of her father.

During one of her trips to claim weapons and supplies, Juana reached the region where Río Santa Cruz nears Lago Nahá, the site of her native village. She had been on a barge making her way toward Monte Líbano, when she was filled with an urge to return to the place where she would find her father, where she would ask him the questions that had haunted her for years. When the boat stopped at Monte Líbano, she got off and walked to the road leading to her village.

On the way, she blended into clusters of people who walked the muddy roads, either making their way to the marketplaces of Ocosingo and Comitán, or traveling in the opposite direction toward the lake villages of Ts'ibatnah, Mesabak, or Ah K'ak, as well as Nahá. It was a long walk, taking her an entire day.

As Juana made her way, she observed her people, taking in the men and women who crowded the intersecting paths in that part of the Lacandona Jungle. She scrutinized the men, those coming toward her heading in the opposite direction and those traveling her route. Some held reins pulling emaciated burros, or oxen; others pushed dilapidated carts loaded with sacks of beans or vegetables. She focused on their worn, wrinkled faces, their eyes downcast in dejection, and she mused how that look became transformed once a person became an insurgent, someone convinced that life could be changed.

Juana looked at the women especially. Some of them were just girls already burdened with hefty loads of goods meant for the market, or by bellies heavy with child, or by children that dangled from a backpack or clutched at a skirt. In each one of those women, Juana, remembering her life, saw her reflection first as a girl carting goods, then as a wife experiencing one ill-fated pregnancy after the other, all the time toiling in the fields or by the river of El Caribal.

Juana trekked along with everyone else, her feet pounding the hardened mud, her throat coated with the fine dust lifted by the tread of countless feet. She felt energized by the sound of thumping *huaraches,* murmuring voices, creaking carts, squalling children, but she was also filled with anger, knowing that such a life had been going on for decades, for centuries, that the pathway she and others now trod had been pounded into the ground by enslaved ancestors whose names were now forgotten.

She wore the long woolen skirt of her tribe as well as a faded embroidered blouse and *huipil.* She knew that outwardly she was just another Tzeltal woman, but inwardly, she was different from them. This thought empowered her and reconfirmed her mission of finding her father. As she neared Nahá, however, her resolve began to falter because she wondered what she would say to him, how she would let him know that he had condemned her to unhappiness for the price of a mule.

When she neared Lago Nahá, Juana's nose picked up the scent of water and her ears caught whiffs of voices that skimmed the lake, reminding her of her childhood. Without having to ask, she took the path that rimmed the lake, heading for her family *palapa,* but when she arrived at the place, she found nothing, only faded remnants of what used to be her family's dwelling.

Juana, astounded and not understanding, looked around, but there was no one; the place was abandoned. What she remembered as a flourishing cluster of huts was now a heap of rotting poles and palm fronds entangled in fetid mud pits. She looked toward the trees that had surrounded the dwellings and noticed that in their place were saplings growing out from under felled trees. Other than that, there was only silence broken by the sound of the breeze, rustling bushes and low-growing ferns.

Bewildered, Juana paced the short distance to the rim of the lake, where she walked until she came across a group of women doing their wash. They gawked at the stranger until the one who appeared to be the oldest spoke.

"Demetria Galván?"

"No, *abuela.* I'm her sister, Juana."

"¡Ahhhhhhh!"

A hushed expression that sounded like a sigh passed through the women's lips, but Juana was not able to interpret its meaning. She noticed that they stared at her, then one after the other, faces turned toward the woman who had taken the lead.

"You're the wife of Cruz Ochoa, who lives in El Caribal."

Juana stiffened at the sound of the name that she never uttered. She knew that, cutting through vast distances of jungle and mountain, there was a tight system of communication between villages and tribes. Knowing this, however, had not prepared her to hear that name thrown in her face so soon after her arrival.

"Tongues said that you left him, but that he found you and brought you back to El Caribal."

"Those who speak say the truth, but only part of it. I left him again years ago."

"¡Ahhhhhhhh!"

"But that is not why I've returned to Nahá. I've come looking for my father and my mother."

The faces again snapped in the direction of the elder woman. After this they glanced furtively at one another, their expressions betraying anxiety. Juana gazed at them in an effort to guess the meaning of those looks, but she decided that asking questions would be more effective.

"Where are they, *abuela?*"

The old woman wiped soap from her gnarled fingers and dried her hands on a faded apron. She was obviously filling time while she thought of her response.

"Your mother is dead, *niña*. Drowned by the waters of this lake."

Juana felt a strange pressure in the pit of her stomach, which quickly spread, becoming a profound sadness. She was also afraid, and she recognized the feeling; it was what she felt after a torrential downpour, when the jungle and its animals fell so silent that she filled with apprehension. Her mother's pained expression, when her father had finalized his bargain with Cruz Ochoa in the marketplace, became vividly clear.

"How did it happen?"

"A deluge of rain came, causing the lake to sweep away the *palapas* and sheds that fringed it. The torrent flooded us during the blackest hours of the night; few down here survived. Your mother disappeared into the deepest part of the water and her body was never found. Everything was gray and wrapped in mist that day."

"How long ago did this happen?"

"Three years ago."

Eager to know her father's whereabouts, Juana forced herself to put aside her grief. She would not, after having journeyed so far to see him, allow sadness to erase the reason for her coming.

"Where is my father?"

"*Niña*, do you see that path? If you follow it through those trees, you will come to several *palapas*. The last one on the path is where your father lives."

"*Muchas gracias.*"

Juana turned away from the group and headed for the trail pointed out by the elder woman. As she walked, she felt her heart race, knowing that with each step she was losing courage. Words she had rehearsed for this moment now, one by one, escaped her mind, making her fear that she would be struck dumb by the time she faced her father. Nonetheless, she walked, following the path to its end, until she arrived at the last of the huts.

Juana paused at the entrance, long enough for her nose to pick up the smell of smoke and tortillas. She knew what was going on inside: the same as in her childhood days. Her father would be sitting cross-legged, silent and brooding, not because he was alone, but because he had always been turned in on himself. She remembered, and for the first time she saw that he and Cruz Ochoa shared an impenetrable isolation. These thoughts threatened Juana's resolve to face her father, even more because they opened the door to her girlhood dread, which returned vivid and strong. All women, she knew, shared this fear of the men in their family. She realized also that this condition resulted in isolation: the men from the women, and the women from the men.

Was that the reason why it was so easy, Tata? Juana heard herself talking out loud. She hesitated for a moment, then instead of entering, she decided to call out.

"*¡Tata!*"

Juana waited, listening for a response, but all was silent in the hut. She called out again, but this time she thought she heard movement. She moved away from the low opening, expecting someone to emerge. When her father stepped out into the light of the early dusk, he seemed shrunken, much smaller than she recalled. He looked at her and responded as if she had been with him that morning, as if the years that had passed had been only hours. After a few moments, he gestured with his head for her to follow him into the *palapa*. Once inside, they both squatted facing each other across the small fire.

Juana was now used to speaking whenever she had something to say. She nonetheless observed the tradition of waiting for her father to speak first. A long time passed before he began to murmur, time during which her thoughts fell into place. As she waited, she felt relief that she no longer lived under the pall of deference to someone who did not return that same respect. Thoughts of other women filled her, people who, like her, had taken one step after the other, leading them to fight for their worth. Her father's voice brought Juana out of her musing.

"You have brought the family shame."

"How?"

"You have abandoned your husband."

"He was not my husband."

"You married him!"

"You chose him!"

Although quiet, their voices were charged with recrimination, with unspoken anger. Juana fought off rising emotions by trying to focus on her reasons for this encounter. She realized that her father had no notion that a new wave was washing over the minds of other women like her. It was he who spoke again.

"It is the duty of a father to choose for the daughter."

"What if Cruz Ochoa had not offered the price of his mule?"

This time his eyes snapped away from the fire to glare at her. She could not discern if what she saw was anger or confusion. What she did know was that she had crossed a forbidden line.

"If I had not found you a husband, you would have starved."

"I left him many years ago and, look, I have not starved."

Her father backed away from the sparring and returned his gaze to the fire, giving Juana an opportunity to observe his face and body. He had aged since she had last seen him, but his face had not lost its bony angles and she realized for the first time that she looked like him. An inexplicable sensation overcame her when she saw that her nose, her eyes, her ears, were repetitions of the same features of his face. She was amazed that she had not seen the resemblance before, and she inwardly asked how he could have so easily traded off his own reflection. Then she looked at his body, seeing that it was emaciated, and his hands were covered with scars, his fingers gnarled. He spoke again, and this time he looked at her, seemingly knowing her thoughts.

"A daughter should not question her father."

"*Tata,* why did you sell me?"

"I did not sell you! It was an exchange!"

"Were you exchanged for the price of a mule by your father?"

"I'm not a woman!"

Juana could not speak anymore. It was clear that her father, like the other men of her people, did not give the same value to a woman as to a man, and that from that conviction flowed their every action.

But knowing this did not help her find a way to contradict or to correct him; she did not know the words to reach him. Juana rose, left the *palapa* and walked in the opposite direction, toward the jungle. She traveled until darkness forced her to take shelter in the nook of a giant *ceiba* tree. There, she spent the night thinking, straining to find words that would ease the pressure draining her mind. She reflected on the motive for which she had returned to face her father. Was it to change him? Was it to make him experience the same misery she had felt? Why had she come?

As night moved toward its end, Juana thought that she had at last found a way out of the labyrinth into which she had been cast after seeing her father. She understood that it was useless to expect him to change or to feel her bitterness or sadness. Yet, to live with anger was bound to destroy her. She also knew that if she was to find peace, another road was necessary; she needed to go in another direction.

How are fathers forgiven? How does it happen? Is it in their time, their world, their thinking?

These questions took shape in Juana's mind, but they remained unanswered. She saw that night had crept by and daylight was filtering through the overhead canopy of branches. Although she had not slept, she knew that she had gained some understanding with the notion of forgiveness. Juana decided that she would reflect more on it. She rose, brushed dried leaves from her rump, and turned toward Ocosingo, and from there, northbound to receive a new cargo of armaments and supplies.

Years passed during which her father's image began to fade as well as the bitterness, liberating her to follow the path of insurgency. Her feeling of freedom was not complete, however, because she remained apprehensive that one day Cruz Ochoa would track her, find her and again try to dominate her. This lingering feeling was realized one day when she was at the river bathing. She was stripped to the waist; soap dripped from her long hair down her neck, shoulders, and over her breasts. As she rinsed the suds out of her hair with a gourd, Juana suddenly sensed something: a presence nearby. Her body tensed, but without betraying her uneasiness, she inched toward the riverbank and reached for the revolver that was always by her side. With her other hand she got a towel and slid it over the weapon. She remained still but poised to spring, if necessary.

"Juana!"

She recognized Cruz Ochoa's voice immediately. It was soft, as always, but still filled with anger. She was not surprised; she had been expecting his return for years.

"Juana!"

She slowly raised her face as the soap continued to drip from her hair to her shoulders and breasts. As she did this, Juana cautiously got onto her knees, gaining balance as she judged the distance between herself and Cruz. Beneath the towel, her thumb cocked the revolver's trigger.

"¿Qué quieres, Cruz Ochoa?"

"You! You're still my wife, Juana, and I've come for you!"

"I'm your wife, but I am not returning to your palapa."

"You are returning with me!"

As Cruz lifted his arm in hostility, Juana drew the weapon with both hands and pointed it at his face. The sight of the gun unnerved him as if he had been struck by an invisible fist. He reeled backward, eyes wide open, pupils dilated. When Juana spoke, her voice was steady, quiet, determined.

"Turn around, Cruz Ochoa, head for your village and never return. If you do, I'll kill you. Te lo prometo."

Cruz was stunned as he stared at Juana. He saw, for the first time, that she had changed, that her face was different and that her eyes were transformed. Her words cut into his brain, convincing him of her determination and ability to kill him. He turned in his tracks and vanished into the bushes.

Juana waited until her heartbeat normalized before she dressed. The sight of Cruz Ochoa's face had filled her mouth with bitter saliva, but knowing that he would probably never return calmed her. To steady herself even more, she reminded herself that she had an assignment to carry out that day. Focusing on this idea helped clear her mind. Word had reached the general command of a photographer, a woman, who was living in Pichucalco. Juana had been given the task to recruit her into their ranks.

∽ ∽ ∽

Dawn was breaking, and early light was seeping into Juana's *palapa*. She was thinking that now she knew the name and face of that photographer. She now realized that she had spent the night reliving important moments of her life while searching for an explanation for the feelings she was experiencing for that same woman, Adriana Mora. Without answers, Juana shrugged it off for the moment and left her *palapa* to prepare for the day.

Chapter 14

Kap jol, the anger of the people.

Lacanjá, a village in the Lacandona Jungle, 1963.

Even before he knew it, Orlando Flores was to be among those who gave energy and life to *tzak' bail,* the armed movement against *los patrones.* In time, his followers would number in hundreds, even thousands, but in the beginning it was his hand alone that first wielded the machete, lifted not to clear the paths of undergrowth, but to bring down the long line of masters who had come to that land centuries before. Even as a boy, when he was known as Quintín Osuna, he would often smell the biting stench of *kap jol,* the anger of the people, as it seeped from *palapa* to *palapa,* as it snaked on its belly through rows of coffee plants in the highlands, as it coiled itself under the green gold of the giant mahogany trees in the heart of the Lacandona Jungle. Even then the boy wondered how long it would take before his people rose in defiance of the masters.

Orlando's first recollections really began when he was fourteen years old, in the village of Lacanjá, where he was born and named Quintín Osuna. The cluster of huts was planted on property owned by Don Absolón Mayorga, a mestizo who sprang from a line of *patrones* dating from the first days of colonization. The Mayorga family lived on a vast estate, a *finca,* known as Las Estrellas. There, the men and boys of Lacanjá toiled on the coffee plantations, or in the jungle as *boyeros,* those forced by the *patrones* to rob the forest of its precious mahogany known as green gold, *oro verde.*

The women labored under similar stress in the household of the *finca*, where they were in charge of cooking, weaving, laundering and

113

caring for the Mayorga children. When a woman was not able to bring enough money to her *palapa* from her work in the big house, she was forced to join the horde of men who daily trekked up the mountain to harvest coffee. Such a woman did this two or maybe three days out of each week. And if she had an infant to care for at the time, she lashed the child to her breast and worked, stooped under the charring sun, as the baby suckled, first from one breast, then from the other. Orlando Flores had been one of those children, and it was from there, from his mother's milk, that he sucked the outrage that coursed first through her veins, then through his own.

When the boy was fourteen, he was called by *el patrón* to serve as a houseboy. That was the day when Orlando's memory began to record his life, because he understood at that moment that his was a privilege not shared by many other boys of his tribe. Most of them were forced to trudge to the highlands to tend the coffee plants, or worse, become *boyeros* in the jungle. Orlando became a good servant because he knew that his was a frail privilege, one that had to be guarded lest it shatter. During the day, he polished countless silver ornaments and dishes, he washed windows twice his size, and he dusted glossy mahogany furniture, rubbing each piece until he could see his reflection peering back at him.

In the evenings, he was instructed to put on a starched white cotton suit and to wait on Don Absolón by bringing him a glass of sherry. The old man routinely took the after-dinner drink in the hacienda's elegant parlor—a vast, ornate room with glittering chandeliers where he sat by the record player, savoring the tasty liqueur and listening to the music of European composers.

After performing this duty, but before he was free to return to his family's *palapa,* Orlando had to report to the kitchen to help mop floors and clear away the dinner pots and pans. Each evening, the kitchen crew waited for the boy with anticipation, knowing that he would make them laugh, something those workers seldom did as they labored during the day. It had become a routine. Orlando would saunter into the kitchen, holding himself in the aloof manner of *el patrón,* pretending to sip his drink, the pinkie of his hand held stiffly in the air. All eyes were on him as the boy acted out, placing an invisible record on the turntable, pretended to raise the volume and dancing as he and the others imagined white people danced. Orlando swiveled, pirouetted and leaped high into the kitchen's saturated air with his arms held gracefully above his head, a snooty expression pasted on his face. Sometimes, because of the strain of leaping as high as he could, a tight, squeaky fart would escape from his rear, sending his audience into convulsions of laughter.

Las torteadoras, women who spent their days kneading *masa* for the production of countless dozens of tortillas meant to feed not only the Mayorga family but the entire army of household servants, clapped their weary hands with each of Orlando's escapades. *Los cargadores,* men who toted firewood for the giant ovens and stoves, and whose job it was to wash griddles and cast-iron caldrons, grinned widely at Orlando's mocking their master, their blackened faces contrasting with white teeth and glistening eyes.

It was during those days that Orlando met Rufino Mayorga, who was his age. At first, when Rufino suggested that they go somewhere, Orlando was hesitant, knowing that it was forbidden for someone like him to mingle with the son of *el patrón*. But despite this forbidding rule, Orlando gave in and the two boys often roamed the fringe of the jungle, playing or hunting small game. Then, as they grew older, they fished together in Río Lacanjá, and when the bites were few, they abandoned their poles and went swimming and diving into the water from high branches. The forest rang with their voices as they shouted, daring one another to do different feats.

"*Epa,* Rufino, I'll bet you can't dive from up here!"

"Hey, Quintín, I'll bet you can't pee as far as I can!"

As time passed, Orlando became more aware of the differences between him and Rufino. The mestizo boy's body was straight, with long legs, and his skin was as white as milk. When Orlando began to notice this, he often glanced down to gaze at his own body, seeing that his legs were not long but short and slightly bent at the knees. He saw also that his skin was dark, like the furniture he rubbed daily.

It happened one evening as Orlando glided on sandaled feet over a gleaming marble floor. He carried a crystal snifter filled with sherry, balanced on a silver tray. He carefully stood in front of Don

Absolón, slightly bent forward as he offered him the drink. As always, *el patrón* was dressed in evening attire with a starched white shirt secured at the neck by a silk bow tie. When he looked up at the boy, Orlando thought that the heavy bags under the old man's eyes were puffier than usual.

Don Absolón gingerly took the glass with thumb and index finger while he riveted his glance on the boy's face. His bulbous eyes narrowed as he studied Orlando's face. He did this in silence, taking his time, knowing that his servant would not move away until he was excused. Seconds passed, but because this was unusual behavior for *el patrón,* Orlando began to sense trouble. He shifted from one foot to the other as he hid the tray behind his back, trying to conceal his hands that were beginning to shake. The boy's growing apprehension eased when Don Absolón finally spoke.

"How long have you been working in this house?"

"Nearly two years, *patrón.*"

"How old are you?"

"Sixteen. I think."

"What do you mean, you think? When were you born? What year?"

"No one is sure, but my *Tata* tells me it was during the years of Presidente Alemán."

Don Absolón lifted the tiny glass to his jowls and sniffed its contents. He was calculating, remembering the dates of the Alemán administration. All the while, Orlando moved his weight from one foot to the other.

"Yes, that makes you sixteen or so."

"*Sí, patrón.*"

The old man drifted off into silence once again, but since he had not made his usual hand motion excusing Orlando from his presence, the boy knew he was to stand there for as long as was necessary. Finally, Don Absolón spoke, but only after draining the glass of its contents.

"Why have you been keeping company with Rufino?"

Orlando froze, his hand in mid-air as he was reaching to take the snifter from his master's fingertips. Although Don Absolón's voice was hushed, the boy heard the rough edge of accusation in the words that had dripped out of the old man's lips.

"We're friends, *patrón.*"

"*Friends?* Since when is someone the likes of you *friends* with a Mayorga? Who gave you permission? What are you thinking?"

The roar in Orlando's ears prevented him from hearing the rest of what Don Absolón was saying, and he found himself struggling against the intense desire to run and not stop until he had escaped those bulging, watery eyes. When he saw the old man get to his feet, Orlando squeezed shut his own eyes, expecting blows to come down on his face and neck. But nothing happened. Instead, he was startled back into opening his eyes. He detected the sound of the soft leather of his master's slippers shuffling on the marble floor. Before disappearing into the darkness of the long corridor, Don Absolón stopped and stiffly turned toward Orlando.

"*En esta vida, siempre hay que guardar nuestro lugar.*"

In this life, it is always necessary to keep one's place. The old man's words echoed, bouncing off the vaulted ceiling, crashing down on Orlando. Once alone in the room, however, he responded to the urge to escape, and turned and fled through the huge dining room with its polished silver and carved furniture. He ran through connecting hallways and parlors, until reaching the vast kitchen. When he streaked by the cooks and dishwashers, they hardly recognized the blur of speed, and Orlando kept running until he crashed through the low entrance to his *palapa,* panting and out of breath.

"*¿Qué pasa,* Quintín?"

"*Nada, Mamá, nada.*"

He knew that his response to his mother, that nothing had happened, would not be enough. He was covered in sweat, gasping through a gaping mouth, and his face was twisted with fear. He knew she would not be satisfied until he told her the truth.

"*El patrón, Mamá . . .* "

"*¿Qué del patrón,* Quintín?"

The boy's heart began to return to its normal rhythm, allowing him to speak. He swallowed a large gulp of saliva before telling her what had happened.

"He knows that Rufino and I are friends."

"*¡Ay, Dios Santo!*"

"But he didn't do anything, Mamá! He just walked away from me when I told him the truth."

"*¡Ay, Dios Santo!*"

"Mamá, don't worry. Nothing will happen. Maybe *el patrón* likes me as a friend for his son."

Orlando watched as his mother slid down onto her haunches and rubbed her hands together. She kept quiet, and her silence scared him. He wanted to hear that she agreed and that everything was fine, that nothing bad would happen because of his friendship with Rufino Mayorga. Mother and son remained in silence for the next few minutes as night drew near, and even until Orlando's father slipped in through the entrance. With a glance, his mother let Orlando know that he should wait outside, and he obeyed without saying a word. Once outside of the hut, however, he could hear the soft murmur of his mother's voice; he even thought that he heard her weeping.

The next day, the boy's ingenuousness was shattered when his father met him as he was leaving for work. Orlando was alarmed when he saw a stranger standing not far behind his father, but curiosity overcame his fear almost immediately. He leaned his head to the side as he peered at the man, who was too tall to be a Lacandón, but too dark-complexioned to be a mestizo. The stranger stared at Orlando out of beady, onyx-colored eyes that appeared not to have eyelids; those marble-like eyes were shadowed by bushy eyebrows that coiled upward like tiny horns. His nose curved downward; it hung over a bulbous harelip through which the man's front teeth protruded. Orlando stared at that mouth because he had never seen another like it, and he saw that although it was fringed by a mustache, the ugliness could not be disguised.

The man was dressed in khaki, with a revolver hanging on his belt. When Orlando looked down at his feet, he saw that the man wore heeled boots with pointed toes. His eyes snapped upward to again look at that scary face, and he focused on the stranger's large, northern-style sombrero, which he wore pulled low over his brow.

Orlando's father finally spoke. He did it calmly, but the boy detected fear in his words. Father and son stared at one another. *"Hijo, el patrón* has assigned you to work as a *boyero,* and this man is here to take you to where you will be working from now on."

"¡Tata!"

"Go, Quintín! Take care of yourself because now you're a man and no one will be there to help you. Come to see us whenever you can."

"¡Tata!"

Orlando saw grief stamped on his father's face. When he turned to look at the man to see if his reflected similar emotion, he saw only hardness and determination in his eyes. Suddenly, the boy was overcome with images of what he had heard about the burden of a *boyero:* labor along teams of oxen that pulled the giant mahogany trunks through the mud of the jungle; the danger of being sucked in by mire to suffer a hideous death, either by suffocation, or by being crushed under the hooves of the straining beasts; the pain of being devoured by carnivorous mosquitoes that tear at human flesh, bit by bit; the agony of indescribable fatigue that can never be relieved because the work is endless. Orlando had overheard grown men weep, telling how even one trunk of mahogany is known as *oro verde* because of its high cost in lives of men and animals, as well as for the high price paid for its lumber.

The stranger gave Orlando a short time to put a few belongings in a pack and to say goodbye to his mother and father. After that, he found himself trekking behind the sullen man, who was to lead him into the heart of the Lacandona Jungle where the mahogany was harvested. Orlando followed his guide, lost in silence, wondering if he would ever see his mother or father again, asking himself if Rufino would try to persuade Don Absolón to bring him back to *la finca.* As he hiked, Orlando felt scared, and the saliva in his mouth was dry and bitter.

When they arrived at the campsite, Orlando saw a few dilapidated huts clustered against a long shed that held more than a dozen hammocks. It was nightfall, and there were scattered campfires, around which the boy made out other young men, most of them close to him in age. He saw by the way in which they crouched, or slouched on the ground, that they were dejected and exhausted.

As they neared the place, the man made a gesture with his hand, and a boy appeared out of the darkness.

"This is the new *boyero*. Take him to your place. Show him what he's to do. If he dies in the first week, you will be held responsible."

"*Sí, señor.*"

Orlando felt a terror he had never before experienced when he heard those words, and he bolted, intending to escape, but several bodies accosted him almost immediately, tackling and knocking him to the ground. The boy who had been put in charge of him grappled with him until Orlando settled down, breathing heavily through his mouth.

"*¡No seas pendejo!* There's no escape from here, so what's the use of being stupid? Come on, I'll show you your *hamaca.*"

Orlando followed the boy, who wore only pants cut off above the knees, taking in his back and spindly legs. He saw that his hair was encrusted with mud and that his ears and neck were streaked with caked slime. Orlando stared at the network of mosquito wounds that showed on the boy's neck, back, chest and arms. He could tell that some of the scars were old, but that others were so fresh that blood still glistened on the scabs.

"My name is Aquiles Rendón. What's yours?"

"Quintín Osuna."

"Come on! Don't hang your head that way. Soon you'll get used to this shit camp and make the best of it. I'll teach you to stay alive, and that's all you have to know. Lots of the *boyeros* that come here don't stop to think that there's only one important thing here, and it's not food, not sleep, not even money. The only important thing is not dying, staying alive. And I'll teach you how to do that, I promise. You know what, Quintín? You're one goddamn lucky *boyero* because El Brujo has put you in my hands."

Orlando, who had been walking alongside Aquiles, listening to what he was saying, suddenly stopped, wondering why the man with the harelip was called the sorcerer. He looked at the other boy with curiosity.

"*Ah, sí,* you want to know why he's called a *brujo.* Well, for one thing, just look at his eyes and you'll see that they're the eyes of a bat.

They're small, beady and black like those of a *murciélago*. Have you noticed that his teeth are pointed? The guys around here all say that he never sleeps, that he's always watching so he can run to the *patrón* with whatever bad things he can say about us. Maybe he is a bat, or maybe he's a *brujo* who knows stinking witchcraft. Maybe at night his arms turn into webbed wings and he flaps over the *caoba* trees, spying on the whole goddamn jungle. I don't know. All I know is that wherever the giant *caobas* grow, that's where he leads us. Another thing about him: If he even begins to hate a *boyero*, that's it for that poor *cabrón*; that guy mysteriously is sucked into the mud never to be seen again. Believe me, Quintín, I've seen that happen many, many times."

Orlando felt frightened by Aquiles' talk of El Brujo and his sorcery. Such things happened, he knew. Knowing this added to his apprehension about the camp and the work he was supposed to do. To fight off his fear, he shifted his attention from the sorcerer.

"What will I have to do? I've only heard of *boyeros,* not what they do."

"Well, *amigo,* a *boyero* is the poor *cabrón* who pushes the oxen to drag the *caoba* trunks through the mud to a river so they'll float away to the nearest port. You and I are *boyeros,* which means we're less strong than an ox, and because of that we're less important. Don't worry. Just do what I do and listen to what I tell you, and you'll be safe."

As Aquiles spoke, Orlando concentrated on his face and head: unruly hair spiked by countless coats of slime; a broad, flat forehead; tiny, slanted eyes out of which a silvery spark flashed; high cheek bones and a broad mouth filled with large white teeth.

"How long have you been working here?"

"I was thirteen years old when my father got drunk and got into a fight with one of the *patrón's* servants. My father disappeared. No one knows where he is. I was sent here because I am the only son and had to take his place. That was three years ago, but I still have five more years because I was sent here for eight. How many years will you have to be here?"

Shocked that he did not have an answer, Orlando gaped at Aquiles. He did not know how long he would have to be in that camp; no one had even mentioned a term. He felt his chest tighten.

"I don't know. El Brujo didn't say."

"*¡Qué chinga, amigo!* I never heard of any of the guys coming here without knowing for how long. You better find out, but not right away. Later on, when *El Brujo* sees you doing a good job, you can ask him. He won't put the evil eye on you that way. Now, we'd better get to sleep because day after tomorrow, we head for the jungle at dawn and we need to rest as much as possible. We'll stay there for four weeks working, and believe me, there are no hammocks there. A *boyero* sleeps where he falls in the mud at night, when he can't walk anymore because he's so tired. Then at dawn *El Brujo* comes with his prong and sticks it into you until you get back on your feet to work for the day."

That night, Orlando hung listless in the swinging hammock as his mind wrestled with unanswered questions: *Why am I here if my only mistake was to be a friend to Rufino Mayorga? Why is Aquiles in this camp if he has never done anything wrong? Are the other boys here for similar reasons? What are the chances of escaping from this place?*

"*Compañero,* don't think of it."

Aquiles' voice cut through the darkness, startling Orlando, who suddenly thought that his companion had been hearing his thoughts. He rolled over on his shoulder to peer across to where Aquiles swayed in his hammock. Orlando squinted in the dark, trying to discern the expression on his face.

"I know what you're thinking. It's what goes through all our minds when we first get here. But the camp is guarded at all times. Even if you don't see them, they're waiting for any one of us who tries to run away."

Orlando felt his chest well up with frustration and rage, anger at something unseen, a presence he could not identify. Then Don Absolón's puffy face appeared in the gloom, its baggy eyes leering at him, his slack mouth grinning. Orlando's stomach ached when he swallowed the bitter saliva that had filled his mouth. He was miserable and confused as he hung in the flat, humid jungle air, not knowing that years would pass before he could free himself from the mud of the *boyero's* life.

Chapter 15

I'll see that he's taken care of.

Young Rufino was standing next to the stone sink taking a drink of water when he overheard the maids gossiping about his friend Quintín Osuna. When Rufino realized that they hadn't seen him because he was standing in a dark corner of the kitchen, he decided to eavesdrop on them.

"They took the boy. Several people saw El Brujo come after him."

"*Comadre,* are you certain?"

"*Sí.*"

"That overseer is a devil. He could only bring harm to Quintín. But then . . . well . . . maybe . . . I think you're mistaken."

"Well, don't believe me if you don't want to, but others were standing near the Osuna *palapa* and even swear that they caught a glimpse of the Evil One's eyes."

"*¡Virgen Santísima!* If that's what happened, we'll never see young Quintín again."

Rufino's eyes widened as he listened to the women's soft murmurs. He could not make sense of their words, but they filled him with fear. The thought of his friend being taken away by his father's overseer overwhelmed him so much that the last gulp of water he had taken was still trapped in his mouth; his throat had clamped shut.

"*¿Por qué?* What could the boy have done to be sent away with that evil man?"

"Not much! Everyone knows what *el patrón* is like, and that any little thing can cause him to do the most terrible things. Remember his sister? If he was so cruel to his own flesh and blood, what can anyone else expect."

In his mind, Rufino also asked the woman's question: Why would his father punish his friend by sending him away from his mother and father? He remembered his aunt and her punishment, but that was different because she had done something bad and deserved what she got. Quintín had done nothing except be a good friend to him.

Suddenly this thought froze in Rufino's brain. He remembered that every time he and Quintín had gone far into the jungle to play, it had been behind his father's back because he had known all along that he was not supposed to act as if Quintín was like him. He had not paid attention to any of the warnings. Shaken, he put down the glass he was holding and dashed out of the kitchen, startling the maids and cooks as he rushed by them.

Rufino found his father sitting at his desk in the study. The day was ending, but there was still enough daylight filtering through the tall windows, allowing Don Absolón to read the document he held in his hands. When he heard the door close, he looked up as he removed the small reading glasses that perched on the bridge of his nose.

"*Hijo.* Come in."

"*Buenas tardes, Padre.*"

The old man squinted as he focused on his son's image. As always, he felt a pang of emotion just looking at Rufino, his youngest, his favorite, the center of his hopes. There were the three older brothers, but Don Absolón had long ago pinned his attention on Rufino as his successor. The old man absentmindedly rubbed his chin with one hand and beckoned his son to come nearer to him with the other.

"*¿Qué pasa,* Rufino? You look upset. Are you feeling sick?"

"No, *Padre,* I'm fine. It's just that I've heard words that I think are only gossip."

Sensing an awkward moment, Don Absolón sat up in the armchair as he motioned to Rufino to sit in a nearby chair. He had expected that his son would require an explanation regarding the Indian boy, but he had not thought that the moment would come so soon. Nonetheless, the old man was prepared.

"What is it that you've heard?"

"That Quintín Osuna was taken away by El Brujo."

"*El Bru* . . . Rufino, the best overseer on our property has a name. *¡Por favor!*"

"I'm sorry, *Padre*, but I don't know it."

Don Absolón was only trying to put Rufino on the defensive while buying time in which to discern his son's feelings. The truth was that even he did not remember the overseer's name. He sucked his teeth and shrugged his shoulders, letting Rufino know that he should go on with what he was saying.

"*¿Por qué, Padre?* Quintín was my friend."

Don Absolón was momentarily taken off guard by Rufino's looks and words filled with emotion. He saw that his face had drained of its usual color, and he thought that the boy might even be close to tears. But instead of moving him to sympathy, this impression of deep affection of his son for the Indian boy only reinforced the old man's decision to have done away with him.

"Precisely!"

"Precisely?"

"Yes, Rufino! That the boy has cleverly made his way into your friendship is *precisely* why he should be sent away. His likes should never forget their place when it comes to mingling with our families. In fact, *Hijo,* we, too, must be held to the same rule. We must not lose the place we have occupied for so many generations by letting those under us believe that they are our equals."

Don Absolón abruptly halted his harangue when he saw that Rufino's face was betraying confusion, and somewhere hidden behind the pupils of his eyes, the old man thought he detected resentment, even resistance to what he was saying. When his son kept quiet, Don Absolón decided to take another route.

"At any rate, *Hijo,* this is really only a trivial incident, one that you'll forget as soon as you go to the academy. As a matter of fact, this letter I'm reading is your acceptance as a cadet. Isn't this what you've always wanted?"

The tactic worked. Rufino's eyes changed almost immediately on hearing that not only was he accepted by the military school in Mexico City but that his father was actually agreeing to it. But he was jarred by the sudden change in his father, since he had always said that he wanted Rufino to stay on the *finca* to learn its ways of operation. Quintín Osuna's absence began to recede to the back of his mind.

"I thought you wanted me to stay here."

"Well, yes, that's what I want. On the other hand, *Hijo,* it would be good for you to mingle with the men that have always been our right hand. Who knows, you might even be a colonel or a general, eh? That's it! General Rufino Mayorga!"

Don Absolón's bloated face contorted into a grimace as he patronized Rufino, humoring and condescending to his boyish wishes. He knew, however, that his youngest son would ultimately be his inheritor; he would assure this against whatever obstacles might arise. He knew that a few years away from Las Estrellas would cure Rufino of his outlandish dream of being an officer. The boy's calling was to a much higher status.

Rufino got to his feet as his heart raced with joy because he would be joining the academy. As he turned to leave the room, however, he remembered the reason he had come to speak to his father in the first place. Quintín's brown face flashed in front of him; it seemed to be waiting for Rufino to do something.

"Padre, what about my friend?"

Don Absolón, who had already returned his attention to his papers, looked up. His expression was neutral, revealing nothing.

"Don't worry about him. I'll see that he's taken care of."

Chapter 16

There was only emptiness.

"Hey, Quintín, tomorrow I go out to do my last four weeks of shit work. What do you think of that, *amigo?* Eight years of this hell. *¡Qué chinga!* And now I'm going back to my *palapa.* I wonder if there's anyone left to remember me."

Orlando and Aquiles were ending a week of rest and ready to undergo another four weeks of harvesting mahogany. Orlando sat cross-legged, leaning against a tree, staring into the campfire that crackled with burning embers. Though he appeared not to be listening to Aquiles, he was hearing every word. As his companion rambled, Orlando felt torn between joy for Aquiles because he would soon be free, and envy because he, himself, was to remain locked into that life of captivity which he had now endured for five long years.

Orlando now remembered how he had worked up the courage to go to El Brujo to ask him the length of his term as a *boyero.* He had dared to approach the man just a day after his arrival, only to be told that *el patrón* was thinking about it and would give word of his decision. When days passed and Orlando received only the bat-like glares of the overseer, he went to him again.

He approached El Brujo, afraid, but his desire to know what was to become of him overcame his apprehension. He swallowed a large gulp of saliva as he neared the man who, as always, stood apart and silent.

"*Señor.*"

"*¿Qué quieres?*"

El Brujo beaked his upper lip as he glared at Orlando, who shifted his feet in nervousness, thinking that the man was deliberately toying with him, pretending to have forgotten their talk of a few days earlier. He breathed deeply, trying to overcome the anger that was welling up in his chest.

"I want to know what Don Absolón has decided about me."

"About you?"

"I mean, how long will I have to be a *boyero?*"

"Until he decides that you have paid for your crime."

"Crime? I haven't committed a crime!"

"Are you defying Don Absolón's wisdom?"

"No, señor. I'm only asking a question."

"The answer to your question is that I didn't ask *el patrón* what he intends to do with you, so I'm sure he's forgotten all about you and whatever you did."

El Brujo's words stunned Orlando, who felt that his legs were about to give out and that he would crumble at the overseer's feet. The boy held his breath, struggling to get control of his racing heart and the overwhelming surge of hatred flooding him. Aquiles' words came to him: *If he even begins to hate a* boyero, *that's it for that poor* cabrón; *that poor devil mysteriously is sucked into the mud, never to be seen again.*

Orlando turned away from the man without a word, knowing that his hatred had leaked out of his eyes, and that El Brujo was now sure to put the evil eye on him. Orlando didn't care, however. Don Absolón and El Brujo had put him there for nothing, and what was worse, he would remain a *boyero* until he died, either with mud clogging his throat or from snake bite. What did it matter if the sorcerer put a hex on him? Nothing mattered now.

It was only his second day in the camp, but Orlando knew he was a dead man. His hatred for El Brujo intensified with each step he took away from the man, and his body grew so cold that by the time he reached the campfire Aquiles had started, he thrust his hand into the burning branches.

"*¡Epa, amigo! ¿Estás loco?*"

Aquiles lunged toward Orlando and yanked his hand from the embers, but not fast enough to prevent it from being scorched. The burn did nothing to lessen the chill that had invaded Orlando's insides.

His teeth rattled one against the other, and his body shivered as if he were buried in ice.

"¡Ese cabrón! ¡Ese cabrón! ¡Qué chingue a su madre!" Orlando stuttered, hurling insults at El Brujo, mumbling profanities that even Aquiles had not heard. His friend, mouth open, stared at his *compañero,* not understanding the cause of his fury, but when Orlando regained some composure, he told Aquiles what had happened, launching into more obscenities.

"¡Ay, amigo! This is not good! This is very bad for you. Be careful because one day that devil will try to kill you."

Orlando could not bring himself to accept the sentence that El Brujo had hurled at him. If Don Absolón had forgotten him, then it would be true that he was to stay at the *caoba* camp until he died, by accident or at the hands of the sorcerer. A separate idea took hold of him: What about his mother and father? If the old *patrón* had indicted him so severely for doing nothing, what about them? Understanding this compelled him to begin a plan of escape. He spent weeks spying on the guards that surrounded the camp. When he detected sloppiness in one or two of them, he concentrated on their every move: how they snoozed while the overseer was not keeping an eye on them, how they were careless with their weapons, how they became distracted when they joked and gossiped while on guard.

After staking out the guards' day shift, Orlando decided that if he were to escape, his best chance would be after dark. So for countless evenings, while everyone slept, he crawled from his hammock and spent hours spying on the night guards. He discovered that they were even more negligent than the day watch, and that they slept most of the time.

One night, after waiting for Aquiles and everyone else to fall asleep, Orlando rolled a *petate,* lashed it to his back and tied a gourd filled with water to his waist. He crawled away from the *palapa,* past circles of fading embers in the center of the camp, past snoring *boyeros,* all the while grazing arms and legs that dangled from hammocks. Orlando slithered on his belly, clawing at the soggy earth with elbows and knees, struggling to muffle his strained breathing, knowing that the sound of a cracking branch might alert at least one of the snoozing sentries.

As he moved, he felt joy surging through him, knowing that each stroke of his arms and legs dragged him further away from the camp, away from the hateful sorcerer. When he judged that he had penetrated the ring of guards, he gingerly got to his knees and looked around him. The jungle was especially dark that moonless night, and there was only the humming of nocturnal reptiles and the occasional whelp of a howling monkey. He got to his feet and began to walk, carefully at first, then picking up pace until he reached a brisk rhythm, in spite of his sandaled feet sinking into the ooze of the jungle floor, hindering his speed.

Orlando's heart beat wildly because of the exertion, but more so because he understood that he would soon be free, that no one would be able to find him once he buried himself in the jungle, that never again would he fear a sorcerer or any *patrón*. His mind raced at the same speed as his heart, thinking, planning, rejoicing, knowing that he was no longer a captive.

He was suddenly yanked from his thoughts when something stopped him, and his legs seemed to be paralyzed as his ears tried to decipher a strange noise, something different, foreign to the night sounds of the jungle. He squinted his eyes as if this would sharpen his hearing. It was a rasping, flapping noise, like that of a bat's webbed wings beating against the humid night air.

Orlando's head jerked upward trying to see, but his vision was cut short by the dense canopy of tree branches. Terrified, his eyes searched, eager to penetrate the gloom from which the whipping sound grew stronger and nearer; he even felt a swirling current of air graze his face. He began to turn in circles, arms outstretched, gnarled fingers groping wildly in the dark as he strained to recognize the sound that was increasing his terror with each moment. His eyes were wide open, pupils dilated, as he scanned the treetops until he thought he caught a glimpse of a bat's silhouette. As he spun full circle away from the hateful image, his mouth open and gasping, his heart beating uncontrollably, a voice brought him to an abrupt halt.

"Boyero, ¿Qué haces?"

Orlando knew who it was. The shrill, hissing voice was unmistakable. When he gained control of his body, he turned toward the voice and he saw the bulbous, onyx-colored eyes of El Brujo shining in the blackness. Even in the dark, Orlando was able to make out the revolver in his hand. El Brujo held it high, pointed at Orlando's face.

"*¡Vámonos!*"

Nothing else was said. Orlando was so shaken that his tongue was sticking to the roof of his mouth. He could hardly force his legs to obey his mind, but he walked, nonetheless, stiffly at first, then at a brisker speed. As he moved, his mind was a swirl of confusion, fear and hatred. He could not understand how El Brujo had caught him, how he had known where to find him in the jungle's density and darkness. Orlando could not account for the flapping sounds he had heard, nor for the bat's image he was sure he had seen. He wondered if it had only been his imagination.

As he marched, he felt the sorcerer's gun grazing the nape of his neck; he could even smell the man's heavy breathing. Aside from that sound, everything was quiet. The jungle creatures were watching in silent awe, as if they, too, were wondering what would become of Orlando Flores.

When Orlando and El Brujo reached the camp, it was bristling with the comings and goings of men, no matter that it was before day-break. At first it was only a rumor that got around that someone had tried to escape, and that it had been the new *boyero* Quintín Osuna. Few men were alarmed because a first infraction by a *boyero* usually received a mild punishment: five days without nourishment, except for water. But it was always El Brujo who decided on the severity.

At dawn the gossiping among the *boyeros* stopped abruptly, when word went from mouth to mouth describing what was said to be Orlando's punishment. It was to be the worst, not the mildest. Aquiles rushed to El Brujo with the intention of intervening for his friend, but he saw that the sorcerer, two armed guards by his side, could not be approached. Besides, Aquiles also saw that Orlando was already being led to the pillory, where he would be flogged until he lost con-sciousness.

The lashing began in view of all of the workers; it was to be a lesson. As the whip cut through the air, each one of those men could feel the steel-tipped leather bite into his own flesh. Orlando at first was able to stay on his feet, but as the lashing increased, his knees began to buckle and eventually cave in, so that he was hanging with the entire weight of his body held up by his wrists, which were strapped into an iron ring at the top of the post.

Orlando's knees had failed him, but his heart continued to burn with hatred for El Brujo and all he represented. Orlando stayed conscious by repeating a promise to never forget what was happening to him, and what happened every day to men like him, and what had happened to his people for generations. His eyes fluttered, opened, fluttered and opened once again, letting everyone know that he refused to surrender to unconsciousness. The guard who was whipping him tired and had to be replaced, but Orlando still would not faint. The flesh on his back was in tatters, yet he would not allow himself to fall into darkness, despite the pain.

The men around him began to shift and move in indignation as the whipping continued; they cast angry eyes at El Brujo, but Orlando remained alert, aware. The sorcerer, urged by the other overseers, finally gave the order to cease the punishment. After all, his intention had been reached: Orlando was pulp and blood; the other *boyeros* had seen and learned their lesson. Yet, he had one more detail to add to that example.

"¡Córtenle un dedo de cada pie!"

To have a toe severed from each foot gave Orlando intolerable pain and even long after the wounds healed, the memory of that agony inhabited his heart and mind, and would do so until the day of his death. He never forgot that his was a solitary pain, but the suffering that anguished his people was universal, and this thought mitigated his own agony. These were the thoughts that caused Orlando to cease being a boy.

Now as he listened to Aquiles, Orlando realized that time had crawled for him since then. He had aged as if more than five years had passed. Only twenty-one years old, his body had taken on the appearance of a much older man. The constant labor of dragging chains through dense ooze while struggling against the pull of oxen had stunted Orlando's growth; only his feet had developed, but they were now out of proportion with his body size, and each foot missing a toe.

His arms were long and sinewy, their veins coiled from elbows to hands like blue snakes trying to slither around untold pockmarks left by relentless mosquito attacks. His face had broadened, flattened; his lips had also changed, clinging to the hollows caused by knocked-out teeth; and his eyes had lost the light that had been there on the day he left his *palapa.*

Orlando's greatest change, moreover, took place within him: somewhere around the heart, in the niche where his spirit lingered. The punishments he had endured, as well as countless unanswered questions, had left him with a growing anxiety, which surfaced masked as bitter rage. He often picked fights with his *compañeros,* battering anyone who would so much as glance at him.

Because his intelligence had been stunted, neglected, his mind often groped blindly for a way out of its dungeon, and he looked for reasons, for answers, but there was only emptiness. Orlando would often howl in desperation. He did this almost always when he was on a team of men, struggling, pulling at the chains that guided straining oxen. At those times, his screams disappeared into the din, swallowed by the clamor of grunting, cursing men, snorting beasts, shouting overseers and groaning, creaking tree trunks.

Now, listening to Aquiles, Orlando's mind drifted; he was thinking of where the mahogany trees grew. His thoughts traveled to the heart of the jungle, where torrential rain and humidity gathered in ravines and crevices, where that moisture penetrated the earth. There, fallen leaves rotted, mixing with dirt, dead insects, and reptiles, becoming impenetrable mud. It was there that for thousands of years, the mahogany had flourished. Their growth had been silent and secret until the *patrones* had discovered its worth: a wood more precious than gold to people beyond the ports and rivers of the Lacandona.

Orlando was thinking of how many boys he had seen perish, devoured by the mud of the jungle. His mind was looking at the gangs of workers responsible for prodding and pushing teams of oxen into dragging a trunk, and how that tree became caked with mud, rendering it heavier with each step. He was used to seeing *boyeros* risk tripping just to goad the oxen ahead, even if falling meant death under the beast's hooves, or asphyxiation by mud.

When the gang of workers finally cleared a section of trees, their task turned to chopping at the jungle to make a path, a *calzada,* from the fresh *caoba* grove to the river. It was only at those times that the overseers, under the bat's eye of El Brujo, armed the *boyeros* with machetes. Because the morass was so dense, this work was just as awful as goading oxen. As each man hacked at stubborn giant palms and undergrowth, he did so not knowing if he might be disturbing a nest of poisonous ants or falling into a snake pit. The overseers coaxed and pushed the workers forward relentlessly, shouting profanities and threats, commanding them to finish the path, never allowing time for rest or a drink of water. Many times a *boyero* collapsed, drained of all energy, and this meant that he would be left behind to die.

Now, as Aquiles chattered cheerfully, Orlando's fingers massaged the sores on his arms, wounds caused by swarms of blood-sucking mosquitoes. As he did this, his memory brought back the image of the pinkish ooze that dripped from a *boyero's* skin, aggravated yet more by the demanding pokes of El Brujo, who used his prodding stick insistently.

"*¡Ándale, cabrón! ¡Jala! ¡Jala!*"

Come on, son of a bitch! Pull! Pull! These words, which he heard coming from El Brujo's mouth, snapped Orlando back to the present and to the awareness of Aquiles' presence. As he looked over to his friend, he tried to smile, but realized that his face was stiff, unwilling to bend to such a gesture. He got to his feet and headed for his hammock, hoping that sleep would erase the intolerable images invading his mind. Dawn came, but time had dragged for Orlando that night because he had been unable to rest. He knew these would be his last weeks with Aquiles, and he was saddened, knowing that his friend would leave, that he would probably never see him again.

When Aquiles and Orlando joined the gang of *boyeros,* they saw that although they had been in the jungle for only a week, they were already exhausted beyond endurance. They sluggishly lined up, listening for El Brujo's shrill commanding voice. The men began the trek into the density of the jungle, followed by teams of oxen that looked as if they, too, sensed their own impending death. Two of them squatted on the ground, refusing to move, and no amount of prodding or pulling could make them get to their feet. The drivers lost patience with them and ordered those remaining in the camp to look after them. When Orlando saw this, he wondered what would happen if he got down on the ground and refused to move.

After a day's march, El Brujo signaled that they had arrived at the harvesting site. As the *boyeros* looked over the surrounding area, they saw countless prime *caoba* trees. Many of the boys secretly exchanged glances which confirmed: *I told you he's a sorcerer.* Other workers scratched their head, wondering how El Brujo always managed to find such rich reserves of timber, when others often lost their lives searching. Someone in the rear muttered, *"¡Cabrón brujo!"*

Orlando always kept his eye on the sorcerer, knowing that he, in turn, was continually spied on by those unblinking eyes. Years had passed since his attempted escape, but Orlando knew that the sorcerer planned to kill him and that Aquiles' prediction would some day come true.

Time passed, but nothing happened until the day foreseen by Aquiles arrived. At dawn, the caravan of *boyeros* and oxen struck a path toward the jungle, El Brujo, weapon in hand, at its head. The shift would begin with their dragging to the river a trunk left over from the night before. It would end with the beginnings of a path. Three men carried the necessary machetes.

"¡Ándenle! ¡Jalen! ¡Jalen!

El Brujo's shrill call to pull the trunk shattered the first rays of light that had begun to filter through the mesh of vines and trees. At his command, men and beasts strained to dislodge the tree that had doubled in weight as the mud coating it had hardened overnight. The hooves of the oxen plowed into the slime beneath them, sinking deeper each time the *boyeros* drove them on. As the animals struggled, the ooze beneath them churned, deepening, thickening. Its sucking sounds struck fear in the men, and they instinctively kept a distance while trying to reach the oxen with their prodding irons.

The struggle was at its peak when Orlando, straining at his section of chain, saw Aquiles slip; one of his ankles had buckled under his weight. He saw that his friend tried to regain his balance but the momentum of the pull worked against him, causing him to plunge headlong into the churning mire. Orlando dropped the chain and rushed to the edge of the mud, so close that he felt the haunches of an ox brush his torso. He thrust his arms into the slime, grabbed one of Aquiles' shoulders and raised him up far enough so that he could gasp air through his opened mouth.

As Orlando did this, the blast of a shotgun stopped all motion; even the animals froze. He looked over his shoulder in time to see El Brujo lower the weapon he held in his hands. In that second, Orlando snapped his face back to look at Aquiles and saw that part of his friend's face had been blasted away. It was at that moment that Orlando realized that the shot had been meant for him.

"¡Boyero Osuna! ¡A la chamba!"

The gang stood in stunned silence as they saw that Orlando refused to obey the command to return to work and that he no longer cared what El Brujo was ordering. They watched as he pulled Aquiles' body from the mire, dragged it to a small patch of solid ground, and there laid the remains of his friend. They followed his movements, watching as he wiped whatever mud he could from the bloodied face, and then gently crossed his friend's arms over his chest.

Orlando got to his feet, still not caring that the sorcerer was watching him, weapon in hand, with his bat-like gaze defying Orlando to do something. But then, with a speed that even El Brujo's eyes could not follow, Orlando leaped at the hold of machetes and, armed with one of the sharpened long knives, he sprang toward the sorcerer, reaching him before he could raise his shotgun.

Orlando's arm, grown tough with five years of hacking and chopping, raised the machete and brought it down on its target. The cut was clean, swift. El Brujo's head hit the ground while his body was still on its feet. Moments passed before it slowly crumbled to the soggy jungle floor, where its blood oozed through severed arteries into the mire. Years later, those who witnessed the execution swore that the sorcerer's blood was not red but white, like the milk of the *yuca*.

Orlando looked around him and saw that the *boyeros* as well as El Brujo's underlings were paralyzed into inaction by what had happened. No one moved or showed signs of daring to apprehend him.

They only stared, mouths agape. Seeing that no one intended to accost him, Orlando, the machete still in his hand, approached Aquiles' body and got down on his knees. He placed the machete by the body, taking its inert hand and closing it around the weapon's handle. He then got to his feet and disappeared into the jungle.

Chapter 17

The night in Tlatelolco had shaken him.

It was late October and the diffused autumn light filtering through tall windows accentuated the reflection in the full-length mirror. Twenty-one-year-old Rufino Mayorga stared at his image and was pleased with what he saw. His hazel-colored eyes took in his blond hair, oval-shaped face, long straight nose, wide mouth highlighted by lips clasped in a jaunty smile. His glance slipped downward, pausing on his broad shoulders, slim torso, long legs planted apart on the tiled floor. Rufino gawked at his mirrored image, gratified with how the officer's uniform, knee-length boots and shiny medals rendered him an exceptionally handsome figure.

He suddenly snapped out of his reverie when he remembered that he and other officers were expected at Los Pinos to dine with *El Señor Presidente*. The 1968 Olympic Games had ended and with those events a turbulent month had just closed in Mexico City. Rufino Mayorga had distinguished himself as a young officer, emerging from the bitter violence of those days with a sterling record, proving himself an enemy of the rabble that had tried to embarrass the country in the eyes of the world. Dinner with the president was his reward.

Rufino sniffed contentedly and looked at his watch, noting that there was still time before the driver was due to arrive. He walked to the window and stared out at the steel-colored sky while he waited. Soon it would be dark, but there was still enough light for him to make out rooftops, and farther away the silhouettes of the Tower of the Americas and other tall buildings. He craned his neck to look down at streets, now eerily silent after the turmoil of the past month.

He turned his gaze north of the Zócalo, to Tlatelolco, and his thoughts drifted back to the mass student demonstration of October 2. The towering silhouette cut into the night by the church of Santiago de Compostela loomed in his memory, its giant wooden doors slowly creaking shut. The square was jammed with people chanting, shouting, singing, protesting. In his memory, Rufino looked beyond the left flank of the church and focused on the building known as El Chihuahua; its balconies were filled with screaming, ranting university students, its walls draped with insulting placards and banners. Over tinny microphones, hysterical voices poured out scorn, all of it aimed at the government, at the ruling class, at the military.

"¡Asesinos!"

"¡Gorilas!"

"¡Puercos!"

"¡Gobierno de mierda!"

When Rufino received the order to be one of the officers in charge of dispersing the crowd, he felt proud, but when he actually confronted that outraged mass of people, he was filled with terror. Face to face, he realized that the troops he commanded were identical to the mob filling the plaza, except that his men were uniformed. Amid the turmoil, Rufino had looked at them as if for the first time, seeing their flat, brown faces, accentuated by slanted eyes, broad mouths with lips that barely covered buck teeth. *What if they turn on me?* His soldiers did not turn on him; they obeyed his orders when he commanded them to fire into the crowd, leaving him wondering why they fired on people who looked just like them.

Rufino, standing at the window, thought he now heard the echo of panic-stricken voices floating in the chilly air, and his eyes conjured images of bodies falling, riddled with bullets, others trampled by those trying to escape the carnage. He remembered looking upward and seeing the scramble of young men and women, leaping from an upper balcony to the one below, some making it, others falling two and three floors.

The battle—his men against the students—lasted the entire night, and when it was over, Rufino felt sickened, not by the deaths and maiming of people, but because he discovered that he detested the sound and stench of violence. He was convinced that the insurgents deserved to be crushed, and that force was the only way. He wondered, however, if it was for the likes of him to carry out such tasks.

Rufino turned away from the window, glanced at his watch, then looked again at his image in the mirror. He absentmindedly fidgeted with the top button of his tunic, then straightened one of the medals while his train of thought returned to the subject of living a military life. He had to admit that the night at Tlatelolco had shaken him and deeply eroded his resolve to be an officer. He had discovered that he found the experience too untidy, too messy—not at all for him.

Rufino stood in the middle of the room, lost in thought; his mind was toying with an idea that had emerged on that violent night: *My father would rejoice if I returned to stay at* Las Estrellas. This thought conjured an old memory of his friend Quintín Osuna, of whom he had heard nothing. Over the years, whenever he remembered to ask his father, Don Absolón would shrug his shoulders or merely change the subject. Rufino, as always when thinking of his boyhood friend, discovered that he barely remembered his face. He imagined that it now might resemble that of one of the soldiers under his command, or he might even look like one of the dead students. Rufino was yanked out of his thoughts by a soft rap on the door, announcing that his car was ready.

Before leaving, Rufino stepped over to the chair where he had laid his cap and gloves. As he turned, he could not help but see his reflection in the mirror once again. He was tall, handsome, refined, soon to reach the prime of his life. The image told him that a life in the barracks was not for him—perhaps for others, but not for him.

Chapter 18

We call him Tatic, Little Father.

Orlando Flores became a fugitive in 1968, the year of the massacre at Tlatelolco. It was also in that year that the Catholic bishops of Latin America met in Medellín to ask one another how the Church was to spread not only the word of God, but also the word of God's people. But those prelates were mostly perplexed; they had only the old ways to talk about God. One of them knew what to do, nevertheless, and it was he who signaled the exodus to freedom of the congregations he shepherded.

Led by a bishop, the journey of the tribes that inhabited the canyons, the highlands and the jungle was difficult; it took years. The spiritual centers of the movement became Ocosingo and San Cristóbal de Las Casas, where teachers, organizers and social workers congregated after heeding the bishop's call to catechize in a new manner, a way in which the people were brought together not to hear but to be heard, not to erase their culture but to remember it, not to disdain their mysticism but to rediscover it.

When this new spirit swept through Chiapas, Orlando was only twenty-one years old, but he, like his people, had already sustained indescribable physical and mental pain; he had also killed a man. He knew that Don Absolón would not be lenient, much less forgiving, of the native who murdered his favored overseer. *El patrón* would not rest until he had Orlando's severed head dangling from a *ceiba* tree.

These thoughts collided with concern for his mother and father. He was torn between the certainty of death for himself if he went back to Lacanjá, and the fear that his family might be punished in retribution if he did not return. He pondered this dilemma and finally decided to flee into the deepest part of the Lacandona Jungle, away from Lacanjá. This choice would gnaw at Orlando thereafter, growing as years passed, filling him with guilt and sadness.

Orlando wandered through the jungle, feeding on fish he captured from rivers or small game he ensnared in traps he constructed. He emerged from the density from time to time, entering villages or *rancherías* where he would accept food or a garment in return for small jobs rendered. In time, people grew to recognize him; they knew that he was a fugitive, shielding himself from a *patrón* or any of the many *catxul* who prowled in search of natives they hungered to punish.

Orlando hid in the jungle for five years, and during that time he became haggard, deep wrinkles surfacing on his face. As time passed, solitude became a burden to him, growing until he decided that he had changed so much that he would not be recognized if he emerged from hiding. He decided to head for Ocosingo, a town with streets and houses, a place where he could more easily disappear into the crowds of Tzeltales, Choles and even other Lacandones. In an effort to make his capture yet more unlikely, he did away with the tribal tunic he still wore and put on faded trousers and a cotton shirt. He cut his hair short around the ears and neck, and combed it back on his forehead, making him look less like a Lacandón and more like an ordinary laborer. It was then that he changed his name to Orlando Flores.

He worked in whatever place would give him a job: in the fly-infested butcher shops that lined the main market street, on construction sites laying bricks and smearing plaster on walls, on plantations picking beans. Countless times, Orlando stood on corners, along with other day laborers, waiting to be picked up by paneled eight-wheeler trucks that transported gangs of men to work places, sometimes as far removed from Ocosingo as Palenque, where luxury hotels were in construction as a result of the flow of tourists.

It was on those long trips when the fatigued men were given a break to eat a lunch of cold tortillas stuffed with beans to be swallowed with gulps of water, that Orlando began to concentrate on the workers' talk. At first, he disregarded their conversations, judging them to be mere babble, tuning them out and taking the moment to catch a bit of sleep. But soon, he began to listen, to take in what he was hearing as well as to witness the impact of those words; such talk had never before reached his ears.

He heard, for the first time, mention of a bishop who had sent out his representatives to help the people, and that changes were happening because of the new ideas being spread by those envoys. Slowly, Orlando began to understand that those men around him were speaking with one spirit, that they were no longer separated by tribal customs and beliefs, but united by the conviction that, together, their lives could be changed for the better.

¡Tierra! ¡Educación! ¡Salubridad!

Land! Education! Health! When Orlando began to take notice of that talk, he realized that his fellow workers were speaking of privileges enjoyed only by the *patrones* and their offspring, and that now the natives were murmuring of the possibility of having those same rights. He felt a mix of reactions: disbelief, yearning, disdain, hope. Soon Orlando began to join in the conversations by asking questions, challenging glib answers, raising doubts. Each time, to his surprise, his queries were satisfied with a believable response.

"Hey, *amigo!* Why don't you come to our meetings? Sometimes we meet in Ocosingo, at others in San Cristóbal."

Orlando eventually did join the meetings, which were held in places not easily observed by the police: sometimes in assembly halls, but mostly in churches. At first, he only listened as the bishop's representatives spoke, leading groups in discussion of different issues and concerns. He especially concentrated on his fellow workers, men and women, who had borne witness to family memories and histories, presenting testimonies and experiences. Orlando kept silent for almost a year; despite his wanting to speak, he felt inhibited. He feared bringing attention to himself. He was afraid that his hatred and bitterness might spill out of his mouth, but most of all he dreaded that he was not intelligent enough to speak. So his tongue stuck to the roof of his mouth.

One evening his *compañeros* and *compañeras* met in San Cristóbal de Las Casas, in the Church of Santo Domingo. Orlando, who had never been in that place before, was staggered by its huge altar and tabernacle. As he swiveled his head in all directions, his eyes reflected the glow of the gold leaf covering the church's massive walls. He squinted as he gazed, first upward at the ornate pulpit, then downward at the stone floor polished smooth over the centuries by bare feet and mendicant knees. As he walked in, side by side with dozens of workers—the men with sombreros in hand, the women with heads covered by rebozos—he knew that they, too, were equally amazed. He saw that they looked up and around, pivoting heads and craning necks to get a better look at the paintings of saints, popes and angels. Next to them, Orlando felt puny, diminished in the presence of such grandeur.

"*¡Órale, compañero!* Don't forget that our people made this place with their own sweat and bent backs."

Orlando swung around to see who had whispered those words to him, but he caught only a glimpse of a short woman who winked at him as she walked by. He tried to catch up to her to speak to her, but she had disappeared into the milling throng of natives. Then someone tapped him on the shoulder, letting him know that everyone was expected to sit, so he squatted on his haunches and concentrated on the first speaker of the evening, the same woman who had spoken to him.

"*¡Hermanas y hermanos!* Tonight I bring words to you that will make our bishop better known to all of us. We will discover that he has been with us before, that he has felt not only our own pain but that of our ancestors of many generations ago. Look! Look up there!"

As she spoke, the woman pointed a short finger at the pulpit that had captivated Orlando; it was lodged in the upper part of the wall and rose high above their heads. A surge of faces turned at once, lifting to observe the small, rectangular box shrouded at that moment in darkness.

"It was from that pulpit that our bishop first spoke out in defense of our anguish. It was from these very stones on which you sit that our ancestors listened to him. This is my testimonial, words which I received from my mother, who received them from her mother, and she from her mother, and so on from the mothers beyond memory, reaching back to the year 1545, when our bishop walked up these steps and spoke. Please listen with your hearts as well as with your ears.

"At that time, one of our *compañeras* sat with our people in this place. She knew that there, close to the pulpit, stood the slave masters, the land and mine owners, the *capitanes,* those who kept order and received favors from those above them, the *maestros* and priests who absolved a man from sin if he paid the proper amount, or excommunicated him if he failed to honor the system.

"Behind those men stood their women, elegant and stiff, fluttering fans, playing with a loose end of lace, or tugging at underwear that was too tight, cutting into soft parts of their flesh. Those women attended mass daily along with their servants, and it was the task of those maids to bring cups of hot chocolate to their mistresses to fortify them during the long ceremony.

"Our *compañera*'s mind wandered during the service; she was thinking, remembering. She had returned to her valley twenty years before, a time when she was searching for her family members who had vanished. They had been among those who chose death by flinging themselves over cliffs rather than being snared into slavery. But she was prevented from killing herself, so there was nothing left for her to do but work for and obey the new masters.

"As our *compañera*'s thoughts drifted, her fingers touched a scar on her arm, and she remembered the searing pain caused by the boiling water, no matter that it had happened years before, when she was only a child. To forget her pain, she stared up at the statues: saints, women as well as men, with faces which resembled no one among her people. Then she shifted her eyes, squinting as she focused on the gold covering the walls of this very church. She let her vision focus on the altar and its golden tabernacle; everywhere she looked there was that yellow metal prized above all things by the masters. Look, *compañeras* and *compañeros!* The gold is still there. Just as she saw it!

"Her attention at that moment was drawn by a boy, dressed in the same garments as the priest, who walked onto the altar with a long pole to light the candles. Soon the front part of the church glowed with the amber and red tones set off by the tiny flames. She looked toward the elevated pulpit, concentrating on its ornate depiction of angels, devils, apostles, virgins, centurions, swords, lances and wheels—all of it snarled together like snakes in a pit.

"Suddenly, the altar bell rang out telling everyone that our bishop was about to begin the mass. Our *compañera* stretched her neck to get a better look, because she had heard the rumor that this priest was different, that he often scolded, even punished those of his own kind for injustices done to the natives.

"'*¡Indios, levántense!*'

"*¡Compañeros!* How well we know those words, eh? The skinny cleric barked out the order for our people to rise to their feet in sign of respect. Sighing and grunting, they got up, most of them struggling to straighten backs so used to being curved and stooped. A young Lacandón man helped our *compañera* to her feet.

"Our bishop intoned the opening of the ritual and he was answered by the congregation. Our *compañera* listened as the masters responded vigorously, loudly, making certain that those around them took note of their presence. Our people, however, could only mumble the words because, like us, they could not understand what they meant, nor could their tongues repeat the strange sounds. But they made sure to move their lips, because the cleric in charge watched them with eagle eyes.

"As the mass moved forward, everyone continually stood, knelt, returned to their feet, and then did it all over again. While the up-and-down rhythm added to our *compañera's* weariness, the motions appeared to invigorate the masters. As our bishop followed along with the ritual, his flock became agitated, acting as if they were at a fiesta. Some whispered, others made eyes at one another, smiling, flirting. Our *compañera* snorted through her nose when she observed how the women shuffled and twittered, slurping loudly as they took their chocolate, making sure that everyone understood that their brew was made from a superior crop of cocoa beans. All the while, the service continued.

"Soon, our bishop ascended that very same pulpit we now see to read from his holy book, but he refused to begin until there was complete silence. Minutes passed before the masters and their women realized that our brother was waiting. When they finally hushed, he began to read. At this point our *compañera* opened her ears, deciding that she wanted to know what he would have to say.

"'A lesson taken from the Apostle Saint John.'

"By now our *compañera* realized that the tone of our bishop's voice was harsh, even intimidating. She was happy when she saw the elegant men and women startled, staring up at the small figure, which seemed to become a giant with each passing moment, and whose eyes were filled with outrage. His purple vestments appeared to darken as he read. Our people listened carefully as well, trying to understand the lisping sounds of that other language, the sounds we all now know so well.

"'Come now, you, the wealthy, weep and howl over the miseries which will come upon you. Your riches have rotted, and your garments have become moth-eaten.'

"Our *compañera* saw the masters shift from one side to the other. When she returned her gaze to our bishop, she saw that he sensed their agitation, and, interrupting the reading, he looked down at the upturned faces; he glared at their raised eyebrows, their pursed lips. Running his tongue over parched lips, he continued the reading; his voice was filled with rising anger.

"'Your gold and silver are rusted; and that rust will be a witness against you, and it will devour your flesh as fire does. You have laid up treasure in the last days. Behold! The wages of the laborers who reap your fields, which have been kept back by you unjustly, cry out; and their cry has entered into the ears of the Lord of Hosts!'

"'¡No!'

"'¡Shsss!'

"'¡Silencio!'

"'¡Abominación!'

"Our *compañera* felt her heart racing when she saw that our bishop went on reading, unafraid of the hissing and the irreverent shouting hurled at him by the congregation. Inexplicably, she understood every word, and she closed her eyes, hoping that he would not lose courage.

"'You have feasted upon the earth, and you have nourished your hearts on dissipation in the day of slaughter. You have condemned and put to death the Just!'

"Our bishop slammed shut the holy book that he held in one hand, and with the other he gesticulated vigorously. He waved his clenched hand in an arc, swinging it from one side to the other, encircling those beneath him. Our *compañera* saw that everyone was staggered, first by the words of the reading, then by the priest's hostile gestures. But he was not afraid. He spoke again, this time with more anger.

"'Before I continue, I ask the maids to remove the cups, saucers and jugs from this House for this is the House of God! I command the rest of you to sit on the floor, just as those who serve you have done, for in this House we are all servants of God!'

"Our *compañera* marveled when she saw that the congregation obeyed him and got down on their rumps, but something in their bodies told her that they hated our bishop, despite their obedience, and she knew the reason. They despised him because he was our protector, and understanding this made her put her fatigue aside. She could only think of what had just been said by our brother. Suddenly her concentration was interrupted by the young man next to her who wanted to know our bishop's name.

"'*Compañera,* who is that priest?'

"'His name is Brother Bartolomé de Las Casas, but we call him *Tatic,* Little Father.'

"Our bishop breathed in deeply, filling his lungs as he prepared to speak out again. He looked toward the rear of the church, and our *compañera* thought that his eyes met hers, but then he returned his gaze to those huddled beneath him, their fine garments wiping the dust off the floor.

"'It is a mortal sin to enslave the natives of this land! Blind cowards, whom Satan holds deceived, put down what you have stolen, or at least stop stealing! I command you to do this now! Otherwise, I shall excommunicate you right here in this sacred House! Almighty God is my witness!'

"Our *compañera's* eyes widened because she understood our priest's words, every one of them, and as she looked around, she saw that the others also had understood. Their eyes, too, were wide open, and filled with expectation.

"'Traitor!'

"'Liar!'

"'Cut out his tongue!'

"'No! Cut out his heart!'

"She heard the rumble of insults and threats, first in low, whispering tones, then louder, and finally they were hurled against our bishop in pitched, shrill voices. The slave masters, *capitanes* and *maestros,* as well as their women, got to their feet, faces red, veins puffed up with the blood of outrage, as they screamed their fury at our priest. Fists were raised in disgust, slashing the heavy air. They shuffled back and forth, like cattle. Soon, several men broke away from the crowd, daggers drawn. They leaped over the altar rail heading for the pulpit.

"Our *compañera* rose to her feet with a speed that she thought her limbs had forgotten and, without thinking, she plunged into the milling, screeching crowd that shoved her back and forth. Suddenly she lost her footing and she fell, pressed to the floor where the heeled slipper of one of the ladies squashed her hand. She let out a groan but got to her feet again, forgetting the sharp pain in her hand. When she looked back, she saw that many of our people had followed her.

"The attackers' lunge toward our bishop had been halted by three soldiers who had been standing behind the pulpit, giving him time to descend the narrow steps onto the floor of the church. He headed for the vestibule, but before reaching safety, his path was blocked by a bearded slave owner. As the man raised his dagger, our *compañera* and the others jumped on him, all of them falling in a heap, rolling in the dust, amid the clamor of curses, obscenities and threats. This break gave our bishop time to escape into the sanctuary at the rear of the church, leaving his enemies infuriated and filled with hatred.

"*Amigas y amigos,* you can imagine how, at that violent moment, our *compañera's* memory must have conjured the years during which she had wandered, looking for what she and our people had lost. She thought of the many deaths, mutilations and floggings which she had witnessed. Now, her thoughts were riveted on the image of our bishop, who had dared to unmask the evils that had gripped our land. She had no way of knowing that he would live many more years, never ceasing to decry what his countrymen were doing, never halting his stinging words that assured the world that she and her people were humans, with souls that wept because of pain inflicted on their bodies and for what was gone from their lives.

"The next day, our *compañera* did not resist when she was strapped to the pillory by a soldier's rough hands. She looked around hoping to inspire the others awaiting punishment, but she saw that she was surrounded instead by a multitude of white faces, some bearded, others partially covered by *mantillas*. To one side was the front of this cathedral, its ornate pillars and niches staring down at her like empty eyes. In the opposite direction, close to where she stood, was the huge cross that still rises nearly as high as the cathedral. Soon its shadow would be cast over her. She waited patiently for its darkness to overcome her.

"And so you see, my *compañeras* and *compañeros*, our bishop was among us then, just as he is living with us now. And then as now, our *hermanas* and *hermanos* were, and are, punished for defending him. In this very place, if one listens, one can still hear his voice raised in our defense, as well as the sounds of whips cutting into the backs of our people. If he has the courage now, as he had it then, to speak against injustice, I ask you: Why do we not have the strength to follow the path that he is again carving out for us? If our *compañera* had the will to defend him then, why are we afraid to do so now?"

The woman ended her testimonial with two images that danced in the church's dim light: a *compañera*, overshadowed by a cross, awaiting punishment, and a bishop who, in his attempt to stand up for the rights of his people, was living a repeated life. The narrative left the listeners stunned by its challenging words that churned up memories of ancestral injustice. Silence prevailed within the ancient walls of Santo Domingo, while the *compañeras* and *compañeros* listened to echoes of words from the past trapped in the church's vaulted ceilings.

Orlando Flores sat as if in a trance. He was remembering the story of the woman who had led the insurrection generations ago—another testimonial learned in the kitchens of the Mayorga *finca*. He was also struck with admiration for the woman who had just spoken. Her memory, her gestures and her way of speaking had unlocked his heart, allowing the fears inhabiting it to spring loose to escape into thin air. He felt strong again, fearless, new, and he wanted to speak out.

Chapter 19

They crush us but we also crush ourselves.

The Las Casas Indian Congress was scheduled to convene in San Cristóbal in October of 1974. It was the bishop who had called together such a conclave, and although he declared that it was in memory of Brother Bartolomé de las Casas, its primary purpose was to hear the voices of the natives, which had been silenced for nearly five hundred years.

The year before the congress, when Orlando Flores had first experienced the bishop come alive in the storytelling of his *compañera* in the Church of Santo Domingo, his own life took a new path. For days, even weeks, he could not stop thinking of the man who was inhabiting this world in a repeated way. The repetition of life was not a new idea for Orlando; his people knew that this was a common occurrence. What baffled him, however, was his own role in the events that were swirling around him.

What am I to do? Should I return to the jungle to protect myself? Should I remain here in the city or on the fincas *to listen, to speak, to help?* These were some of the questions that robbed Orlando of sleep despite his weariness beyond words from hard days' labor. His body and legs ached from carrying loads on his back, or from countless hours spent stooping over bean plants.

He decided the least he could do was to become a part of the excitement that was taking hold of the people: the Tzeltal, Tzotzil, Chol, Lacandón. Despite his fatigue after work, he joined the groups of men and women who got together in back rooms or in churches. He found that at those times people talked without restraint; everyone

151

seemed to have something to say—except for him. Although he had wanted to speak right from the first meeting he attended, he found himself surrounded by the masses and listening to the inspiring stories of others. Orlando still found himself tongue-tied.

As his reticence struggled with his desire to speak, his attention was riveted on the organizers whose presence became more apparent each time a meeting took place. Orlando saw that among them were women, as well as men, and that they were mostly mestizos educated in cities, who were responding to the bishop's call to prepare the people for the Indian Council.

He observed those persons closely, listening to their words, scrutinizing their moves and gestures, because he distrusted them. He noticed that at first they visited workers only in the field or on the job site. But as 1973 moved on, they became bolder, appearing at evening meetings as well. Their presence, Orlando realized, spurred everyone into questioning, planning, even expecting changes in their lives, and this disturbed him because he saw that the organizers did not give solutions but only gave short sermons about Christ and his apostles, and often about Bartolomé de las Casas. This forced Orlando to wonder where such words would lead. He listened to the questions and remarks often provoked in his companions by the organizers, but he thought most of their talk was essentially without direction.

The pressure caused by hearing so many things and not speaking up intensified in Orlando. With each meeting, he came closer to telling everyone that he thought that they were on a mistaken path. The truth was that in his heart Orlando doubted that any one of those organizers, with talk alone, could change what centuries had given to his people as their burden.

Yet the misery experienced by his people was undeniable and growing with each day. So he listened to the voices of the women and men who were like him, and he remembered the years he had spent dragging mahogany trunks through impenetrable mud while being prodded and driven as were the oxen. He remembered El Brujo and his severed head and its staring eyes. He remembered his days of wandering in the jungle and Don Absolón's face.

"*¡Compañero!* What about the land the mestizos stole from our ancestors? When will we get some of it back? They have the best land; we get rocky *barrancas* in which to plant our seed."

"I get paid only seven pesos a day for working like a burro, and most of the time I don't even get money, just a paper that I can exchange for a kilo of beans at the company store."

"And what about us women who have to work like oxen, along with our children, for even less than that?"

"That's right! Don't forget us women! We want education for our children. We need medicine for them when they're sick. We want to be heard!"

Men and women uttered afflictions which cycled and repeated. People used different words but said the same thing over and again until the time did come when Orlando was finally able to put words together to say what he wanted. This happened when one of the organizers again spoke of Brother Bartolomé de las Casas.

"I tell you, *hermanas y hermanos,* he walks among us."

Orlando felt a knot of words coursing from his heart toward his mouth, and got to his feet. He stood quietly, sombrero in hand, but the organizer saw him almost immediately. The man interrupted what he was about to say as Orlando spoke.

"No! That bishop died many generations ago!"

Orlando's voice rang out with such vigor that it bounced off the vaulted ceiling, echoing through the church. Everyone turned in his direction. Many twisted on the rickety pews on which they sat, trying to look at the face of the one who had uttered such a terrible thing.

"*Hermano,* why do you say that?"

"Because we all know that Brother Bartolomé died many years ago."

"Do you not believe that our lives repeat?"

All eyes were pasted on Orlando. He felt their rounded pressure pushing in on his skin. Instead of feeling intimidated, however, he experienced a surge of energy moving through his body. During the first seconds it was hot and slow, but then, as if it had broken through a barrier, his courage soared.

"I do believe that we repeat ourselves, but just as the bishop left us the first time, so will he leave us again with empty hands."

"*¡No! Cabrón mentiroso.*"

"*¡Fray Bartolomé se ha repetido!*"

"*¡Él está con nosotros!*"

The gathering shouted, hurled insults at Orlando, protesting what he had said. Many of them got on their feet; the shorter ones even jumped on chairs and pews to look at Orlando and to contradict what he had said.

Orlando would neither be intimidated nor silenced. "*Hermanos, hermanas,* don't be offended, for I am one of you."

"Then why are you trying to discourage us?"

"No, *compañera,* I'm not trying to dishearten or to make any one of us back down or turn away in fear. I'm only trying to find a way in which we will have a true chance to overcome the *patrones.*"

"If that's so, why are you saying that our bishop is dead?"

"Because he *is* dead. But, *hermana,* listen carefully to me. To understand that he's dead is not a bad thing. We all know his spirit is still with us. What I'm saying is that now it is *our* turn."

Orlando paused because he saw that the *compañeras* and *compañeras* were baffled by his words. He was searching his mind for the words needed to say what he meant. He wrinkled his brow and licked the dryness from his lips.

"What I mean is that we must be new Bartolomés. We must now take his place, stop our talk and do what he did. We must be the ones to care for one another, and defend one another with words, yes, but with actions as well. We must begin by loving ourselves and stop thinking of ourselves as stupid burros born to be slaves."

An uneasy silence followed his words as they reverberated in the transparent, warm air. The *compañeras* and *compañeros* were amazed at what Orlando had said and by the conviction of his ideas. They gaped at him, some with open mouths. The organizer narrowed his eyes and pursed his lips as he concentrated on what he had heard. An expression of admiration rapidly replaced one of disbelief.

Even Orlando was astounded by the words he heard flowing from his mouth, because they gave life to thoughts that had nestled deep inside of him since his days as a *boyero*. He now realized that each time he had wanted to describe what he felt inside, rage would render him speechless, and because of that, he had become as silenced as the oxen that churned their hooves in the mud.

"*Amigo,* come here where we can all see you. Tell us who you are and encourage us with more of your words."

The organizer walked toward the rear of the crowd where Orlando was standing. The man beckoned with both hands, inviting him to come to the front of the group. Shyness, however, overcame Orlando, and he hesitated, not wanting to bring yet more attention to himself. Apprehension also crept into his mind as he thought of the possibility that Don Absolón might have spies among those gathered in the church. But the organizer would not back away. He approached Orlando, gesturing all the while for him to come closer.

After a few moments, Orlando put aside his timidity. He began to move, and, twisting his sombrero in his hands, he made his way to stand in front of the group. There he saw, for the first time, a sea of brown faces upturned toward him. He took in the brightness of those eyes, the high cheekbones, the flat foreheads, many covered with the straight overhanging bangs of his own people.

"My name is Orlando Flores. I am a Lacandón, born close to the Lacanjá River. I am one of you. I may not have suffered as much as some of you, but I, too, have been hurt."

Silence followed his words. Eyes were riveted on him, telling him that they were expecting more from him. Those looks were filled with such intensity that Orlando felt himself losing his nerve, and he began edging toward the rear to regain his seat.

"Wait, *hermano* Orlando! How are we to become new Bartolomés, if our stomachs are so empty and flat that they cling to our backbones? How are we to defend one another, when we are so weakened by hunger ourselves? How are we to see ourselves as more than burros when the *patrones* crush us with labor and disdain us each day?"

Orlando returned the look that was in the woman's eyes. He understood the meaning of her words and recognized the suffering in her plea. He experienced doubt and hesitated, because, although he wanted to answer her question, he did not know how to do so.

"*Compañera,* I don't have a cure for such pain, but I do have the beginning of a response. Everywhere I look these days I see unity. When I'm laboring in the field or building a wall, when I sit to eat my tacos or to take a drink of water, I see harmony and *hermandad* in my *compañeros.* I can forget that I'm a Lacandón, or that he is a Tzeltal, or that she is a Chol. I see only that I am like them, and that they are like me. I believe that if all of us can think this way, we'll form a strength never before seen by the *patrones.* Yes, they crush us, but we also crush ourselves by thinking of ourselves as they do. We must stop thinking that way. If we come together, remembering that our ancestors were good and powerful, we will be the new Bartolomés."

Orlando held his breath when he saw that most of the men and women in the crowd turned to one another in heated talk. Some got on their feet, trying to reach someone in the rear, or farther up the aisle. There was hand waving, wagging of heads and pointing towards Orlando, who stood, feet planted apart on the stone floor, as he tried to decipher his own words. He looked over to the organizer, who stood a few paces away, and saw that his eyes were focused on him. Orlando tried to discern the man's thoughts, but his expression was blank. The organizer blinked, as if trying to clear his vision, and walked over to Orlando's side.

"*Amigo,* you have said important things."

"Others have said the same thing."

"Not as you have done. Look, the *compañeras* and *compañeros* have understood you."

Orlando did as the organizer asked and turned again to look at the crowd. This time it was clear to him: They were happy, excited, nodding and smiling. Now and then, glances were thrown his way, looks that told him that he was trusted and that where he would lead, they would follow.

"*Compañero* Orlando, why don't you join our group of organizers? We need you."

"Why do you need me?"

"Because already you are trusted."

"How do you know that, *amigo?*"

"I have eyes and ears. I can see and hear."

"I'll think more about what has happened here."

Orlando pondered the events of that evening for days. At the time, he was working as a bricklayer with a gang that was trucked from Ocosingo to Palenque, where the laborers stayed for up to a week on the job. As he worked, he revisited his life, as if each brick he laid marked a different moment of experience. He saw himself as a boy, playing childish games with Rufino, then serving Don Absolón. This memory made Orlando's stomach churn as he realized the power of that *patrón*. He asked himself, *What if Don Absolón had not sentenced me to the* caoba *camp?* Brick by brick, he repeated this question over and again as his mind erected a wall of understanding: it was not the sentence itself that was significant to Orlando. The important thing was that Don Absolón *could* do it, that he held that authority in his hands, that there was nothing to rein in the power he held over people like Orlando.

When the job was done, he returned to Ocosingo with his mind determined to accept the organizer's invitation. That evening, he reported to the meeting and began training as a leader of his people. In the beginning, he accompanied one or another of the organizers on trips out to remote villages and settlements as well as to less distant communities. Orlando observed his companion as he or she spoke to the people in preparation for the Indian Congress, which was now scheduled to take place in San Cristóbal de las Casas. He listened to words used, reflected on them, making them part of his own language.

More importantly, he took in ideas regarding equality and ownership, health and education. The name of Emiliano Zapata was often invoked when speaking of land and liberty, and Orlando was gratified when he was told that a native of the state of Morelos, a man like him, had fought and died so that his people might have a piece of land and the freedom to farm it.

Orlando caught on quickly and became an organizer himself, taking care to stay far away from the Lacanjá region. He gained confidence knowing that his looks had changed almost entirely. Don Absolón, he was certain, could no longer recognize him, and he believed that even Rufino would not be able to identify his boyhood companion. Nonetheless, Orlando journeyed westbound, in the opposite direction of Lacanjá, concentrating on the Tzotzil region.

He went to the larger places first: into the northern areas of Simojovel, then down to Ixtapa, and over to Chamula. In between those centers, Orlando visited small villages, settlements and even clusters of *palapas,* with his message to unite and to prepare for the congress. He reached out to those men and women who hesitated, some in fear, others in skepticism. He knew when to back away, if necessary, hoping that when he returned, his words would be better understood. He spoke convincingly to anyone who would listen, reminding them always of their worth as men and women, stressing the power and organization of their ancestors, often invoking the legends of his people.

He met with serious resistance several times from overseers of *fincas* and haciendas. He often had to cut off whatever he was saying to a gathered group just to duck into a hiding place out of sight of a lackey of a *patrón.* Only once did Orlando come close to being captured. At that time, he was in the community of Santa Marta speaking to a cluster of young women.

"The gods made men and women of maize, but the *catxul* became envious."

Orlando had just begun to speak about the origins of their people, intending to push his lesson to the point where his listeners would understand who were the maize people and who were the *catxul.* Suddenly, a woman ran to him, and even though out of breath, she stammered a warning.

"*Hermano,* someone is looking for you. Run!"

Orlando dove for cover but not before he was spotted. He heard several blasts of a shotgun as he disappeared into a thicket of bushes and from there into a wide span of trees. As he ducked and crawled, vivid memories returned to him of the time when he was hunted by Don Absolón Mayorga. Orlando was saddened and angered by those recollections because he wondered if his life as a fugitive would ever end. Despite these thoughts, however, he did not give up, and after that incident, he always made certain to have a companion with him to watch his back, to warn him of any impending danger.

After that, Orlando plunged deeper into his mission of bringing more natives into the preparations for the congress. Primary in his strategy was the recruitment of leaders who were members of the different tribes: men and women who felt what was being said, who knew what suffering meant. The people trusted those native organizers, recognizing them as their own; and they followed them, wanting to be part of the congress. The barriers that separated the city-bred mestizo organizer from the trust of the people melted away in the face of someone who spoke of similarly experienced afflictions, in their language. This tactic proved effective, especially over the long run, since it was from this group that leaders would emerge twenty years later: women and men who would follow Orlando into the Lacandona Jungle, from where they would mount the new struggle.

Chapter 20

There cannot be equality in a false peace!

The debate was heated but orderly as the members of the Indian Congress took their turns in explaining their positions regarding health, education, land and commerce. Orlando Flores sat at his place, listening, pondering what the other delegates were submitting. He felt proud of having been elected to represent the Ocosingo delegation, but because he did not know how to read or write, he felt intimidated. He knew, however, that sooner or later his ability to speak would lead to his participation in the deliberations.

He followed as the various views were explained by women and men representing different tribes. He felt moved to hear the clarity of those voices reading declarations and summaries, or simply speaking from the heart, proving what the organizers had always said: The natives of those lands had a mind with which to think, a tongue with which to speak, and given the opportunity, they would let their ideas be known.

The hall was large. Its seats were placed in rows so that everyone could see the main stage where the speakers sat on either side of the president. The place was packed there were no empty chairs. Orlando looked around, concentrating on the delegates' faces and expressions. He saw men and women, most of them wearing tribal garb, who appeared uncomfortable in the enclosed environment of the hall. Their eyes squinted, unused to the harsh glare of neon lights. Their hands fidgeted with a sombrero, or the fringe of a *huipil,* and they sat awkwardly on the metal folding chairs to which they were assigned. Despite this, they seemed eager to adapt, to listen, to be heard. It was only when the time came for each sector to forward their grievances, that the members grew restless and the environment in the hall became tense.

"We are treated like slaves!"

"Our customs are trampled on!"

"We get the worst land."

"Our children are sick and uneducated."

"We women are excluded from all planning!"

Many times voices became shrill, and some people even got to their feet in frustration, babbling or waving a hand to get the attention of the speaker. Whenever that happened, the president of the congress hammered his gavel on the table and repeatedly reminded the members to respect the speaker's right to be heard.

"Hermanos, hermanas, please remember our goal: *Equality in peace!* We see it written above the entrance to this auditorium as we enter. We must respect each other if we are to be respected."

Those words cast a pall over the members, and Orlando was disappointed; he thought that the president should allow voices to rise and be heard, even if they were speaking out of place. Otherwise, what good was the meeting? Each time a woman, or a man was silenced, Orlando became increasingly impatient, and he wondered what direction was being taken by the congress. He was also displeased to see that after the first sessions, words seemed to be repeating, spinning, and their importance fading.

Discussions dragged on, and after several days Orlando felt that little was being accomplished. He had anticipated the opportunity to be one of those who would speak out as he had in the past, but that chance never materialized. He waited patiently, hoping to be pointed out by the president whenever he raised his hand to speak, but he was not acknowledged. As he waited, he became distracted and his mind wandered; thoughts swirled, entangling with memories.

"I say that there cannot be equality in a false peace! That's shit!"

Orlando was yanked from his thoughts by the harshness of the voice as well as by the crude expression. So far everyone had been careful not to use vulgar words. His face jerked toward the direction from which the words had come and he saw a man who stood in the middle of the audience. Orlando narrowed his eyes as he concentrated on the figure. He saw that everyone else was doing the same. He took in the man's shirt, trousers and even the hat, which he had not removed from his head. What he saw told Orlando that the man was from the city, that he was a mestizo, and that more than likely he was educated.

Everyone gawked at the speaker, some open-mouthed, but they were startled back to attention when the president smashed his gavel on the table. Its crashing noise had never been so loud or explosive; it forced all faces to turn to the stage.

"*Amigo,* we're all here to listen and to be heard, but your words are disrespectful. I will tell you not to express yourself in that manner again!"

"*Señor Presidente,* I'm here in good faith, so I beg your pardon, but what I've been hearing during the past few days has made me lose patience."

"Identify yourself before you say any more."

"My name is Pedro."

"And your last name?"

"I'm only Pedro. May I speak?"

The president went into a huddle with the other speakers who shared the table, some wagging their heads negatively, other shrugging their shoulders. They whispered and interrupted one another until the president spoke up.

"We agree that at this meeting all the *compañeros* have a right to speak. Say what you must, but you must be brief, and watch your language."

The man looked to the uplifted faces that were concentrating on his words, turning in a circle as he spoke. Orlando saw that the man was assured in his manner, relaxed but intense. He plunged his hands into the pockets of his khaki pants as he spoke.

"Whatever accords you offer, whatever agreements you reach, if you do so in so-called *peace,* you are fooling yourselves into believing that your lives will change. What here is being called *peace* is a false peace. It is the condition that keeps you bound to the yoke, like dumb beasts. It is your masters' tranquility, not yours! They will never share their prized land with you! They will never erect schools for your children! They will always cheat you when you sell your beans and coffee to them. Your sweat, your silence, your suffering is your masters' *peace!*"

The gavel slammed on the table once again, signaling the protest of the president, who now got to his feet. He circled around the table and stood at the edge of the stage.

"Do you speak against the plans we're making because we propose to carry out our action in a peaceful manner?"

"Yes, *Señor Presidente.*"

"What do you propose in the place of that plan?"

"War!"

The man hurled the word at the president and it exploded in midair, as did the assembly. That word triggered an energy buried deep in the hearts of those people, shattering any semblance of orderly debate. The forbidden, feared, yet desired word had at last been uttered! Men and women got to their feet, shouting, wagging heads, craning necks, stumbling over each other as they strained to move from one place to the other. There was pandemonium. Orlando, lips pursed and scowling, glared at the man who had dared to articulate the word. The man stood without moving. His calm demonstrated that he had expected, and even wanted, the chaotic response to his proposal.

"This session is closed!"

The president shouted above the din and banged his gavel repeatedly, bringing an end to the day's meeting. People hardly heard the gavel as they argued with one another, already engaged in the debate of war versus peace. The ushers opened the doors of the hall and the delegates plunged toward the exits, shoving and pushing while excitedly engaged in feverish talk.

Orlando, still seated, waited for the hall to empty. He did not want to be dragged by the crush, but most of all he sat quietly as he wrestled with his thoughts, which were in turmoil. The idea of armed resistance was not new to him; he had pondered it many times, but especially when he became impatient with incessant talk and little action. More recently, the reality of being hunted by the Mayorga people had incited him to think of ways in which to fight back, to defend himself. Somehow, negotiation and bargaining did not provide the answer to his own dilemma.

At last, the auditorium had emptied but Orlando remained seated, lost in thought until he was interrupted by a voice that startled him.

"*Amigo,* are you thinking about what I said?"

Orlando turned in his seat to see the man who had almost thrown the meeting into a riot. At close range he saw that he was in his mid-twenties, of medium height, and that his eyes were shrewd.

"Yes. I'm thinking that maybe you're right. That maybe we're stuck in the mud of injustice, and that the only way to free ourselves is to raise the machete and cut off the head of the beast that keeps us down."

Orlando stopped abruptly, surprised at the intensity of his words, which had come straight from his heart. As he spoke, he relived having cut off El Brujo's head, he relived the mud he had wiped from Aquiles' face, he relived the feeling of having placed the machete in his friend's dead hand. The other man nodded, seemingly reading Orlando's thoughts.

"Come. Join us."

"Where?"

"In the Lacandona, where we've been gathering for years."

"What do I have to do?"

"Recruit for us."

"I'll think about it."

"We'll be waiting for you."

The man walked away from Orlando, but before he exited, he looked back at him and said, "You're a good recruiter. I've seen how you work. Instead of people from towns and streets, you can help us gather men and women from the villages and canyons. They're the ones who are suffering most."

"How can we stand up to the power of the *patrones?*"

"With an army of men and women."

Orlando gazed at the man, doubt stamped on his face. But his racing mind was already beginning to accept the man's proposal as the way to self-defense and survival, his people's as well as his own.

"When you've made up your mind, go to our camp in the Lacandona. Tell them El Bombardero sent you. That's me."

Chapter 21

He wondered if he would ever see her again.

Orlando did not join the guerrilla forces right away, as The Bomber would have liked. Instead, he took time to consider what path he would take. Four years passed before he became disenchanted with the direction the activists had taken. He had finally concluded that their words and advice would not change anything, much less transform the misery of his people. Everywhere Orlando looked, he saw hunger, sickness, ignorance. Men sank deeper into debt and drunkenness; women became more oppressed by constant pregnancies and battering. And no one did anything. To speak of liberation and not provide a way seemed to him cruel and futile.

During the four years of his discernment, Orlando taught himself to read and write. He mastered those skills to the point of being able to understand newspaper articles as well as to compose simple pages expressing his views. This made it possible for him to follow the guerrilla movement that had sprung from the ranks of university students, mainly in the city of Monterrey in the state of Nuevo León, and had spread to other parts of the country. By reading newspapers, he learned of reports damning those men as traitors and insurgents—enemies of the state.

Orlando discovered that the movement was not new, that it had begun sometime in 1971, had grown and spread from city to city. He learned that police had recently arrested culprits in a clandestine cell somewhere on the outskirts of Mexico City, then in Veracruz, and also in Tabasco. One of the accounts asserted that other centers were suspected as far south as the Lacandona Jungle in Chiapas, and that it was only a matter of time before those, too, would be discovered and erad-icated by the army.

One of those newspaper articles in particular attracted Orlando's attention because it was accompanied by photographs of two men sus-pected as leaders of the Puebla cell. When Orlando took the paper in his hands, he stopped what he was doing to concentrate on those pic-tures. One displayed the corpses, mutilated beyond recognition by multiple gunshot wounds. As he held the page to the light, he made out dangling arms, ruptured stomachs, protruding intestines, shattered and bloodied faces. To the side of that grim scene, the photos of the same two men, still students, were printed.

The culprits, stated the article, were university-trained, one in biology and the other in political science. One of them stirred Orlan-do's memory. He did not recognize the man's name, but despite the passing of four years, his face riveted Orlando. It was El Bombardero, the same man who had confronted the Indian Congress and declared that war was the only way to change. Orlando stared at the picture, whispering the man's fictitious name: The Bomber.

Instead of being frightened, Orlando felt that what he was reading and seeing was a message indicating which direction he should take. He saw that there were people already fighting a war, already dying for what they believed, and that it was a national movement with a name, with leaders, and that those people were ensconced somewhere in the Lacandona Jungle. At that moment he decided to abandon the organizers' mission and join the guerrillas. He did not know where to find them in the vastness of the Lacandona, but he had no doubt that he would encounter them. He was determined to become part of the force, so he journeyed to the Lacandona in search of his insurgent *compañeros*.

He returned to wearing the white tunic of his people and left behind the khaki trousers and cotton shirts typical of the organizers. After months, his hair was finally long enough to dangle from his forehead to his eyes and the back of it reached toward his shoulders. He wandered, sometimes visiting villages where he exchanged fish or small game for tortillas or a bowl of beans, but Orlando mostly stayed hidden in the jungle. Whenever he asked villagers about the camp, his questions were answered with blank looks or shrugged shoulders. He did not know if those people were uninformed or unwilling to give him directions, but after a while, he stopped asking.

It occurred to him that he was not looking in the right places, nor was he asking in the right way. He remembered that The Bomber had singled him out as a recruiter. This led Orlando to believe that others would be doing the same thing, and that those recruiters would be concentrating on the villages and canyon settlement most likely to respond to their message. He then began going into those places that he judged to be ripe to listen and respond to the insurgents' message. When he found such a settlement, he stayed to mingle with the people for days, hoping that a recruiter would appear and lead him to the guerrilla compound.

It was in El Caribal that Orlando noticed a group of women and men clustered around a man dressed in the Lacandon way. His plan had finally worked. As he approached the gathering, Orlando caught snippets of the man's speech.

"I tell you, *compañeros,* we have to band together and fight back! There's no other way."

Orlando looked at the villagers and saw that the recruiter's words were not having the effect he expected. The men and women barely looked at the man, and most of them fidgeted distractedly.

"Do you want to go on living like burros?"

One or two in the group walked away; others began to talk among themselves, losing interest in what the recruiter had to say. The man appeared frustrated to the point of following those who were leaving the circle. He neared one man and put a hand on his shoulder.

"*¡Compañero!* Aren't you at least going to ask a question? Why aren't you interested in what I'm saying?"

The man, annoyed at having been stopped, pushed the recruiter's hand away. He glared at him, hostility stamped on his face.

"Do you think we're fools? It's easy for you to tell us to fight back, but how can we overthrow the *patrones?* They're the ones with the power. They have the *catxules,* too. Those jackals are ready to kill all of us and take what little we have."

Orlando saw that the recruiter had lost his audience because he was not delivering his message in a manner that might be understood. He sensed that his time had come, that he had at last found his way into the insurgents' group. He stepped forward as he raised his voice.

"*Amigos,* I have heard what this man is saying and I believe in his message. We must fight if we are to free ourselves from the burden that the *patrones* laid on our ancestors. It will not be an easy task; many of us will die, but we must fight and not give up."

Although Orlando had spoken almost the same words as the recruiter, something in Orlando's voice captured the group's attention. Those who were about to leave turned to look at him and listened to what he had to say. Others, men and women, seemed to come out from the shadows of the trees and from behind huts. The recruiter, at first taken by surprise, soon regained his composure, recognizing an ally in Orlando. He walked up to him, reached out his hand and shook it warmly.

"*Compañero,* I'm Rodrigo Vázquez. Who are you?"

"Orlando Flores. The Bomber sent me."

Orlando saw Rodrigo's eyes narrow suspiciously and he realized that the man was backing away from him even while his hand was still in Orlando's grip. Orlando tightened his grasp.

"I know that The Bomber is dead. Don't think I don't know, but I say that he sent me because it's the truth. I've come because of him. We met at the Indian Congress in San Cristóbal de las Casas four years ago."

Rodrigo relaxed with that, backed away and allowed his new *compañero* to take over. The task came effortlessly to Orlando as he applied the technique and style that had won him so much approval when he was organizing. He spoke to the villagers and they responded, wanting to know more, asking questions, speaking among themselves. There were some questions that Rodrigo had to answer, but Orlando's listeners neither lost interest nor confidence.

The day was turning to evening, but Orlando and Rodrigo were still in conversation with men and women who were now so interested in joining the ranks of the insurgents that they had forgotten about time. When they realized that it was nearly night, the women ran off to put together campfires, to heat *comales,* to knead *masa* for tortillas. The men, in turn, headed for their *palapas,* where they would sit by the fireside waiting for the food that was being prepared.

Orlando and Rodrigo accepted the villagers' invitation to stay for one more night so that their conversations could continue. After eating, they sat around the center campfire, shoulder to shoulder with the others—men in the inner circle, women in the outer one. The talk went from expressions of grievances to tales told by elders, remembered and passed down from generation to generation.

Orlando told of his work with the Las Casas Congress, of his disappointments but also of the many things he had learned. Rodrigo spoke of how he had joined the insurgents, who were still so new that they hardly had a dozen guns to go around, and he told of their plans to expand as they organized for an uprising. His honesty finally won him the people's confidence.

When the talking ended, both men were given a *petate* on which to sleep by the smoldering fire, but Orlando stayed awake for a long time, listening to the jungle, staring at the sky, which was intensely black and studded with glittering stars. He knew that his life had taken yet another turn, and that it was the right one. Knowing that, he was content. Finally, he rolled onto his side and drifted into a dreamless sleep.

At dawn, Orlando was awakened by the comings and goings of women carting water and snapping twigs to set fires, men moving silently around the camp and babies crying. He rose, rolled up the *petate* and headed to the river, where he took off his clothes and bathed. As he was drying himself off, he saw a man nearing the center of the village; a few paces behind him followed a woman.

Orlando dressed quickly and followed them, his curiosity aroused by the woman's dejected appearance. As he walked, he saw that she held her head erect despite the villagers, mostly the women, glaring at her and pointing. He was able to overhear whispering and mumbling as he moved along, trying to keep up with the couple.

"Evil woman."

"She deserves to be punished."

When Orlando saw the man and woman disappear into a *palapa,* he turned to someone standing next to him. He feared it was rude to pry, but an inexplicable feeling of compassion for the dejected woman urged him to ask.

"Who are they?"

"That's Cruz Ochoa and his wife, Juana Galván. She ran away some time ago, but there you see—he's found her."

After, as Rodrigo led the way into the jungle toward the insurgents' camp, Orlando thought of the woman and others like her. Years later when working side by side with Juana Galván and Adriana Mora, Orlando would remember this encounter, knowing that it was then that his mind had turned to the possibility of recruiting such women as part of the insurgent force. It was at that moment that he realized that women were more oppressed than the men. As he marched behind Rodrigo, Orlando reserved his idea for another time, but he remained curious about Juana Galván, wondering if he would ever see her again.

Chapter 22

It was quick. It was merciful.

After leaving the military academy, Rufino returned to Las Estrellas. Don Absolón welcomed his arrival with days of fiestas filled with displays of horsemanship and bull riding, as well as dancing and music. His other sons had not surprised him in turning out to be failures; he had expected that since their youth. When each one chose to drift away, the old man did not object nor resist; he was relieved. Hidden in his heart was the hope that young Rufino would return to take his place. When that happened, Don Absolón ordered every man and woman on his vast properties to celebrate with him.

Rufino adjusted easily to the life of his class in Chiapas. He mingled with the best families of San Cristóbal de las Casas and even with those across the southern border, whose daughters were prime for marriage. He did not miss the military life; on the contrary, he was grateful that he had received the wisdom to see his way of life as necessary. In a short time, Rufino married and began his family, never leaving the company of Don Absolón.

As years drifted by, the old man's trust in his son deepened, seeing his capacities and eagerness not only to maintain the Mayorga properties but his evident ambition to expand and modernize them. Don Absolón now invited Rufino to join him daily during his evening drink. It was during those moments of comradeship that both men exchanged views and plans. One night, Don Absolón abruptly brought up Rufino's nearly forgotten boyhood friend.

"Hijo, have you ever again heard from Quintín Osuna?"

The question was so unexpected by Rufino, so out of context of their conversation, that the younger man gawked at his father, trying to recall who it was that his father was mentioning. When Rufino finally focused, he got to his feet and went over to the record player to lower the volume, then he returned to the armchair facing his father. *"No, padre,* I haven't heard from him. Not ever. Why do you ask?"

Don Absolón puckered his bulbous lips, savoring the tangy sherry taste coating his tongue. He leaned his head against the back of the chair, eyes half closed, evidently weighing his thoughts.

"You probably are unaware that he murdered our best overseer, El Brujo. It happened during a day of work in the *caoba* fields."

Surprised and shaken, Rufino put down the glass he had been holding and shifted his weight forward to the edge of the chair. His father's words were so blunt and hard that he had difficulty dealing with their power.

"Quintín? He murdered an overseer? How long ago?"

"Not only *an* overseer, but *the best* overseer Las Estrellas has ever claimed, and it happened years ago, shortly before you returned home."

Rufino retreated into silence for a few moments in an attempt to process what he was hearing. Quintín's boyish face flashed in his mind as did their pranks, their games, their swimming, their competitions. But as he allowed these thoughts to fill his memory, other considerations pushed them aside: *A murder had been committed. A great loss and affront had been dealt to Mayorga family integrity. A common Indian had defied their authority.* Rufino leaned back and crossed his legs.

"Why didn't you tell me this before?"

"To be honest with you, it's not something that preoccupies me."

"Then why are you telling me now?"

"Because I believe that these people, these *indios,* are rancorous, vengeful creatures. I would not want you to be caught unaware."

Rufino again took the drink in his hand. This time he drained its content, then he stood up to go refill his glass. When he returned to his place, he cleared his throat.

"What did you do about it, *padre?*"

"When I mounted a search for the murderer, it proved futile. We came up with empty hands. When I offered a reward, we received only blank stares in return. When I threatened reprisals, there was only silence. The murderer slipped through our fingers into the vastness of the jungle, where I'm certain he still survives."

"After that, what did you do?"

"I did the only thing left for a man in our position. If a son must pay for his father's sins, then the contrary is also true. In this case, Quintín's mother and father paid for their son's vile act."

"How did you punish them?"

"I was kinder to them than Quintín was to our overseer."

"Were you a witness?"

"No! I don't like seeing such things."

"Then, how can you be certain?"

"Oh, I'm certain. You know that I put only those whom I can trust in charge of important matters."

"Were the Osunas shot to death?"

"*Hijo,* why are you asking for details?"

"Because I must know how Quintín's mother and father died. I can't explain it, *padre.*"

"Very well. They were executed as their son would have been had he been apprehended. They were marched to the mud fields of the *caoba* camp and drowned. It was quick. It was merciful."

"What about their *palapa?*"

"It was burned, the earth dug up and turned over until no sign of the dwelling was left."

"Are there other family members?"

"None that we could find."

"Someone must have helped Quintín; someone must have fed him, given him clothing. Did you investigate thoroughly?"

"Yes. But you know these people. They're silent, just like burros and mules. They're stubborn and too stupid to understand what is right and wrong."

"Have you thought that Quintín more than likely will be looking for you to take revenge?"

"The thought has crossed my mind."

"He's my age. He's a man now, no longer a boy."

"Hijo, if he returns, it will be to join his mother and father's bones buried deep in the mud pit."

Chopin's piano concerto was ending; its poignant last notes combined to express deep romanticism and sentimentality as the two men paused to listen. When the long-playing record came to an end, a scratching sound filled the empty air that bonded father and son. Neither paid attention to the noise; instead, they sat in silence, looking at each other, weighing the significance of their words and deeds. Finally, it was Rufino who got to his feet, approached the record player and turned it off. He did this in silence, without emotion. Then he went to Don Absolón, put his hand on the old man's shoulder, and nodded in affirmation.

"I'll see to it that Quintín Osuna is caught. I promise you."

"Gracias, hijo."

Rufino began to leave the room, then paused to look at his father.

"From now on, let me be in charge of these duties."

"Ah, yes. I like that very much. However, the *boyeros* are still my responsibility. Remember that."

"Sí, padre. Buenas noches."

"Buenas noches, hijo."

Chapter 23

In these parts the only thing that matters is a signature.

Orlando had recently experienced an encounter that had left him nervous, and his thoughts returned to it time and again, no matter how much he tried to concentrate on other things. Orlando had overheard gossip about Don Absolón Mayorga's death after being gored by an ox.

"I'm telling you it was the old *patrón* of Las Estrellas."

"No!"

"Yes, I tell you!"

"Don Absolón Mayorga?"

"That's the one. I heard that the beast penetrated him first in the stomach, then down there, right through the big ones."

Orlando, attracted by the name Mayorga as well as the mention of Las Estrellas, edged discreetly closer to the two men exchanging news from the territory they had recently covered. He listened carefully, hungry for details.

"I heard that he was out in the field, overlooking a team of *boyeros*."

"Oh, that's bullshit! Why would he do that? That's what overseers are for."

"That's how I heard it! People were saying that ever since someone called El Brujo was murdered, the old man never trusted anyone else in his place. But maybe this is all gossip. What matters is that he was where he shouldn't have been. He was old, fat, and he could hardly move. I mean, what's an old iguana like him doing out in the field, anyway?"

Orlando's mind raced as the image of powerful hooves and sharp horns appeared in his mind. He remembered Aquiles' false step and how he had plunged into the deep mud churned by those beasts. He could see the hairy monsters slashing into Don Absolón's obese gut, plunging once, twice, until finally ripping open and mangling his vulnerable groin. Orlando could not restrain himself. He moved closer to the men.

"*Amigos,* forgive my intrusion but I used to work on that *finca.* Are you sure it was Don Absolón who died?"

"I'm positive. In fact, everyone was talking about the new *patrón,* Don Absolón's son, Rufino."

This news surprised Orlando for several reasons. For one, Rufino was not the oldest of the Mayorga brothers. For another, Rufino had always said that he wanted to be a general in the army, not a landowner.

"What about the other sons? There were three boys who were older than Rufino Mayorga."

"Well, *compañero,* of that I'm not sure, but everyone knows how it is with those rich families. Who knows? Maybe the old *patrón* disinherited one or two of them. Or maybe someone drank himself to death. But I'm certain about this: Don Rufino Mayorga is now the owner and new *patrón* of the Mayorga estates. And that means nearly all of the Lacanjá region."

That conversation had turned Orlando's mind again to thoughts of returning to his village. After that he began to move closer to Lacanjá. He made his way to the town of San Quintín, which was as close to Las Estrellas as he dared to go. He kept his ears and eyes open for news of Rufino Mayorga, but especially hoped to find out something about his parents.

Orlando's reputation as a recruiter had preceded him, gaining him the trust of the local *cacique* and other native leaders. At the evening gatherings, he spoke of preparation for the uprising, but he also took time to ask questions regarding Las Estrellas and its new owner. Orlando received more information than he had expected. He was given photographs, written documents and newspaper clippings. But when he asked about Domingo and Ysidra Osuna, no one could tell him anything. This made him uneasy, but for the time being, he decided to concentrate his efforts on Rufino.

Orlando discovered that Rufino Mayorga had indeed stepped into his father's role as the patriarch of the family, and that he had done so with an energy and a ruthlessness that even the old *patrón* had not possessed. He found out that he had been absent from his family as a youth; some of the articles explained that he had been sent to the United States. One newspaper stated that Rufino had been studying in Mexico City at the military academy.

Rumors abounded regarding the fate of the three older Mayorga brothers. One tale claimed that the oldest one was poisoned. Another brother was killed in an airplane crash, and since he was the pilot, tongues speculated that he had been a victim of foul play. Gossip had it that the engine had been damaged intentionally. The last of the Mayorga boys had turned out to be a drunkard who mysteriously disappeared from Las Estrellas. Once again, gossip had it that *someone* had murdered him. Orlando discovered different versions of these stories, but all had one element in common: Rufino's unspoken name was at the root of the explanation for the deaths and disappearances of his brothers.

Soon after Orlando's arrival in San Quintín, the city clerk was called away on business, but he told Orlando that he was welcome in his office to use any files that he needed. He accepted the offer one evening, when he took time to go through files looking for photographs. When he stumbled upon a thick dossier filled with pictures of the Mayorgas, he took the top sheets and slipped them into his knapsack. After that, he focused on pictures of the Mayorga family.

Orlando thumbed through black-and-white prints, most of them yellowed and fly-speckled. He recognized the one of Don Absolón with his wife and children, all of them seated on the vast lawn in front of the main house. Orlando narrowed his eyes as he concentrated on the image of Rufino, guessing that he was fourteen or fifteen years old at the time. Orlando wondered if the photo had been taken before or after his exile into the jungle.

He sifted through the pile of pictures until he came across a more recent one of Rufino. In it, he appeared tall, dressed in white casual but elegant trousers, and a loose-fitting shirt, and he had his head to one side as Orlando remembered he used to do. By Rufino's side was an aristocratic-looking woman with blond hair, also elegantly dressed, and between the two of them was a child dressed in white knee pants.

"*¡Mierda!*"

Orlando snorted the disdaining word through his nose as he experienced a deluge of disgust for Rufino, for his wife, and for the child with the round, overfed face that stared at him from the picture. Feeling overcome by the intense heat and flickering dingy light of the office, Orlando pushed aside the pile of photographs, got to his feet, and headed for the door, where he clicked off the naked bulb and left the place.

Once outside, Orlando stepped down off the uneven curb and began walking at a brisk pace. He turned the corner, crossed the cobblestone street and headed for a small room with a light glowing in the window. He knocked.

"*¿Quién?*"

"Orlando Flores."

The heavy wooden door creaked open to let him in. His eyes squinted as they adjusted to the light of the small room that was shared by other recruiters. He nodded to two women and a man that were bent over documents; one was reading out loud and another was transcribing notes. Not trusting his own interpretation of the papers he had gathered, Orlando turned to one of the recruiters.

"*Amiga,* I have some papers here that I would like you to read to me."

"Now? We're almost finished with this project. Can you wait?"

"Of course."

Orlando plopped down on a chair as he extracted the sheets from his bag. He waited patiently, still thinking of the images he had just seen. After a while, one of the women approached him, sat on the floor and extended an open hand. Orlando handed her the short stack of papers.

"Let me see. This one says that a certain Bonifacio Zaragosa owes the Mayorga *finca* ten sacks of coffee beans. This other declaration states that the son of a Berta Espinoza was caught trying to steal food from the *patrón*'s kitchen. And this one . . . hmm . . . this one is more serious."

"What does it say?"

"It's a warrant for the arrest of a certain Quintín Osuna. He's charged with murder. It doesn't state the name of the victim, only the date of the crime. 1968."

Orlando stared at the woman. She looked up at him, startled by the expression on his face. His pupils dilated, and she thought she saw dark rings forming around his sunken eyes.

"1968. Is that the date of that paper?"

"No, *compañero*. This document is recent. It's dated only three months ago."

"But if it doesn't name the person who was killed, or any witnesses, or other details—doesn't that make the paper invalid?"

"Maybe somewhere else, *compañero*. In these parts, however, the only thing that matters is a signature. And here it is: *Rufino Mayorga*."

"What if this paper disappears?"

"Another copy will surface. Tell me, why are you so interested in this document?"

Orlando shrugged and rolled his eyes without saying a word. He got to his feet, and without retrieving the reports, he excused himself.

"Buenas noches, amigos."

"Adiós, compañero Orlando."

Orlando walked out of the tiny room into the darkness of the night. The village was quiet, and its only light came from the small yellow bulbs that hung from spindly posts located at each street corner. His sandaled feet sometimes tripped on the cobblestones as he walked aimlessly. Finding that paper had triggered new emotions and thoughts in him. Orlando realized that, despite the passing of the old Mayorga, he was still a hunted man. Rufino would not allow his father's hatred to disappear; he had inherited the rage and vengefulness from *El Viejo*.

Orlando asked why this had to be: Why did a son take on the hates of a father? To understand this, he knew, would explain why families repeated what their ancestors had done before them. It was the same with his people; they followed in the steps of their fathers and mothers.

This thought evoked the images of his own mother and father, and fear for them filled him. The idea that they might come to harm because of him was more intolerable than ever for Orlando, and he did not know how to deal with what he was feeling. He finally stopped pacing and took refuge from his anxiety under the yellowish circle cast by one of the street lights.

Chapter 24

They were innocent!

Orlando went on with the work of recruiting for the insurgents. During that time he enrolled men and women, from regions covering the length and breadth of the Lacandona. When he finished his east-west trek, he began a campaign taking him from north to south and back again. When this was completed, he crisscrossed the paths leading him to untouched areas of the jungle. As the months turned into years, Orlando grew to know the floor of the jungle by heart; he could recognize trees and distinguish one from the other.

His work yielded a profit as the insurgents' ranks grew almost daily when men, as well as women, trekked into the camp and pledged to follow. The unique quality of Orlando's work, compared to that of the other recruiters, was that the people who followed him stayed. Rarely did they experience a change of heart, no matter how difficult they found the life of a guerrilla. Not one of Orlando's recruits wavered in the conviction that one day they would rise, weapons in hands, to shatter the yoke that had oppressed them from birth and even before that time.

Most of Orlando's anguish during his first years as an insurgent was rooted in the disgust he felt because he had not had the courage to return to Lacanjá to his mother and father after his escape from the *caoba* fields. His moment came, however, when he was in Yaxchilán, a village close to Lacanjá. It happened when he was recruiting a group of Lacandones and one of them approached him.

"*Compañero* Flores, you must be careful."

At the moment, Orlando thought that the man was warning him because of his message to rise against the *patrones*, but he was struck by the look in the recruit's eyes; it was different from that of all the others who had cautioned him. Instinctively, Orlando stepped closer to the man. When he spoke, his voice was a whisper.

"What do you mean, *amigo?* Of what should I be careful?"

"Are you not the son of Domingo and Ysidra Osuna?"

Orlando was startled to hear his parents' names. He had not identified himself as being an Osuna since the days when he was an organizer and he had changed his name.

"Why do you ask?"

"Because my father remembers you. He was a *boyero* with you in the *caoba* fields of the Mayorga family. Are you not Quintín Osuna?"

Stunned into silence, Orlando took hold of the man's arm and nudged him over to a place far removed from anyone who might overhear their conversation. He was silent for a while as he wrestled with a decision: to be honest with this stranger and risk capture, or to be false and save himself, yet miss the opportunity to discover news for which he had spent years of his life waiting. Orlando's desire to know at least something about his mother and father compelled him to decide on a middle road.

"I once knew a Quintín Osuna, of these parts I believe. What I don't know is why he should be careful."

The man nodded, and with an understanding smile, played along with Orlando. Now it was his turn to walk toward an even more secluded fringe of the village so that both men might be able to speak openly.

"I understand the caution you show for that man. My father was a witness to the murder of the Mayorga overseer, a sorcerer often called El Brujo. My father has told me this story from the time when I was just a boy. He swears that the sorcerer received justice on that day when Quintín Osuna cut off his head, and he also swears that El Brujo's blood was white, like the milk of the *yuca.*"

Orlando had turned partially to one side so that all the man could see was his profile, chin jutting out, eyes clamped into slits. He held one hand, fingers outstretched and palm flat against his throat; he did this to disguise the wild beating of his heart, which was making the thick vein in his neck throb visibly.

"*Amigo,* what does this have to do with me?"

"Since you know Quintín Osuna, it might be a good idea to tell him what old Don Absolón did to Quintín's mother and father, when, after searching, he was unable to find him and punish him."

The mention of his parents made Orlando flinch. He turned to face the man. He wanted to speak, but he felt heat racing up from his stomach. He feared being sick in front of the stranger, so Orlando chose to keep silent. His silence, however, signaled the man to continue talking.

"The villagers of Lacanjá were witnesses to *el patrón*'s rage when he burned the Osuna *palapa* to the ground. Then he sentenced Domingo and Ysidra to death."

Orlando felt that his knees were buckling, but reminding himself that he had long feared what he was hearing, that it was really not unexpected, revived his strength. He spoke despite an overwhelming urge to vomit.

"How did they die?"

"They were dragged to the site of a *caoba* camp by overseers. There the *boyeros* were forced to witness the fulfillment of the sentence."

"I asked you, *how* did they die?"

"They were drowned in a mud pit."

Orlando kept silent, weeping inwardly as he remembered the last day he saw his mother and father. He knew the cruelty and pain of dying in a mud pit, and the thought of their torment was intolerable. He waited until he regained his composure.

"How long ago did this happen?"

"Only a few months had passed since the death of El Brujo."

Shortly after finding this out, Orlando returned to Yaxchilán, and from there he made his way to Lacanjá. Keeping cover in the jungle, he traveled secretly day and night. He was clear as to what he intended to do, and he understood the risk involved. The worst that could happen, he reminded himself, was death by execution, an end that was certainly his destiny anyway. Memories of Don Absolón, of his son

Rufino, of El Brujo, and even of his friend Aquiles, filled him with an insatiable desire for vengeance, making him forget his commitment to justice, to freedom—all the ideals that had led him to join the insurgents. He was accosted by regret, knowing that years earlier, when he had been so close to Lacanjá, when he had discovered that he was a wanted man, his mother and father, unknown to him, were already dead and he had done nothing. Above all, he was filled with disgust, knowing that old Don Absolón was now dead, ripped apart by an ox, and that he, Orlando, had been cheated of the pleasure of executing the old man.

It was dusk when he arrived at Lacanjá. As he skirted the village, he felt some comfort in seeing women stoking campfires, men and children carting water from the river; the fragrance of fresh tortillas made his mouth water. But, he could not stop to visit; it was too dangerous. He pushed on toward the fringe of the village, heading for Finca Las Estrellas.

It was past the family's dinner time when Orlando quietly made his way onto the property. He moved stealthily over the darkened parts of neat, manicured lawns, gingerly stepping over plush flower beds, avoiding the areas where he remembered watch dogs were kept. He moved cautiously, slowly, crouching, as if walking on brittle telltale twigs. He halted every few steps, eyes peeled wide open, ears tense and vigilant for any noise that would alert him to his being discovered. Nothing. The dogs, bellies filled and asleep, ignored him as he stole closer and closer to the room with the glittering chandeliers.

The entrance used by house servants was open. There was no one in sight. Orlando paused to remove his *huaraches* and made his way barefoot through the kitchen, heading for the parlor. He still remembered the way. The house was wrapped in silence; Rufino's wife and children were already asleep or elsewhere on the *finca*.

He rounded a corner and entered the dining room, now shrouded in shadows. From there he caught a full view of Rufino Mayorga sipping from a tiny goblet. Seeing how much his boyhood friend now looked like old Don Absolón, Orlando's memory zoomed back in time. In the same brocaded armchair, he sat dressed in similar white linen trousers and shirt. Orlando took his time to observe his prey, savoring the moment, taking in the details: graying blond hair that had begun to thin, well-fed paunch not yet as pronounced as the old man's, polished fingernails, white leather slippers, one of them dangling from a leg elegantly crossed at the knee.

Orlando then moved his gaze away from Rufino to scan the surroundings, remembering the elegance and rich security each piece of furniture and ornament conveyed. He saw himself, still a boy of fourteen years, dusting, rubbing, carting. He envisioned that boy courteously bending to offer the small tumbler of sherry carefully placed on a silver tray.

Orlando had time, and so he looked and remembered. Rufino was listening to music as did his father, and there was yet plenty of time before he would begin to make his way toward his bedroom. As the minutes passed, Orlando looked down at himself: his overgrown bare feet were callused and mutilated; his legs were bowed; his belly was flat, emaciated, as was his chest; his tunic was frayed and threadbare. He put his hand to his face and felt the scars he had received during his years as a *boyero,* laborer and insurgent. He took a hard look and saw the difference between himself and Rufino. He reflected on how both of them had been born close to one another in date and place, yet how the similarity ended there. He now saw why the old man and his kind forbade intermingling; the differences were so vast that only the blind could ignore the gap. *Someone might get ideas when the truth was realized.* With this thought, Orlando moved toward the armchair, the music covering the sound of his naked feet treading the marble floor.

"Rufino!"

Orlando's voice was drowned out by the music, which had reached a loud crescendo of shrill piano notes backed by even louder violin chords filling the room, floating upward to linger on the vaulted ceiling. Suddenly, the concert ended and only the repeated scratching of the needle on the disk could be heard. Rufino stood and headed for the record player.

"Rufino!"

The man's body jerked, turning abruptly. He was so startled that his hand, midway to lifting the arm of the record player, froze. A scratching, hissing sound filled the space separating the two men as the record spun, the needle yawing from one edge to the other. Para-lyzed, Rufino gawked, confusion and fear dilating his eyes.

"Who are you? What are you doing here?"

Orlando had now taken the pistol from his waist and he held it, not pointed at Rufino, but hanging from his hand. He moved toward the frozen man slowly, putting one foot in front of the other, knees slightly bent. His slanted eyes narrowed, allowing Rufino to see only the flint of their pupils.

"Who are you?"

Rufino's voice had grown thick with apprehension, intensified even more by Orlando's silence and constant motion toward him. He began to back away, knocking a vase to the floor and almost losing his balance. When his back touched a wall, Rufino knew he had nowhere to go.

"Don't you recognize me, *amigo?* Is it because we all look alike? Do you see the same miserable face on all of us?"

Rufino's skin had paled to nearly match his white shirt. His lips began to turn blue as his breathing became more and more irregular. Orlando's words seemed to confuse him even more because he could not remember; he could not identify the angry-looking native who stood confronting him with so much hostility.

"Domingo and Ysidra Osuna. Do these names remind you of any-thing, Don Rufino?"

Rufino's face crinkled like a mask, aging him, nearly transform-ing him into his father's image. Now he knew who it was he was fac-ing. He knew what awaited him. He followed the unspoken order when Orlando jerked his head toward the back, to the kitchen, where the servants had entered and exited the mansion for decades.

Orlando was calm as he followed Rufino out the door. He took time to slip into the *huaraches* he had left at the entrance. With the pistol in one hand, he nudged Rufino with the other until they were standing under a moonless sky.

"Move!"

Rufino moved as if in a trance, mechanically putting one foot in front of the other. He kept silent, his breathing thickening as they headed toward the darkness of the jungle. Feeling Orlando's prodding hand, Rufino marched in the direction of the *caoba* camp, but as they approached it, Orlando grabbed Rufino's shoulder.

"Turn! Go in that direction!"

"There's nothing there."

"There's mud. Go!"

Rufino, knowing what was coming, could not contain himself. He coughed time and again, evidently trying to suck air into his paralyzing lungs. Once, he halted and emptied his stomach; his vomit glistened white against the blackness of the moist earth. Submitting to Orlando's thrusting hand, he tried to speak as he moved forward.

"It was justice!"

"This is justice!"

"You murdered a man!"

"Your father murdered a man and a woman!"

"Why me?"

"Why my mother and father?"

"You're guilty!"

"They were innocent!"

The two men exchanged angry accusations as they moved until they came to muddy ground; a few paces more and both of them sunk to their thighs unexpectedly. Rufino looked at Orlando but saw only the glint of his eyes and a portion of his large white teeth. Orlando pushed the barrel of the pistol brusquely against Rufino's stomach, shoving it in and out, causing the man to retch again. Orlando then waded to one side as he spoke.

"Taste the food eaten by so many of your *boyeros!* Know what my mother and father were given to breathe!"

"You'll pay for this!"

"*¡Muévete!*"

With unexpected swiftness, Orlando stretched and lifted his arm, bringing down the weapon squarely on Rufino's neck. Rufino yelped with pain and began to back into the center of the quagmire. He was shaking so violently that his hair stood on end with horror. Orlando lifted the pistol and aimed it at *el patrón*'s face.

"*¡Muévete! ¡Más!*"

Rufino was up to his neck in mud and sinking inch by inch. His chin was now grazing the surface of the slime that nearly reached his mouth. Then, without uttering a sound, he closed his eyes and disappeared into the ooze, followed only by the slapping sound of mud closing in on mud.

Chapter 25

Why is the day moving in reverse?

The Lacandona Jungle, 1993.

Orlando Flores stood facing the firing squad; he was afraid but calm. He wanted to etch those faces into his memory. But no matter how much he squinted and focused his eyes, all he could see were blurs in the place of eyes, noses, mouths, chins. He tried to see, realizing that soon a blindfold would be wrapped over his eyes, and then it would be impossible for him to identify his executioners.

He struggled against the growing mist that interfered with his vision, but day's end was approaching and everything was growing darker. Suddenly he became confused, remembering that it was dawn, not night. He mumbled to himself, despite his having been instructed not to say a word: *Why is the day moving in reverse?*

Orlando swiveled his head to one side when he perceived that the commanding officer had approached to give the final order. This time Orlando's vision was clear, focused, precise, and he saw that it was Rufino Mayorga, dressed in a captain's uniform, who was to give the word. He twisted his neck to one side to look, blinking over and again because he thought that his eyes were deceiving him.

At that moment, he realized that Rufino was still a boy, and that the uniform he wore was that of a man; it was too large, giving him a comical appearance. He saw that the adult-sized cap on his head had slipped to his ears, almost covering his eyes. The tunic hung nearly to his knees, as if its medals were weighing it down, and his trousers were rolled up to compensate for the boy's short legs. When Orlando looked at Rufino's shoes, he burst out laughing because their over-sized toes curved upward.

"¡Epa, Rufino! ¿Qué pasó, amigo? ¿Eres ahora payaso?"

Clown! The word became the order to fire and Orlando's eyes bulged as he saw the bullets flying toward him; they were missiles from an unknown world. They wiggled, pirouetted, shimmied, as they traced their course toward him. Suddenly, everything stood still, and he had time to jerk his head to the side to take one final look. The last thing Orlando saw before his chest was blasted open by the torrent of bullets was that it was not Rufino after all. In his place stood the bloat-ed figure of Don Absolón Mayorga, covered in gleaming medals, baggy eyes concealed behind green-shaded dark glasses, mouth twist-ed in a grin. The ugly visage smirked at him.

        ∽ ∽ ∽

    Orlando awoke, panting and covered in perspiration; it took sec-onds before he realized that his hands were desperately massaging his chest. When he saw what he was doing, he clenched his fists, forcing himself to stretch his arms rigidly into the darkness. Slowly, he allowed himself to roll off the hammock onto the earthen floor, where he remained for several minutes, trying to separate the nightmare from reality. He sat, legs sprawled out in front of him, while his breath stabilized. All the while, he pressed the palms of his hands against his chest, still feeling the intense pain caused by the nightmare bullets.

    Trying to anchor himself to what was real, Orlando blinked and rubbed his eyes. Then he looked to the sides, downward and upward, but it was still so dark that he was barely able to make out the sup-porting beams of the *palapa* he shared with the other *compañeros.* As he ran his fingers through the sandy dirt, he wondered if anyone had awakened, but he saw that everyone was asleep and that some of the men were even snoring.

    Orlando needed more assurance of where he was. He forced his eyes to adapt to the gloom. He took in the stand where a gourd was placed next to a tin basin; that was where he washed. His eyes shifted along the side of the *palapa,* concentrating on the sleeping forms of his fellow insurgents, then stopping at the narrow, low-cut entrance; through it, he could make out a piece of the jungle, still bathed in moonlight.

As soon as he was able to get a grip on his surroundings, Orlando rolled to the side where he could rest his back. He concentrated on the present, on the *palapa,* and beyond it to the jungle. Still inundated by the fear caused by the nightmare, his thoughts shifted from the past to the present, then back. He again looked out through the *palapa*'s opening and saw that it was still deep night. He was grateful because he needed time to think, to decipher the bad dream that had just accosted him.

His mind drifted back to the time of his childhood, to the village where he lived with his mother and father. Orlando remembered that before falling asleep, instead of saying *buenas noches,* his mother or father would say: *Be careful of what you dream tonight.* He thought now of those words and of their meaning, and he longed to speak to someone who knew how to explain dreams. But there was no one. That he would be executed sooner or later was clear, but the other parts of his nightmare, what did they mean? Orlando closed his eyes and meditated, listening for a voice that might explain what he had experienced. His mind drifted, neither awake nor asleep, as words formed.

Why were the faces of my executioners blurred?
Because evil has no face.
Why was the day moving in reverse?
Because time is round and curls in on itself.
Then time stood still.
No. It only appeared to do so as it repeated itself.
Why was Rufino still a boy?
Because he died unchanged.
Why was he wearing clothes that were not his?
Because he clothed himself in the identity imposed on him.

Orlando opened his eyes and sucked in a large breath; he held it for a few moments as his mind settled. He exhaled slowly, thinking that now the dream was clear. The one question that continued to haunt him was whether he would always feel like an animal, constantly tracked by a predator.

Still sitting on the ground and leaning against the side of the *palapa,* Orlando finally dispelled the fearful feelings caused by the nightmare. He looked toward the entrance and saw that daylight was beginning to seep through the mesh of palm fronds and treetops. He got to his feet, wiped his hands on his shirt and looked for his sandals as he prepared to go down to the river. He did this silently, although he knew that his *compañeros* would soon be milling around the campfire, getting ready for a day of maneuvers and tactical planning.

Orlando made his way toward the water, listening to its cascading rhythm as it crashed against muddy banks. He breathed in deeply, smelling the river's dampness mixed with the pungent fragrance of decaying flowers. When he was not away from the camp on recruitment, this was where he liked to rest and spend time.

At river's edge, he pulled off the tunic in which he had slept. He sniffed it, taking in the sharp odor of his sweat, and the nightmare unexpectedly returned with its phantom firing squad. He shook his head to erase those images, and he plunged into the warm water, where he abandoned himself to its current and to thoughts of the winding path that had brought him to that place and time. He had begun as a servant on the *finca* of Don Absolón. He had been condemned to the life of a *boyero.* He had killed a man and experienced the life of a fugitive. He had organized and recruited. He had become an insurgent. He had settled the score with Rufino Mayorga.

Wanting to dispel this last thought, he shut his eyes and conjured the image of Juana Galván, who, he thought, had grown more beautiful over the years. Nothing in her life as a soldier had hardened her spirit, he mused. Her face had changed; this he acknowledged, but on the inside, she was tender and joyful. There was a time, in the beginning, when he had desired her as his companion, even loved her, but the hope that she would ever return his feelings had vanished years before when he realized that her heart, trampled by Cruz Ochoa, would never belong to any man.

Orlando then concentrated on the day's order of business as planned by the general command. There would be discussion and decision regarding the crisis that had arisen from the murder of two military policemen; discussion and drafting of a declaration of the insurgents' position; discussion and decision regarding the bishop's proposed mass demonstration. The list was short, and when his mind came to its end, Orlando's thoughts drifted to the previous day, when Juana had returned to camp, bringing with her the photographer named Adriana Mora.

He thought of the photographer for whom he had felt some distrust. He had voiced this sentiment when the general command had initially discussed recruiting her. He feared that she would betray them if she were captured, and now that he had seen her, his apprehension was even stronger. She was frail and foreign, but that alone was not what bothered Orlando. There was something else. He shook his head, gave up thinking about Adriana Mora and climbed to where he had left his clothes. It was time to join the *compañeros* for breakfast and to prepare for the meeting.

Chapter 26

What about me?

Insurgent Training Camp, Lacandona Jungle, August, 1993.

Adriana Mora concentrated on the faces of the members of the general command as they drafted the declaration of war that would be read to towns and cities, once the offensive began. Her camera clicked time and again, capturing the expression of El Subcomandante; his large nose dominated his face. The lens moved from Major Ramona over to Colonel Orlando, then on to the other officers.

Click! Click! Click! The repeated sound merged with muffled words, paper scraping against the rough table top, someone sneezing. Adriana circled the table to focus on the opposite side of the panel. When she pointed her camera toward Juana, she felt her heart beat faster, and she stopped what she was doing. Still aiming the camera, she saw that Juana had tilted her head; her eyes were looking at her. Adriana lowered the camera and returned the intensity of her gaze.

Suddenly, a deafening explosion tore the air, nearly rocking the shed off its foundation. Seconds of stunned surprise followed the blast, but before anyone could make a move, more detonations shook the ground. Adriana hit the floor on her rump, the camera still gripped in both hands. As she tumbled backward, she saw others dive under the table and benches, weapons already in hand.

El Subcomandante signaled everyone to leave the building and go on the defensive. Orlando was the first to crawl out; the others made their way through a panel in the floor boards. The room had filled with dust and smoke, and Adriana lost sight of Juana. She rolled over, slithered on her belly, and tried to escape the asphyxiating fumes. All the while she felt panic gripping her heart as her lungs constricted.

Without letting go of the camera, Adriana thrashed around, flinging her free arm in space, inching her way on her hands and knees until she discovered the exit. Throughout, she was aware of a torrent of bullets, signaling that the camp was under siege. When she emerged, she stretched out on her back, mouth agape gulping air, hoping to regulate her breathing. She could hear the searing noise of bullets cutting through bark and leaves, then she was shaken by another blast that she could not identify.

Voices clamored. Orders were shouted. Muffled groans were beginning to emerge. Adriana finally regained composure, realizing that she was missing the moment for which she had joined the insurgents. She scrambled behind a tree, breathing through her mouth, trying to forget her asthma and deflating lungs. She moved her head slowly to catch a glimpse of what was happening and she saw that she was positioned at a vantage point.

Adriana felt her hands and fingers trembling as she raised the camera, pointed and focused. In the center of the lens were two men garbed in government army fatigues; their arms blurred as they jerked back and forth, piston-like, while their weapons repeatedly blasted flames from reddened cylinders. Click! Zoom! Click! Zoom! Adriana twisted her head and body to pan the camera from one angle to another, capturing images of insurgents, who returned fire with as much ferocity.

The air was polluted with the stench of burnt gunpowder as well as with an ear-shattering din. Snap! The camera recorded the picture of a body slammed against a tree. Click! That frame captured Major Ramona, sawed-off shotgun held against her small frame, blasting fire with both barrels. Everywhere Adriana turned to focus her camera, it snapped weapons firing, smoke streaming toward treetops, *palapas* engulfed in flames, soldiers falling, running, insurgents firing their weapons at will, ripping bodies.

Gaining courage, Adriana ventured more and more into open space, fear receding from her mind with each second. She focused, clicked and refocused, oblivious to the danger of being shot. She turned in different directions, pointing upward, sideways. Her body became a blur of motion. Somewhere in the back of her mind, she was already processing the pictures, already sending them to journals and newspapers; names and addresses of publishers surfaced clearly in her mind.

Suddenly, she caught sight of forms, shady figures running through the trees. She looked around, camera held mid-air and ready to shoot, but everything had become silent; everyone was gone except the apparitions she had just glimpsed. Confused, Adriana turned in circles, her eyes wide open, her mind trying to decipher the sudden silence as well as the transparent shadows.

Without knowing from where it came, she heard the racket of three loud blasts; she felt hot, searing pain ripping open her stomach. The camera fell from her hands as she looked down at her abdomen. It was bloody, and her shirt was ripped to shreds. Her legs lost all strength as she crumpled to the ground.

Knowing that she was about to die, Adriana closed her eyes and waited, but nothing happened; there was only stillness. When she sensed that someone was beside her, she opened her eyes and she found herself cradled in Juana's arms. Adriana raised her head and saw that the camp was serene, orderly; there were no signs of battle, except that she knew that she was dying. The sun was setting when she felt the pressure of Juana's lips on hers. She opened her mouth, matching Juana's passion.

Adriana's head swirled and she began to lose consciousness as she rolled her knees up to her bloodied stomach, but she was startled back to alertness when she realized that she was sitting cross-legged facing Chan K'in; he was seated and listening to her. Adriana saw that they were no longer in the camp but in the jungle; its shade and sounds wrapped itself around them. Dumbfounded, she stared at him, waiting for him to speak. Instead, he signaled with his eyes for her to look to her side. Adriana did as he asked. When she turned, she saw her mother seated next to her. She, too, was on the ground, cross-legged, and she looked at Adriana with sad eyes.

"Adrianita, I've been looking for you. Have you not seen me?"

Adriana stared at her mother, not understanding what was happening. She was confused. She felt strange emotions seeping through her heart, sentiments that she could not identify, but she did not feel fear—of that she was certain.

"No, Mamá, I haven't seen you."

"I've been with you many times, because I know that there is something you want to know."

This time Adriana turned to Chan K'in, yearning for direction, wanting him to explain to her what was happening. The old man, however, only looked down at the earth in front of him as he etched a design.

"What happened that night, Mamá?"

"Don't you remember anything?"

"Only the noise."

"I killed your father."

"I know, Mamá. What I don't know is why."

"He betrayed me."

"Why did you kill yourself?"

"I had no reason to live."

"What about me?"

Adriana's question was filled with longing and pain that turned into anger. When she saw her words seep out of her mouth, she saw that they were enraged. They left her lips and furiously crept upward, leaping like monkeys from branch to branch, tree to tree, climbing higher as they made their way to the highest parts of the jungle. Up there her words reverberated as they elongated, widened, deepened, finally bursting into an echo that floated away, out of Adriana's hearing.

∽ ∽ ∽

Adriana awoke. Her eyes snapped open to see pale light coming through the *palapa*'s entrance. She had been dreaming again. Adriana forced her body to be still while her brain raced, trying to understand the meaning of the dream. She concentrated on the fleeting shadows, the same ones that had inhabited her other dreams, but this time one of them had been her mother. *What about me?* Adriana put her hands to her ears, trying to retrieve the echo of her words, but instead her eardrums vibrated with the blasts of gunfire and bomb explosions.

She wiggled her nose, feeling it scorched and plugged up with the odor of gunpowder. Then her head jerked downward because the pain of the wound was still on her mind. She examined her stomach, rubbed it, heaved it up and down, testing its strength, but she saw that it was intact. It had all been a dream. The violence of men and women slaughtering one another, the conversation with her mother, her own unflinching determination—it had all been a dream.

Adriana stretched, then rolled off the hammock exasperated and mumbling under her breath. She felt shaken and near tears, aware that her dreams were becoming an inexplicable obsession. She longed to speak to Chan K'in; he would know what to make of her dream. Unanswerable questions swirled in her head: *Had she already experienced such violence? Was it a portent of what was yet to come? Did Juana kiss her? Was her mother one of those shadowy figures always tracking her? Why had her mother abandoned her?*

Adriana's head ached, but she put her pain and nervousness aside, hoping to anchor herself in reality by reminding herself that a council had been called for seven that morning. She had been commissioned to record it on film as well as in her notes. While she bathed, and later on as she ate breakfast, her mind could not erase the images of her dream; they were etched on her brain as clearly as those she captured on film.

When Adriana entered the room, the members of the general command were already at their places. Loaded down with camera, film and note pads, she made her way to an empty seat, trying not to disrupt the discussion. She noticed, however, that all eyes were on her. She smiled sheepishly as she put her gear in a corner and then greeted the committee.

"*¡Buenos días!*"

"*¡Buenos días!*"

The response was simultaneous but uneven, male voices outweighing the female. She looked around, taking in faces and other details, marveling at how her dream had constructed such a different scenario. In her dream, the room had been large, with smooth plastered walls, its ceiling high and vaulted. In reality, the room was small, its ceiling low, and its walls nothing more than rough poles lashed together. In the dream, there were only a handful of insurgents: El Subcomandante, Major Ramona, Colonel Orlando, and Juana. Now, as Adriana scanned the room, she saw that the committee was much larger. When she looked toward Juana, she saw that she was looking at her, just as she had in the dream; Adriana got the impression of warmth in Juana's gaze. Before she could give it any more thought, however, her attention was taken away from Juana by the murmuring of voices, low-pitched but intense. Some of the officers seemed agitated, others restless.

The whispering stopped when El Subcomandante spoke. As he did he nodded his head in Adriana's direction, signaling his permission for her to begin her work. She stepped to the rear of the room and began shooting as she moved to take in different angles: first, individual faces, then in twos and threes. As she worked, the committee went on with its discussion.

The camera's shutter clicked so frequently that it soon became inaudible to everyone in the room: El Subcomandante, one hand bracing his jaw, the other holding an unlit pipe; Colonel Orlando, head leaned to one side, a drooping mustache emphasizing the slits of his eyes; Captain Juana, profile turned toward the camera at such an angle that the half-moon scar over her eyebrow appeared to glow; Major Ramona, unconsciously holding the fringe of her *huipil* to her mouth and nose. Click! The shutter opened and shut, capturing faces, profiles, hands, furrowed foreheads, blinking eyes, pinched lips.

Adriana lowered her camera. The film had run out and she needed to reload. As she did this, she was aware of the heated discussion that was going on. It was agitated but orderly; no one shouted nor argued. Opposing points of view were listened to and then responded to as necessary.

The demonstration by the bishop's priests and missionaries.
Military policemen captured, murdered, mutilated.
Compañeros *accused and arrested.*
The review of insurgent troops by El Subcomandante.

Hours passed and the committee continued its work, allowing interruptions only when the officers needed to go out to relieve themselves. Other than that, no one left or took time out to eat. Adriana decided that she would follow that example, using the time to take notes and to snap more photographs.

Her headache persisted, growing worse as the day passed. Although she tried to resist, she continued thinking of her dreams. Chan K'in's words, vividly clear, came back to her. The heat of the jungle became oppressive, and she felt stifled inside the room. Adriana left her gear behind and walked out onto the compound. Suddenly, she felt a little lightheaded and she began to ache. Without warning, nausea overcame her. She ran to the edge of the jungle and emptied her stomach. Fatigued and sweaty, she sat on a fallen tree while she tried to gather her thoughts.

"Compañera."

Adriana whipped her head toward the voice and discovered Juana standing beside her. She could not help herself. She stared at her without inhibition, scanning her face, then down to her uniform shirt, her trousers and boots.

"I'm sick, Juana."

"It's the heat."

"No!"

"Then what is it?"

"It's dreams that hound me and don't let me sleep."

Juana sat by Adriana's side and they remained in silence. The heat had by that time saturated the jungle. The animals were also silent, as if sleeping, only the faraway murmur of cascading water breaking the afternoon languor. In that quiet, Adriana felt an inner door opening, letting out a flood that had been trapped there, and tears rolled down her cheeks. Embarrassed, she tried to turn her face from Juana, but before she could turn completely, Juana took hold of her shoulder and placed her arm around her.

"Talk to me."

"This morning I woke up from a dream in which my mother came to me. She spoke to me."

Juana released Adriana's shoulder and put her clasped hands in her lap. Her face tilted to one side so as to look fully at Adriana. She lifted her eyebrows inquisitively.

"She died when I was a child, and I was left alone. I've always felt that she abandoned me."

"But she died, Adriana. She didn't abandon you."

Adriana looked at Juana but feared revealing what she had never before dared to tell. She had never told anyone of her memories of being locked in an apartment with her dead mother and father, of her childhood rootlessness, of her fear of abandonment.

"She didn't just die, Juana. She killed my father, then she killed herself."

Juana again put her arm around Adriana's shoulders to communicate her understanding of what she had heard, and remained silent. Adriana turned her head toward Juana, thinking that perhaps Juana had somehow experienced similar feelings and truly understood her pain.

"Last night she came to me for the first time. I think that she was trying to explain why she did what she did, but because I felt anger at her, she disappeared. I awoke before she could speak."

Juana listened to Adriana's words, apparently understanding her emotions. She tightened the grasp on her friend's shoulders.

"My people know that dreams say something to us; their words and actions are explanations. We take them seriously. Your anger has meaning; maybe it's a discovery."

Now it was Adriana's turn to look at Juana. She stared at her, again unabashedly. She was thinking that, until the dream, she had never felt anger at her mother. At least, she could not remember experiencing that sentiment.

"Discovery?"

"Maybe it will lead you to understand, to forgive your mother for killing your father."

Adriana pulled away from Juana. She needed to explain to her the real reason for her anger.

"It was not her killing my father that filled me with anger in the dream. It was that she killed herself, abandoning me, leaving me alone."

"Adriana, no one knows what was in your mother's heart. Perhaps that is what she's trying to tell you. Maybe that is why she cannot rest until you accept that she had a reason for what she did."

"But to accept it, I must first know the reason."

"You'll know. Your mother will reveal it to you."

Adriana thought of Juana's words. She closed her eyes, returning to the embrace that had given her strength and pulled her away from the gloom of abandonment. She was not yet ready to accept what Juana had said; she needed time to ponder those words, to understand their meaning. Buried in those sentiments was the explanation for what her dreams held.

That evening, while mingling with the women, Adriana was finally able to dispel the shakiness caused by her dream. There was tension in the camp caused by a sense of approaching conflict. People talked of nothing else, and no one doubted that war was close. They wondered what day would be determined by the general command for its beginning. In the meantime, orders were given for some insurgents to leave the camp to gather intelligence.

Chapter 27

Emboldened, Juana mingled with the crowd.

As far as Juana's eyes could see, a multitude of people covered the sides of the canyon. The beaten paths that marked the hillsides had disappeared under the throngs which had come and were still arriving, responding to the bishop's call for dialogue and prayer. From where she stood, she was not able to see where the mass of people ended; she could only focus below, on the floor of the canyon, where an altar had been erected.

Adriana stood beside Juana. She spotted Orlando Flores nearby, when she occasionally glanced back. They had been assigned to join the demonstration, mingle with the crowd and get a sense of the people's mood. With that instruction, Juana, Adriana and Orlando had trekked from the jungle campsite to the highlands, blending in with the pilgrims as they made their way to the convocation.

Juana scanned the swarm of people, identifying tribes by their dress: the black woolen skirts of the Tzeltal women; the white cotton tunic of the Lacandón men. There were other groups represented; even city people had come. The cut of their dress and shoes gave them away.

Juana had replaced her uniform with her native dress. She inwardly admitted that she was happy to kick off the heavy boots and replace them with *huaraches*. It was not so easy, however, when the time came to transform Adriana. Her hair was too curly and short, her legs were too straight and unblemished, and she was so gangly that Juana had a difficult time finding a skirt long enough for her. The other *compañeras* had giggled when they first caught sight of Adriana dressed like a native, but when they saw her sincerity, they patted her on the back and said she looked fine. Sharing in their humor, Adriana laughed with them as she made sure that she had a camera tucked under her *huipil.*

Looking down on the color-speckled sea of people, Juana felt herself in turmoil, mainly because she, like the other insurgents, knew that war was now inevitable. There had been too many tortures and killings, too many breaches of agreement. Fear of war was the reason for the bishop's call to the people; he hoped to prevent through dialogue a bloody explosion.

It's too late, Tatic, too late. Five hundred years have passed and now we're armed and angry. Nothing can stop the torrent that is about to fall on us all.

Juana's thoughts were so intense that her lips mouthed what was going through her mind. But there was another reason why she was so inwardly stressed: her conversation with Adriana of the previous day. From the beginning, she had felt deeply moved by affection for her, and now her sentiments were drenched in sympathy because she, too, had been uprooted and alone during her life. Juana longed to tell Adriana about herself, about her life with Cruz Ochoa, about her father and how she had returned to him looking for an explanation, but she was not used to speaking about herself or such personal things.

She glanced sideways to look at Adriana and saw that she was taking furtive shots with her camera. She felt apprehensive, but sensed that this was a special moment and that Adriana should capture whatever she could. Juana again turned to examine the growing crowd, guessing that there were thousands of men, women and children, and that the massive convocation might be critical to the insurgents' war. She knew in her heart that no matter what the bishop preached, his words would not halt the momentum of insurgency. It was too late.

Led by seminarians standing in a circle around the altar, each with a portable microphone in hand, the people began to sing hymns. At first, the singing was thin, tinny, but as the swell of voices joined in, the chanting rose and flowed, at times becoming thunderous as the petitions of the people elevated beyond the mist, soared up to the mountain heights.

¡Alabaré! ¡Alabaré! ¡Alabaremos al Señor!
Juana stretched her back, and stood on tiptoe in order to see more. She was moved by the faces of her people, especially the women. In the crowd was a girl, no more than thirteen or fourteen years old, who reverently held a bunch of wildflowers. Next to her stood an old woman, perhaps the girl's great-grandmother; both of them were singing piously, offering their voices in prayer.

Everywhere Juana looked she saw faces worn out before their time by misery and overwork, bodies covered with threadbare cotton and frayed woolens, feet shod in raggedy sandals or even bare and callused. She looked at children's bloated bellies, ill-fed and ruined by parasites, and her own stomach sickened as she relived her childhood when she was weighed down by burdens meant to be carried only by burros. Juana wanted to pray, but she could not because her guts were on fire with anger and rancor.

"The poverty of our people and their deplorable living conditions, which are even more serious in the indigenous areas of our diocese, are explained by the structures that have been formed over the length and breadth of five hundred years of history."

A deacon, making time for the bishop's arrival, had begun to read from the prelate's pastoral letter. The words, nasalized by the sound system, mixed with the continued praying and chanting of "*¡Paz! ¡No Violencia!*" The shouting swelled as lines of people crowded down the sides of the ravines, snaking their way across the mountainsides, closer to the altar.

"For the Indian peoples, the conquest meant that the colonizers brought subjugation and exploitation, as well as varying degrees of brutality and the violation of the dignity of the indigenous."

Juana turned to Adriana and saw that she was riveted by the overwhelming sight and sounds. Again, she turned to look at the girl with the flowers, wondering if she might have looked like her that day when her father had exchanged her to Cruz Ochoa. She returned her attention to the bishop's letter and the people's response to his words. She wanted to discover the real mood of the congregation, wondering if their shouts in favor of peace were sincere.

"Our communities have discovered that, united, they have the capacity to solve the problems that affect them. In the end, they will be the ones to decide their own history."

Juana listened carefully, puzzled as to why, despite the meaning of the bishop's words regarding her people's unity and their obligation to forge their own future, he still advocated peace. Her mind filled with questions.

Is he not recognizing the enormity of grief suffered by our people for so many centuries? Is he not acknowledging that we are the ones to ultimately take control of our own lives? Why can he not admit that war is the only way to solve the grievous problems afflicting our people? War is the only way that will lead to defining our own history.

She was nearly talking to herself when the deacon abruptly stopped the reading and joined the other seminarians as they moved toward a mass of people churning in expectation. The bishop, vested to celebrate Holy Mass, had arrived. He had been transported by car from San Cristóbal de las Casas, but had chosen to walk the last miles down the mountain into the canyon. As he penetrated the crowd, uproarious cheering arose.

"*¡Tatic! ¡Tatic! ¡Tatic!*"

The bishop was jostled back and forth, and countless hands, hungry to touch even the hem of his vestment, reached out to him. He was patted on the back and his hands were kissed or shaken. As he inched his way through the multitude, making the sign of the cross in every direction, hymns were again entoned and led by the seminarians, and the people sang with their hearts. Now, their chant rose yet higher than the ravines and mountain peaks. Behind the sad-looking prelate a long line of priests, also vested for the service, followed smiling, waving, nodding, blessing.

When he finally arrived at the podium, a hush fell over the multitude. The only sound to be heard was the hum of the wind as it snaked its way from the mist-covered peaks down through the ravines. Juana surveyed the right and left sides of the canyon and again was struck by the upturned brown faces, all of them filled with hope.

"*¡Viva Tatic!*"

"*¡Viva!*"

A massive response followed the lone voice that had shouted out its tribute to the Little Father. Minutes passed while the crowd opened its heart, cheering and shouting support for the man most of them believed had lived among their ancestors and who had returned to defend them.

Juana squinted, trying to focus on the tiny figure clad in white vestments. The day was ending; the northern wall of the canyon was now shrouded in a purple mantle. Torches were being lighted around the altar and beyond it. She saw that the breeze was ruffling the bishop's thinning hair and that he patted it down with his right hand from time to time. She waited as did everyone for his words as he adjusted the microphone that had been pinned on his shoulder. Then he cleared his voice.

"I am your shepherd and I say to you that dialogue is one of the conditions for fraternal relationships. Let us speak to one another, not kill one another."

A thunderous roar of applause and shouting ripped through the early evening. Here and there small groups sang; others prayed Hail Marys and Our Fathers. Juana shook her head in disagreement. She wanted to reach for a microphone and bring her people to their senses, but she saw that most of them were nearly hysterical in their approval of what he was saying.

"*En nombre del Padre, del Hijo y del Espíritu Santo.*"

"*¡Amén!*"

The bishop turned to face the altar and began the prayers of the mass. When Juana heard the response from the crowd, she turned away, nearly convinced that her people saw the resolution to their misery through the eyes of the bishop. As she began to move toward the fringe of the throng, she thought she heard voices speaking. Curious to know why they were not praying, she edged closer to the mumbling.

"I tell you, the time for praying has passed."

"What do you mean?"

"I intend to arm myself and fight."

"*¡Estás loco!*"

"The overseer of my *patrón* took my last pesos a year ago. I had nothing, and my two little sons died of hunger. You say I'm crazy because I want to kill that overseer. Well, then, I'm crazy!"

"*¡Shsss!*"

"*¡Cállense! ¡Tatic está rezando!*"

Juana neared the knot of men and women who were whispering despite the ongoing prayers. Behind her was Adriana, and Orlando was another few steps away. Taking a chance of being put off, she tapped the man who had been speaking on the shoulder.

"*Amigo,* you're right. Praying will do no good. It's time to fight. Are you ready to leave your *palapa* and follow us into the mountains?"

"*¡Shsss! ¡Qué vergüenza!*"

"*¡Respeto para Tatic!*"

Juana, undaunted by the complaints, looked at the man who returned her gaze. He was surprised but not put off. He looked around at his companions, then back to face Juana.

"What's in the mountains?"

"Others who think like you. Women and men preparing to fight the *patrones*. Come! Follow us! It's time."

She moved slowly, knowing that the man would follow her as she headed toward more voices. This time Juana did not look, she merely stood still and listened.

"What did you think of the demonstration in Tuxla the other day?"

"How should I know?"

"Because you were there. I saw you."

"No, I wasn't."

"I saw you!"

"How could you? There were more than a thousand *compañeros* and *compañeras* there."

"Ha! So you *were* there!"

"So I was there! So what?"

Juana aimed an ear toward the two men who were nearly arguing, and she approached them close enough to whisper. As she did this, she looked over to Orlando, then to Adriana and yanked her head in her direction.

"Why are you afraid to admit that you were at Tuxla, when so many of your own people were there?"

"Afraid? Yes, I'm afraid. The *patrones* are filled with anger and they will be unleashing the *catxul* on us. That's why I'm afraid!"

"Join us up in the mountains and fight back. The *catxul* are afraid of us."

"Who are you?"

"We're insurgents, but first we are the natives of this land. Don't forget that our ancestors—yours and mine—have inhabited this land since before the *catxul* had memory."

"Memory is not as important as power. The *catxul* have power."

"They have power because you give it to them. Without that they are cowards! They fear the insurgents because we will take away that power. Follow me!"

Emboldened, Juana mingled with the crowd as prayers were chanted and hymns entoned, realizing that she was in the midst of a sea of discontented, lost people who had nowhere to go and who were longing for direction. She listened to whispering men who bitterly cursed their burden but who were disoriented as to what to do about it. She knew that she had been mistaken; nonviolence was not what her people wanted.

Juana moved toward women speaking about laws needed for their defense. She looked at them, knowing that despite the prayers that swirled above their heads, they whispered about change. They were now gesturing energetically, head to head, obviously agitated by their own words.

"They say that we can take part in the revolution, even if we are women."

"What about our children?"

"Those same laws say that we have the right to have others care for them."

"*¡Dios mío!*"

"I hear that there's even a law against anyone beating us."

"Even a husband? A father?"

"Even they will be punished."

"*¡Santa María!* Is that possible?"

While this was happening, Orlando nervously kept Juana and Adriana within sight. He listened to the words of the pastoral letter, along with the singing and other muttering that was going on, while his eyes focused on Juana, who moved from group to group, cautiously at first, then with more ease, saying words that apparently encouraged people. He saw that sometimes she held Adriana's hand when she changed direction.

Orlando frowned, understanding that Juana was developing a special feeling for the foreign reporter. He had never seen Juana so interested in anyone. He thought of Adriana, and his earlier reservations about her returned. When the council had discussed bringing a photographer to join the insurgents, he had objected because he believed that no one except one of their own, someone who had suffered the blows of a *patrón*, could understand their cause. In spite of his disapproval, he had been overruled, and she had been brought to the insurgents by Juana.

On the other hand, Orlando was now experiencing mixed feelings because he saw Adriana's willingness to risk danger for their cause; her commitment was becoming clear to him. Also, the thought that people suffered in different ways—*patrones* and their world were not the only oppressors—pushed him toward accepting her because, although he did not know her story, he sensed that she had already undergone her own unhappiness.

Still, he worried, believing her too frail, too unused to their ways in the jungle. Adriana appeared to have difficulty speaking, even in Spanish. Despite all of this, Orlando had already begun to accept Adriana, especially since his mind had changed regarding the need to compile a photographic history of the events they were facing. He only wished that someone else had been chosen to do the work.

He was thinking about this as he watched her and Juana moving in and out of small groups, speaking and listening, while the mass was proceeding. Then, something drew his attention away from the women, and he focused on two men who seemed intent on following the prayers. Something about them caught his eye, and he watched them as they made the sign of the cross, mumbled responses, knelt and stood at the right times; they even joined in the singing of hymns. Something about them was not right, but Orlando could not decipher what it was.

When he saw one of them looking at him out of the corner of his eye, Orlando cautiously slid behind a group of women. He forced himself to look in another direction while mentally reviewing the men's appearance. They were dressed like laborers, yet there were details that did not fit in. Orlando took another furtive glance, just enough to gather new impressions. The shirt on one was new; the creases where it had been folded were still evident. The other wore boots with pointed toes and elevated heels; those were not the shoes of a laborer. Orlando, pretending to participate in the religious service, considered the discrepancies. When he glanced in their direction again, he was startled to find them gone. He spun around and scanned the crowd; this time he spotted them behind him. Convinced that they were stalking him, Orlando plunged toward Juana and Adriana.

"Juana! Adriana! Some of these people are spies. We must leave immediately."

With Orlando at the head, Juana, Adriana, and several men and women recruits followed as they pushed their way through the crowd, heading up toward the ridge of the mountain. Orlando kept his eye on the rear, but the spies had disappeared. He continued to move at a steady pace. By the time the group reached the highest point, the blaring voice of the microphone had receded, becoming almost inaudible, as had the prayers and singing. When Orlando glanced back for a final look, he saw a squirming mass of people, and he imagined that the canyon was a bowl filled with ants; the countless torches were sweets that had attracted them.

No one spoke as they made their way deeper into the jungle; only once did they stop long enough for Orlando to pull out the pistol he had concealed under his tunic and adjust it around his waist. Juana did the same with the weapon she had hidden under her *huipil*. The new insurgents looked on, amazement and apprehension pasted on their faces, while Adriana jotted down notes with only the light of the moon to make out her writing.

"*¡Vámonos!* Juana, I'll bring up the rear."

Orlando looked at Juana and Adriana, then at the recruits; he was still feeling jittery because of the encounter at the rally. He did not want to admit it, but he was shaken because of the spies, who were most certainly on his trail. He hated this apprehension because it recurred frequently, to the point that sometimes he wondered if it was his imagination playing tricks on him. He also detested feeling weak and vulnerable; his concentration shattered, distracting it from the plans of the insurgents.

These experiences had been going on since the day he had killed El Brujo, forcing him to become a fugitive. The nightmare he had experienced recently only confirmed his feeling of being stalked and one day being captured and executed. Now, following the small troop through the jungle, Orlando plodded in the dark. His breathing was heavy as he walked, nervously looking back to assure himself that no one was following. Nearly impenetrable darkness, hissing insects and screeching monkeys intensified Orlando's apprehension, forcing him to clench his jaw painfully.

Trying to shake off his agitation, Orlando turned his thoughts to the day he had faced Rufino and watched as he died. He remembered the gratification it had given him, how it had relieved him of the burden of guilt for having abandoned his mother and father. But his satisfaction was short-lived. Each time he remembered, he was forced to admit that even while still elated, he had realized that something inside of him had drowned alongside Rufino, that the death of his parents had not been vindicated after all, that a hollow would always remain inside him, like a wound refusing to heal. Orlando understood that taking vengeance had transformed him into the image of Rufino and Absolón Mayorga; he had become like them. As always when remembering this period in his life, he became saddened and isolated. The memory filled him with hatred for the way of life that created such wickedness.

It was dawn when Orlando, Juana, Adriana and the new recruits made it to camp. The women went in one direction, the men in another. The camp was still poised for war.

Chapter 28

You are my blessing.

Ocosingo, January 1, 1994.

The day came. Juana, with an M-1 carbine held in the assault position, crouched behind a corner facing the plaza of Ocosingo. Next to her stood Adriana, a camera in her grip, and across the street from them stood Orlando, a weapon also in his hands. It was nearly two in the morning on the first day of 1994, and the insurgents had been placed to cover strategic points by their commander, Insurgent Captain Irma. They were waiting for word from Insurgent Major Ramona, commander of the column taking San Cristóbal de las Casas; the plan of attack pivoted on the successful capture of that city. The insurgents, males and females, waited with apprehension. They were eager to fight, and although the night was frozen, perspiration slid down their spines, and minutes felt like hours.

"We have recovered the flag."

That was the signal. Juana, Orlando and Adriana, along with their squad, followed their commander as she moved to execute the double-pronged attack on Ocosingo's central radio station, as well as its main garrison, which was located inside the municipal palace.

With the element of surprise on the insurgents' side, everything proceeded smoothly. The federal soldiers guarding the radio station surrendered their weapons without resisting, and the same happened at the garrison. By the time sunlight flooded through the cobblestone streets of the town, Captain Irma had reported full command of Ocosingo. Las Margaritas, Altamirano, Chanal, Huixtan and Oxchuc had also fallen into the command of the insurgents before daylight awakened their inhabitants.

In Ocosingo, it took only a few minutes before the federal soldiers were herded into the central patio of the building. There, surrounded by ornate balconies and columns, Captain Irma faced the commander of the garrison. Juana stood behind, watching her take command, observing how she turned a full circle, assuring herself that her troops were with her. She was backed by her force, all holding their weapons, all masked. Stunned and frightened by the covered faces, the commander handed the rebel leader his weapon.

"*¡Feliz Año Nuevo, cabrón!*"

Juana saw that the officer was sickening. She knew that it was because the insult of that moment would haunt him for the rest of his life. How would he explain that it had been a woman who had disarmed him, reviling him, calling him a son of a bitch? Even more humiliating, how would he admit that she was an indigenous woman? Juana discerned the turmoil stamped on the man's face and felt pride that her *compañera* had been the one chosen to disarm him.

The man cleared his voice, apparently wanting to say something, and the insurgents, whose attention had been riveted on the scene, moved in closer, not wanting to miss what he was about to say.

"How old are you?"

Someone sucked on his teeth, others muttered, showing that they had expected words regarding the officer's loss of power. Instead, they heard a question they considered stupid. Captain Irma, known for her humor and boldness, looked at the officer. She stood with her feet spread apart, showing disdain for his question.

"I'm five hundred and two years old, *cabrón!*"

Her voice was strong, filled with mockery, and her troops chuckled when they saw that she was playing with the man's fear. Embarrassed, the officer frowned as he lowered his eyes.

"We all know our positions. Let's take them. We'll wait until we get new orders."

Captain Irma spoke concisely as she moved toward the central office of the garrison, while the commander was whisked away and the insurgent column was ordered to wait. Adriana, left to move at will through the vast patio and its porticos, took shots continuously, stopping only to reload the camera. She concentrated on the faces of the federal officers, capturing expressions of disbelief and disdain, but mostly fear. She also took portraits of the insurgents, men and women who demonstrated by the way they stood, looked, moved, that this was the moment for which they had prepared.

Several hours passed, during which Orlando and others left the garrison to gather people in the main plaza. There, they read the *"Declaración de la Selva."* When they returned, they reported that the townspeople had fled; word had come to them that federal troops were on the way.

Adriana, in the meantime, realizing that everything had suddenly become quiet, stopped what she was doing. Concerned, she made her way toward Juana, who was sitting on a stone bench.

"What's happening, Juana? It's too quiet."

"Yes."

Juana tensed, holding her weapon as if she were about to fire. Adriana looked around and saw that the other rebels were also taut, expecting something. Captain Irma reappeared and fixed her eyes upward, looking through the open roof of the palace. Without warning, the sudden whirring of helicopters canvassed Ocosingo, growing louder each second. Soon the sky was speckled with the flying scorpions that descended lower and lower over the rooftops.

Irma did not have to give an order; the insurgents dove for cover anywhere possible: under heavy office tables, behind ornate corners. Knowing that the open roof provided targets for the helicopters, Juana and Adriana had time to slide under the stone bench.

The choppers hovered over Ocosingo, their mounted guns launching rounds of ammunition and even rockets at whatever target came into their range. Plaza, cathedral, marketplace, municipal buildings, every structure considered a shelter for the insurgents was strafed and bombed, and the attack went on for hours. The blasts and detonations shook the ground, sending civilians and insurgents alike scurrying for cover. The air was filled with an impenetrable stench of sulfur and burning; everywhere people screeched, and children cried out in terror. But the assault would not cease, as one helicopter wave followed the next one.

The patio was by now littered with chunks of stucco and fragments of sculptured angels and animals. Shards of colored glass were strewn everywhere. Suddenly, the terror stopped, and there was only silence, shattered by whimpering and weeping. Still under the shelter of the stone bench, Juana and Adriana looked at one another, wondering what was happening. They were startled when Orlando appeared by their side; he had crawled from the other side of the patio.

"More than likely, government soldiers are on the way into town."

"What about our installations?"

"We've lost communication. We're isolated. Irma has passed the word that each one of us should head for the mountains on our own."

Juana and Orlando whispered, as if spies were already prying close to them. Orlando removed his mask from his sweat-and-dirt smeared face. Adriana's face had traces of smoke around the eyes and nose. Juana unmasked and put her hand to her forehead, trying to imagine what she looked like, but all she could feel was the scar over her eye.

"Orlando, I think we should find a place to hide until night, when escape might be easier. Adriana, what do you think?"

"The same thing!"

Orlando rolled over on his back, thinking of the countless times he had been in Ocosingo for meetings and rallies. He knew the place, its side streets and alleys, as well as the different school rooms and assembly halls that could provide safe hiding places. He looked around and saw that most of the column had already abandoned the building.

"I think that's a good idea. There's a church, not far from here. We can hold out there till things calm down. Follow me."

The three got to their feet. Juana and Orlando put their masks on again, despite this marking them for the enemy. They were still in uniform, which was just as much a telltale sign. If they were spotted, nothing could hide their identity, anyway. Adriana, in the meantime, strapped her gear to her back. Orlando led them down to the cellar of the ancient building, where they would make their way out of one of the countless doors. The women followed him in single file.

Adriana, while filled with apprehension, was not so frightened that she did not see the antiquity of the halls and floors through which they were making their way. At one point, the ceiling was so low that Orlando and she had to crouch. Juana was the only one who could walk upright. Small cells lined one corridor; tiny windows with wrought-iron grates told her that they had been holding pens for prisoners at one time or another. The odor of mildewed stone permeated the air.

Orlando chose one of the exits, a small door with a rounded top. When he tried to open it, however, he discovered that it was padlocked with an antiquated, rusty lock. He reached into his belt for a knife and pried its point into the lock, pressing until the iron snapped. The three pulled at the door several times until it creaked open. From there they made their way through deserted streets covered with rubble.

The two women followed Orlando on the trek that took them through curving streets that intersected with alleys. They encountered no one; houses were shuttered and doors were bolted shut. There were signs of the attack everywhere: walls pocked from strafing, chunks of concrete blown away and scattered in every direction, windows shattered, burning cars reduced to frames of molten iron. Once they saw a goat skitter by, frantically trying to find its way out of the violence that had terrorized it. There were no humans. Silence hung over Ocosingo in a mournful pall.

It was dusk by the time Orlando had led Juana and Adriana down a flight of narrow stone steps that ended at another tiny door. Once again Adriana saw that it would open into an ancient stone building. She looked up and made out a cupola housing giant bells. They had arrived at one of Ocosingo's many churches, all dating back to the early days of Spanish rule.

"We'll be safe here until later in the night."

Orlando stepped forward to enter the dimly lit chamber, which was mostly underground. Juana and Adriana followed close behind him. Showing them that he had been in that place before, he gestured for them to follow him into the cavernous chamber, leading them to a corner where a window showed high above them.

"Let's rest here. We'll know when to leave."

Adriana unstrapped her backpack, placed it against the wall and squatted with her back pressed to the wall. Orlando and Juana yanked off their masks, showing heavy perspiration coursing down their foreheads and cheeks. They followed Adriana by also leaning against the stone wall. Orlando closed his eyes, appearing to doze off to sleep, but Juana, resting her head on the wall, looked at Adriana, who returned her gaze. Their eyes shared their secret. They had become lovers. It had happened months before on a trip from the campsite to Pichucalco. They looked at one another, wondering if they would survive this day of war. They closed their eyes remembering.

෧ ෧ ෧

Juana and Adriana clung to the seat as the dilapidated bus made its way over potholes in the road. The passengers, those seated but especially those crowding the center aisle, were jostled back and forth, up and down, round and round. The two women were picked up on the road heading toward Palenque after having trekked through the jungle on foot. From there, the bus would stop at Pichucalco, where Adriana planned to drop off film and notes.

They traveled in silence, each woman focused on the events of the past weeks and months. Juana and Adriana had become inseparable during the recent weeks. They were drawn to one another by preparations for the impending war, but also by the powerful attraction one had for the other. The only times they separated was when Juana journeyed to meet with fresh supplies, but other than that, the two women always worked together.

When Juana led practice maneuvers, Adriana followed her, taking photographs, talking to the insurgents, jotting down notes. She was fascinated by the presence of women among the ranks; they made up nearly half the force. She admired their confidence in what they did, whether it was practice shooting or exchanging ideas. She frequently thought of the many village women she had met during the past months, of their reticence and passivity, and she wondered how it was that the women of the force had transformed themselves, how they had built the bridge necessary to cross such a huge separation. It seemed to Adriana that she was seeing two species of women, each one from a different people, from a different land, from a different time. These were the thoughts that filled her note pad during that time and that became part of her conversations with Juana.

Now on the bus, Adriana, thinking of these things, turned to Juana. She saw that her *compañera* had her eyes closed, but she knew that Juana was not asleep; she was lost in thought. Adriana edged even closer to Juana before she spoke, taking care that no one would overhear what she was saying.

"Juana."

"Yes?"

"I'm thinking of you and the other women of the force. How is it that you've made such a change in yourselves?"

Juana smiled wryly as she gazed at Adriana, her expression lingering for a while as the swaying of the bus forced her head to wobble comically.

"It's difficult to answer your question. I think every woman might have a different answer."

"How was it for you?"

Juana moved slightly, giving a little space between herself and Adriana. She was no longer smiling; her face had taken an expression that reflected seriousness as well as recollection. Despite the closeness of their everyday activities, Juana and Adriana had not yet exchanged the stories of their lives. Now, as she looked at Adriana, she felt a powerful desire to bring her into her confidence, to take her back to her girlhood, to her years with Cruz Ochoa, when she had felt betrayed by her father, and to her later encounter with him. She looked around, suddenly becoming aware of the cluttered bus and the countless ears that were undoubtedly tuned in, eager to catch whatever gossip might be floating in the air.

"I want to tell you that, and even more, but let it wait until later, when we're alone."

Adriana nodded, leaned back in the seat and stared out the cracked window. She looked at the sights that whizzed past as the bus picked up speed: here and there a cluster of *palapas;* chickens, ducks and sometimes even a stray pig rummaging in the undergrowth skirting the road; small groups of laborers, hoes and shovels propped on shoulders, silently walking in single file; kneeling women scrubbing clothes as the bus turned the bend overlooking the river.

"Pichucalco!"

The cranky voice of the bus driver shouted out their arrival. Juana got to her feet and waited while Adriana reached to retrieve her bag from the rack above the seat. Then, both women made their way towards the exit of the bus.

"*Gracias, señor.*"

"*No hay de qué.*"

They waited until the bus had disappeared, followed by billows of dust, before making their way toward the path leading to the village. Juana took the lead as they walked in silence, each woman aware that they were exchanging thoughts. In a few minutes, signs of the village began to filter through the growth: children shouting and laughing, women's voices, aromas and sounds. All of a sudden, Adriana and Juana walked into a clearing and encountered Pichucalco, where Adriana felt at home.

As they walked, people became aware of them, smiled and gathered around them. The women, especially those who had been photographed by Adriana, expressed excitement at her return. They brought out gourds filled with water and invited the visiting women into their *palapas* to sit and refresh themselves with a serving of beans and *yuca*. With each invitation, Adriana explained that they were heading for Chan K'in's hut.

Adriana and Juana finally arrived at the *palapa*, but found that Chan K'in was not there. It was Juana's idea to go to the river's edge to find him; and that is where he was, sitting on a large rock as he whittled a branch. When he saw the women, he unsteadily got to his feet to greet them.

"*¡Hola, viejo!* I've returned."

"*¡Buenas tardes, niña! ¿Cómo estás?*"

She accepted his hands outstretched in greeting. At the same time, he looked at Juana and nodded his welcome.

"*¡Buenas tardes te dé Dios, niña!*"

"¡Buenas tardes, abuelo!"

Chan K'in sat down again on the rock as he gestured to the women to sit by his side. They kept silent for minutes, listening to the rushing current of the river, which mingled with village sounds and jungle murmurs. He spoke first.

"Niña, you've returned from the mountain. You're different, I see."

Adriana was taken by his words. It had only been a few months since she had left the village with Juana on her way to join the insurgents, and she really had not detected a change in herself.

"In what way have I changed, *viejo?"*

"You are close to finding that which you lost. Your spirit knows it even if your mind does not."

Still baffled and a bit embarrassed, Adriana looked at the old man, then at Juana, who was looking at her; her expression was a mix of curiosity and affection. Not knowing what next to say, Adriana turned to Chan K'in and changed the subject.

"I've come with these things, which I want to leave with you. Will you take care of them along with the others I left you?"

Chan K'in smiled wryly, letting Adriana know that he noticed the change in conversation. He nodded in affirmation as he pointed a bony finger in the direction of his *palapa,* indicating that she should deliver her bundles there. After that, he returned to his task of whittling.

The women got to their feet and headed toward the *palapa,* where Adriana stacked the bag containing film and notes next to her other bag. From there they joined other women, who shared food and water with them. At nightfall, Juana and Adriana went to the fringe of the village, where they made a place to sleep under a grove of young *ceiba* trees. The night was illuminated by a full moon. Its light cast fragile shadows and shapes that danced on the women's faces and arms as they reclined on the *petates* they had spread on the ground.

They spoke to one another in soft tones. Juana talked first about why so many of the women of her people had chosen to be part of the insurgency, even at the risk of their lives, even at the cost of leaving families. Adriana, entranced by Juana's voice and words, listened carefully, admiring her views. In light of what Juana was saying, Adriana felt she had little to say about her own experiences, so she opened herself to what she was hearing.

Juana's words suddenly shifted from speaking of other women to her life. She spoke of her girlhood; of how her father had contracted her to marry a man whom she came to hate, the one who had inflicted the scar over her eye; her failed pregnancies; the confrontation with her father, which she considered also a failure; her joining the insurgents. She sighed, then edged her body closer to Adriana, who was now on her side, reclining her head on her hand.

"Tell me about yourself. You see how I've told you about myself. You're the only person I have ever spoken to in this manner."

And so Adriana opened her heart to Juana, telling her about being witness to the death of her father at the hands of her mother, of her entrapment in the apartment for days until being rescued by a neighbor, of her life with one family after the other, of being scarred with boiling water; of the dreams in which she felt pursued by fearful dogs; of her search for what she had lost; of Chan K'in's wisdom. She paused for a moment before going on with her thoughts.

"Have we lived together before?"

Juana appeared perplexed by Adriana's abrupt question, and she wrinkled her brow inquisitively. She looked at Adriana, thinking that her beauty was such that even the moonlight diminished as it bathed her face. At this point, Juana recalled Orlando's words regarding the sister of Don Absolón Mayorga and how she was brutally beaten and shamed by him because she was the lover of another woman. Juana remembered this, causing her to fear her own intense attraction to Adriana.

"Perhaps. My people believe that we repeat ourselves, but I'm curious. Why do you ask?"

"Because I feel deeply for you. I can't explain it. It's as if we have known one another from another time, another place."

Still trying to appear unperturbed, Juana stretched out her legs and folded her arms behind her head as she looked up at the moon, its light dancing on the tallest branches. She was still listening.

"Just before you came to Pichucalco, Chan K'in told me the tale of a woman of your people who lived centuries ago, when the

Spaniards first arrived. In that story, the woman witnessed events of great importance, and later on, in her wanderings, she even attempted to join others in taking their lives. That happened nearby, in the valley of Ixtapa."

"Yes, I know that story. We all know it."

Adriana, captivated by the thought that Juana also knew of the woman of whom Chan K'in had spoken, went on with what she was saying.

"The woman in Chan K'in's story had a scar on her arm caused by boiling water. Like me."

"We repeat ourselves, Adriana. Listen to me. When I was a girl, my mother often told me the story of one of our sisters who lived in the early years of the Spanish masters. She, along with countless other women, toted stones that went into the construction of the Church of Santo Domingo. That woman, the story says, had a moon-shaped scar over her eye, like me. At the time my mother told this tale, I didn't have this scar; that came later.

"After that, when I was a woman and fled to the mountains to join the insurgents, Orlando Flores continued the story of that same woman, the one with the scar on her forehead, but this time she appeared as the leader of an insurrection. That happened generations later, when the Spanish masters thought they were secure. When the masters overcame our people, that woman fled to the jungle, where she was pursued by ravenous dogs."

Adriana tensed at the mention of the woman running through the jungle. Flashes of her dream returned. She was the one desperately running, trying to escape the baying dogs, conscious of other women fleeing alongside her.

"Even Orlando tells of a time when he was an organizer. One of the *compañeras* told the story of a woman with a scar on her arm. That woman saved the old bishop, Bartolomé de las Casas, from being torn to pieces by greedy Spanish masters. Orlando describes how that woman plunged into a crowd of bearded white men in defense of Tatic, and how she was followed by others of our people."

Adriana was now completely taken by what Juana was saying. She concentrated, trying to tie the threads together in a way that would explain the possibility that she and Juana had inhabited the world together in other times.

"That woman had a scar on her arm?"

"Yes."

"Juana, my head is spinning."

Adriana flopped onto her back as she pressed her head between the palms of her hands. Her eyes were closed and her forehead was furrowed as she concentrated on what Juana was saying.

"Why can't it be true that we have been together before, Adriana, and that we're now living repeated lives . . . and that I was by your side when you tried to take your life but went on to live as a slave? Now, as I think of it, I can tell you that I believe it. You were by my side when I was bent under the weight of stones, and when I led the insurrection. You were with me, I know, when I ran through the jungle pursued by dogs. Even you have felt this. You have dreamed it, haven't you? I believe that you and I together scratched and pulled and bit at the hairy skins of the masters in futile defense of the bishop. I believe this to be true!"

Almost out of breath, Juana again stretched out on the *petate*. They both fell into a long silence, listening to their thoughts and to the cacophony of jungle sounds. They were experiencing an inexplicable emotion that elevated them as it shed light on the dark moments of their lives.

"Tell me about this."

Adriana broke their silence as she put her finger on a bracelet Juana always wore. It was a narrow strip of woven wool colored in hues of blue and purple.

"This is a gift from a young Tzeltal woman who was standing at the entrance of the Church of Santo Domingo in San Cristóbal one day as I passed. She looked impoverished, and since I had a few extra coins in my purse, I gave her half of what I had. As I walked away, I heard the soles of her feet treading against the stones as she ran after me. When I turned to look, she took my arm and tied this bracelet around my wrist. She said, 'This is a blessing!' I have never taken it off."

Adriana looked at Juana, feeling a surge of emotion. She admired how Juana shared whatever she had with those who had less, even when she, too, faced need. She was not surprised that the other woman had blessed her, and secretly she wished that it had been she who had given Juana that bracelet. Adriana was thinking this when Juana touched her.

"*You* are my blessing."

Adriana slowly moved her hand close to Juana's face, grazing the scar over her eyebrow, now knowing how it was inflicted. The two women drew closer, softly touching each other's face, breasts, until Juana raised her mouth to Adriana's, who responded with the same passion, and she embraced her, clung to her, feeling that she had finally found her lost treasure. Adriana knew that never would she allow that richness to drip through her fingers, that never again would she lose what she loved.

That night, Juana and Adriana made love to one another, exploring their naked bodies, wrapping themselves around one another. The jungle celebrated their love with the murmurs of cicadas and cascading water, while the moon spilled its light on them as it climbed towards its pinnacle and from there to its descent. The passing hours intensified their passion, making them understand that neither had ever experienced such happiness. A sweet joy flooded their spirits, shedding light on their loneliness, expelling it forever.

Metallic rattling followed by the blast of an explosion shook the foundations of the church where Orlando, Juana and Adriana waited. They had been resting, eyes closed, expecting the night to give them cover as they escaped the city. The new round of explosion now told them that Ocosingo was under siege and that a battle for the streets was in progress.

Orlando scrambled to the window, where the women saw flashes of explosions and fire reflected on his taut face. The night was ripped apart by blasts of grenades, blaring sirens and staccato of machine guns. The din was intolerable, forcing them to cover their ears with their hands. They knew that government forces had returned to regain their tarnished honor. Now everyone would pay for the affront that had embarrassed the government in the eyes of the world. Orlando muttered as he adjusted the weapon on his waist. Juana silently slipped her mask back on her face.

They went out into the night, realizing that they were targets, but also knowing that others of their own were battling to save their lives. Juana, Adriana and Orlando crept through streets, dodging and returning fire aimed at them from machine-gun nests perched on rooftops. No one spoke, but each one was appalled at seeing bodies slumped against walls, others trapped in doorways, some still moving. At one point, they crouched under the cover of a low archway, unsure of what to do. They spoke briefly, then decided that they needed to first make contact with the insurgents' position, then double back to Ocosingo to assist the living. After that, they moved on until they made it to the outskirts of town, and from there they struck toward the Lacandona.

Chapter 29

The leash snapped!

The muttering and undertone of rage lifted toward the opaque sky as the throng walked nearly shoulder to shoulder, seemingly locked in step, feet pounding dust high into the air, still polluted by the stench of spent ammunition and the unmistakable foulness of decaying human flesh. Frightened, but forced to return to look for fallen relatives, the men and women of Ocosingo revisited the devastation. Planted among them were countless insurgents, indistinguishable to government troops because of their garb and brown faces.

Juana, Orlando and Adriana joined the stream of men and women who were returning to Ocosingo only hours after the firing and blasting had ceased. They were dressed ordinarily, he in the white tunic of dozens of other Lacandón men, Juana in the Tzeltal woolen skirt and *huipil,* and Adriana, walking separately, in fatigues that distinguished foreign reporters, journalists and photographers. Their mission, and that of other disguised insurgents, was to rescue their own, those left behind, the dead as well as the living. Orlando, Juana and Adriana had agreed that if separated, they would meet in the crypt of the same church where they had taken shelter during the battle.

As a foreigner, Adriana had more freedom than anyone. The government was anxious to prove that it was the insurgents who had caused such chaos and was inviting foreigners to the scene to record the mayhem. Her camera was welcomed; her photos were supposed to show to what extent the rebels had punished their own people.

As she walked, she looked up to see walls crumbling from bombings, strafing and fires. Streets were empty of civilian cars; only military vehicles clogged the intersections and plazas. Her nose filled with the stench that had polluted everything, putting her on the verge of retching. People's faces, she saw, were stiffened by fear and rage. No one spoke or looked up, and there were hardly any children to be seen.

Adriana, nevertheless, was not entirely free to wander the streets of the town because she and the other foreigners were closely watched. Once, when she neared Juana to exchange a quick word, an officer appeared from seemingly nowhere, making her freeze and turn away from what she was about to do. The man's glare was intimidating, full of suspicion.

"There's no need to speak to the natives, *señorita.* Let me assist you."

She struggled to normalize her pounding heart by pointing her camera at a small statue that had been reduced to rubble. After several shots, she felt in control of her voice.

"*¡Gracias!* I would like to take photographs of the town and perhaps even of people."

Taking her bag in hand, the man steered her in the direction of the center of town. Adriana, knowing that Orlando and Juana watched her every move, felt confident, not fearful.

"*Teniente* Palomón Cisneros at your service. May I ask your name?"

"Adriana Mora."

"A good name, but you're not Mexican, are you?"

"No, I was born in the United States. It was my mother and father who were from Mexico."

"Ah, yes. There are many like you. Even I have family up there. Let me show you the way, so you can take as many pictures and ask as many questions as you wish. You'll see for yourself the atrocities the rebels have committed, even against their own people. Do you have a strong stomach?"

Adriana paused to study the man's face before responding. It was that of a native: dark, leathery skin, oblique eyes, high cheekbones, a stringy mustache that shadowed a wide mouth with thick lips. She wondered why he allowed himself to be instrumental to the misery of his own people. She turned away before responding to his question, knowing that she would never forget his face.

"Yes. I've seen terrible things. I'm ready."

Over and again Adriana glanced back furtively whenever the lieutenant was not looking; she wanted to assure herself that Juana and Orlando were not far off. But the last time she had a chance to check, they were out of sight, and she realized they were separated. As they moved, she saw that the place was teeming with other foreign reporters, each of them with an escort, and this returned her confidence.

The officer guided Adriana past the central plaza, through streets leading to the marketplace. As they approached the open square, she became aware of the rank odor of decaying flesh saturating the air. She abruptly stopped walking, as if riveted to the cobblestones. A flashback had pushed her mind back to a locked apartment.

A little girl is standing on a chair, feeling overcome by the vile smell clogging her nose. She pounds on the door, but no one hears the thumping of her small fists.

Adriana reached in her pocket for a handkerchief to hold against her nose and mouth. Despite the handkerchief's protection, she was forced to open her mouth to take in air.

"*Señorita,* I told you that you had to have a strong stomach. Do you want to return to the palace, where there's more calm and where you may take whatever shots you need?"

The little girl runs to hide under the bed, trying to escape the foulness that follows her with its sickly fingers, creeping into her nose and trickling down to her throat.

Adriana's eyes had begun to water as she struggled to suppress her nausea and the painful image of herself as a child. Saliva gathered in her mouth, forcing her to gulp it down until she knew that she could no longer hold it. She turned away from the lieutenant and spit gobs of it onto the curb.

"Are you sure you want to go on?"

"Yes. I'll be okay in a minute."

She realized that they were approaching a killing field and no matter how horrific it was, she could not turn away. Adriana pressed herself to close down her memories and take control of her sickening stomach. The officer took the lead as they turned the corner onto the main marketplace, where she saw a ring of photographers, people jotting notes in pads, armed men in uniforms, all of them staring at something under a canvas canopy. The lieutenant stopped and glanced sideways at Adriana.

"Look for yourself! This is what the *liberators* have done!"

Adriana nudged her way through the onlookers until she came upon a scene so terrible that she felt her breath catch in her throat and an impending asthma attack. As she tried to regulate her breathing, she struggled with the horror brought on by images of her dead mother and father.

Stretched out side by side on the ground were fourteen cadavers, females as well as males. Their hands, fingers painfully gnarled, were bound at the wrists, and each victim had a gaping wound in the forehead. The heat of the day had already brought on advanced stages of decomposition so that flies and insects buzzed around the bodies, some feeding on distorted, stiffened mouths, wide-open or clamped-shut eyes. The bodies looked hard, limbs rigidly twisted in grotesque ways.

The little girl looks at her mother's puffy face. Its mouth is purple and hard, and she has a big red hole in the side of her head. The girl runs to the kitchen and sees her father's dangling arm.

Adriana turned away from the scene she found intolerable. Then, on the verge of running away, she forced herself to stop and waited for the strength to get a grip on her crumbling nerves. She thought of Juana, of Orlando, of her mission to record the events of the war. These thoughts gave her a measure of control, and she returned to the site, feeling more in control.

When Adriana focused, she saw that an attempt had been made to put items on each body that could be construed as an insurgent's uniform: a cap, a gun belt, a hastily slipped on shirt. Despite this artifice, it was obvious to the onlookers that the dead had been civilians and that they had been executed, one by one, with a shot through the head. She pulled her eyes away from the grim sight and saw countless spent casings littering the ground. She bent down and picked one up and held it in a fist.

"These bodies are not insurgents."

"No. They are the victims of the insurgents."

"Then why has someone tried to make it look as if they are rebels?"

Momentarily taken by surprise, the officer remained silent. He rubbed his eyes in an effort to gain time to come up with an answer, so as to explain the blunder, but chose instead to side-step the issue. He sucked his teeth, letting Adriana know that he was irritated by her question.

"*Señorita,* this is war. Strange things happen. I guarantee that these poor souls were murdered by the insurgents."

"Are these not army casings?"

Adriana held the spent bullet up to the officer's face who, without answering, took Adriana by the elbow and began maneuvering her away from the site. She resisted, and as she pulled away from him, she took hold of her camera and began snapping photographs of the murdered men. She had taken several shots despite the officer's displeasure. There were too many witnesses present for him to force Adriana to stop.

"I'm finished. I'll return now to the municipal palace. I know my way, thank you."

Adriana left the man standing as she walked away at a brisk pace. She turned back to look at him several times and she saw that he was standing, feet planted apart, in a posture of indecision. Before he could make up his mind to follow her, she sped around several corners, picked up speed until she was jogging, heading for the church where Orlando and Juana would be waiting for her.

Adriana took some wrong turns, but finally she found the church and went down to the door leading into the crypt. She tried the latch; it was open, and she cautiously entered the darkened room. Adriana stood with her back to a wall, so still that she hardly breathed while her eyes became used to the gloom.

Pale light filtered through the window, cutting through the darkness, and forms slowly began to take shape: a table with a broken leg in the far corner, two mismatched chairs to its side, other broken things strewn about the floor. When her vision finally adjusted, she made out a bulky object. She realized that it was a sarcophagus. The stone coffin sent a chill through her. She forced herself to look elsewhere. Her eyes scanned the room, stopping at the wall where Juana, Orlando and she had waited out the attack. The objects she was now making out had been in the chamber when they were there, but she had not even noticed them.

After a few moments, Adriana was certain that neither Juana nor Orlando was in the room. She went to the far wall and sat down on the floor, relaxing her back against the stone wall. She had to be patient, she told herself. Fatigue began to overcome her and she closed her eyes, just to rest them, but the dreadful scene she had just witnessed replayed behind her eyelids. Distorted faces grimaced; split, purple lips opened in silent screams; gnarled fingers clasped and unclasped as they appeared to reach out from the stone coffin. These forms were pushed aside by the inalterable memory of her dead mother and father, of herself as a child trapped and terrified. One by one, the images paraded behind her closed eyes, and though she did not want to look at them, their invasion would not stop.

Horrified, Adriana curled her body, in defense against the grim forms that floated above and around her. She prayed that Juana and Orlando would soon come. She needed to be with them, to weep with them for the loss of those innocent women and men, for the memory of her dead mother and father. When her eyes snapped open, she looked up to the window and realized that it was dark outside. She looked at her watch and confirmed that the evening had moved toward night and her *compañeros* still had not appeared! Suddenly cold and numb from sitting on the stone floor, she shifted her body, bringing her knees up against her breasts, where she reclined her head to think of what to do next.

Adriana was folded in on herself when she heard the creak of the door. She quietly rose to her feet, alert and waiting to see who had come into the chamber. Her eyes were adjusted to the dark, so she was able to make out Juana's form as she moved forward.

"Juana?"

"Yes."

The women embraced for a long time, feeling each other's heart pounding, until Juana abruptly separated herself from Adriana. She gestured for them to sit down. When she spoke, her voice was husky.

"Orlando has been captured."

"Are you certain?"

"Yes. I saw it happen."

"How?"

"He was betrayed."

"One of our own?"

"No. Someone else. I don't know who, but not one of our own. We were heading in this direction; he was a few paces in front of me when three men approached him. They were dressed like civilians, but I could tell they were spies. After they stopped him, I heard one of them say, 'Aha! We finally found you. Did you think you could murder Don Rufino and live to be an old man? ¡Indio desgraciado!'"

"When did it happen?"

"Hours ago. I followed to see where they put him. A long time has passed."

Adriana sucked air through her teeth. She looked at Juana and saw fear etched on her dark face. It was the first time Adriana had detected dread in Juana, and that, in turn, frightened her.

"What are we going to do?"

"We have to stay close to him."

"Where is he?"

"In the garrison. In the municipal palace."

"Let's return for weapons so we can free him."

"No. We're better off looking like ordinary women. Besides, there's no time. We know how to get into that place from the bottom chamber, so that's what we'll do. There's a chance we can get to him."

The women got to their feet and embraced, trying to inspire courage in each other. Then they left the crypt to retrace the path they had taken the night of the battle. It was past midnight when the women finally reached the side of the municipal palace. It was dark, but they saw at a glance that it was thick with guards and military police. When they crept around to the other side, they found the same fortifications, so they decided to approach the front of the palace. They sped around the corner only to bump into a throng of people milling in fear and confusion. Towering neon lights had been erected to flood the plaza so that people appeared to multiply as their shadows darted back and forth, churning like agitated insects.

Juana, no longer caring about her own identity, took hold of Adriana's hand and led her into the crowd. The situation was chaotic; neither woman could make out the babbling and gesturing that was going on all around them. Juana, still holding her partner's hand, moved close to a Chol man and tugged at his sleeve.

"*Amigo,* what's happening? Why are there so many people here?"

"Haven't you heard? The *chingones* captured a prisoner."

"A rebel?"

"I'm not sure. All I know is that they're calling him a traitor, and he's going to be executed."

"A traitor to whom?"

"To them. Who else?"

Juana backed away from the man and turned to look at Adriana. The women knew that they were too late, that nothing could save Orlando. Caught up by the press of the crowd, they allowed themselves to be swept to the inner fringe of the square, where a squad of shooters was already lined up, waiting to execute their task. Adriana and Juana looked, trapped in the horror of knowing that their *compañero* was about to die. They stared, helpless to do anything except to stand by him.

A drum roll silenced the mob, which gawked in shock as they saw Orlando Flores appear between two soldiers. They were pushing him forward, but his body demonstrated his disdain and hatred for them. By the way he walked and held himself, he showed that he was not frightened, even when the same soldiers ordered him to stand against a wall. He shrugged off the blindfold that was offered him.

The presiding officer came on the scene and stood to the side of the firing squad. He was a short, malformed man whose uniform was oversized, and he wore green-shaded glasses even though it was night. It was apparent by the way he held out his chin and sucked in his belly that he desired to appear taller. As he was adjusting his posture, Orlando's voice rang out; it was so powerful that it silenced the murmur that had begun to sweep over the horde. So compelling were Orlando's words that the presiding officer stopped in the middle of straightening his jacket, and the shooters slackened the hold on their weapons.

"*¡La cuerda se reventó, cabrones!*"

A shocked silence floated over the onlookers because Orlando's words had said it all, all that was burning in their hearts. *The leash snapped, you sons of bitches! It's over! Your grip has been broken!*

In an attempt to silence the prisoner, the officer raised his hand to get attention. He held a sheet of paper in his other hand, from which he began to read.

"Orlando Flores, because you are a communist intruder from another country . . ."

"*Cabrón,* since you're going to murder me, call me by my true name: Quintín Osuna!"

Nearly unnerved, the officer looked around, first toward the shooters, then toward the crowd, then straight at the prisoner. He frowned, confused about the name, and not knowing what to do next. He brought the document closer to his face and removed the shaded glasses, squinting his myopic eyes. He chose to ignore the prisoner's name and continue reading.

"You have been found guilty of instigating . . ."

"*¡Pendejo!* Don't you know anything? If you're going to assassinate me, do it for the right reason. I am Quintín Osuna, the executioner of one of your masters, Rufino Mayorga!"

Mention of the death of the Mayorga patriarch stunned the officer, who finally demonstrated that he understood that the prisoner was the hunted murderer of Rufino Mayorga. Within seconds, the man squared his shoulders, drew his pistol, aimed it at Orlando, and shouted his order.

"*¡Fuego!*"

Orlando's riddled body reeled backward against the wall, where it remained propped up for a few seconds while spots, like black roses, blotched his white tunic. The body teetered, then plummeted face forward onto the stones of the plaza floor.

"¡No! ¡No!"

Before his face crashed against the ground, Juana's voice rang out, emitting a grief-filled howl that so rattled the throng it momentarily froze in fear, then suddenly snapped, panicking, screaming, pushing, tugging, running in every direction. The pandemonium became huge, frightening the military police, who knew they were outnumbered and that control was out of their hands.

Juana and Adriana pushed blindly through the frenzy, through legs, torsos, arms, everything moving and churning. They shoved, using the confusion that had gripped the soldiers, trying to reach Orlando's body. When they did, they took hold of him by the underarms and dragged him, inch by inch, along the wall of the building, aiming for its corner, searching for cover.

The chaos escalated, and the thrust of the crowd overturned the towers supporting the neon lights on one side of the square. The structures crashed to the ground, wounding and frightening the swarm of people even more. That side of the plaza became darkened and it was into that blackness that Juana and Adriana dragged Orlando's corpse.

The women pulled at the body of their *compañero,* but its dead weight became increasingly unmanageable. Suddenly, the burden became lighter, easier to carry and Juana looked back to see the same Chol man to whom she had spoken; he had plucked up the body's legs and was helping the women. Neither Adriana nor Juana paused to speak, or to thank the man. They knew only one thing: that they had to remove the body as far away as possible from the streets of Ocosingo. They halted when the man suddenly spoke.

"*Hermanas,* wait! I have a wagon nearby. We can use it to take our *compañero* from here."

The women looked at him, relief and gratefulness stamped on their faces. They did not know his name, nor did they ask. Juana and Adriana agreed and followed his lead to the cart, which was stationed behind a small chapel at the edge of town. Between the three of them, Orlando's body was placed on the flatbed of the wagon, which was hitched to an emaciated mule. With a jerk, they began their journey.

Hours passed as Juana, Adriana and the Chol man walked beside the creaky cart in silence. So much grief filled them that they found it impossible to speak. Adriana grieved because there was so much death around them. She mourned for Orlando and for all the innocents who were suffering and dying, and for all those who had lost and searched for a fallen loved one. Juana relived the years in which she had walked in Orlando's path, the early days when he spoke of the people of maize and the woman who had led the first insurrection against the *patrones*. She thought about his feelings for her, and she knew that, although he had never said it, he had understood her love for Adriana.

The blackness of the night slowly turned into the milky light that awaits the first rays of the sun; by that time, the cortege had entered the fringe of the Lacandona Jungle. They moved steadily without stopping for any reason, not even their own bodily needs. Neither thirst nor hunger nor the urge to relieve themselves halted the sad journey that was leading them to where they would stop to mourn and say their final farewell to the man they had loved and respected.

Without knowing when, Adriana and Juana realized that others, men and women, had joined the funeral march. No one spoke nor asked questions, yet they knew whose body it was and where it was being taken. They walked the distance in silence. Morning turned to afternoon, then to evening, and it was not until they reached the edge of a river, when the sliver of a new moon appeared over the treetops, that Juana signaled a halt to their journey. Without question or murmur, the cortege stopped.

Juana, Adriana and several other men and women assisted in taking Orlando's body from the wagon to lay it on the damp earth, near the water's edge. There the women disrobed the body and anointed it with water cupped in palm fronds. Juana and Adriana wept silently, their tears bathing Orlando's wounded body. Many of the mourners murmured prayers that would accompany him on his journey to the other side. Then, with fresh branches cut from giant ferns, the body was wrapped and fastened with vines until it was shrouded against insects and other predatory creatures.

Together, men and women carried the body to the river and waded to its center, where the current was strongest. They held on to Orlando Flores for a few minutes, cherishing the feel of his weight against their bodies as they prayed in their native languages: Chol, Chamula, and Lacandón. Juana chanted in Tzeltal. Adriana did not grasp the words of that soft prayer, but she understood their meaning. Then the mourners released their grip and allowed the current to take possession of Orlando's body, leading it downstream towards the land of his birth.

Chapter 30

In lak'ech. You are my other self.

The insurgents went into negotiations with the government after ten days of war. Countless agreements and accords were devised only to be discarded. Promises were made only to be broken. Documents were developed, then rendered obsolete. The insurgents' ranks diminished as men and women returned to their settlements, attempting to halt the collapse of what was left of their lives.

Juana contemplated returning to Lago Nahá, but she knew that her father was still alive and she did not want to live under his shelter. It would have been her obligation as would have been the tasks of weaving and planting and selling goods in the marketplace. She could no longer do this; she was different. The years of fighting and leading others had transformed her. Most important of all other considerations was the presence of Adriana in her life. Juana knew that she could no longer live without her.

After much reflection, Juana saw that the struggle for Chiapas was not over. People were still living in misery; in many ways they were worse off, because multitudes were now uprooted and lost. Juana realized that the only thing that had changed was the place of battle, that it had shifted from the shootings and bombings of the streets to the mountain peaks that sheltered those fleeing for their lives. She decided to ask Adriana to join her as she went on fighting against the misery that was devouring her people.

Adriana could not conceive of a life without Juana, either. She followed her *compañera* wherever she went, working with volunteers and agencies that had swarmed into Chiapas to assist the victims of the conflict. She knew that with her photography she had a special way to be part of the struggle. Hers was a unique way of alerting the world to the anguish that was tormenting Chiapas. She had no doubt that the portraits she brought forth were a graphic and undeniable testimony of truth.

Shortly after the war, Adriana submitted her work outside of Mexico, establishing connections with journals and newspapers hungry to disseminate her prints. She wired and mailed her work from San Cristóbal de las Casas to publishers in New York, Houston, Chicago, Los Angeles. Her portfolios included action pictures of the war, the insurgents, the embattled cities, the refugees as they clogged roads, hopelessly roaming the countryside in search of sanctuary. The publication of her work spread, opening promising doors for her work beyond the United States, extending to Europe, Canada and Australia, all of which resulted in stipends on which she and Juana were able to live.

After 1994, the two women migrated from one refugee camp to the other, staying mainly in the highlands north of San Cristóbal de las Casas. They focused on Chenalhó and Acteal, where they ministered to people who were living under deplorable conditions. There, famine had led to disease, which in turn caused plagues. The extreme cold and fog of the mountains exacerbated the refugees' misery, leading to the deaths of infants and children and to widespread anguish among adults.

Juana and Adriana traveled back and forth between San Cristóbal de las Casas and the camps, bringing food, blankets and medicines. The trek was not easy. Sometimes they walked, other times they were taken aboard dilapidated vehicles slowly meandering from one village to the other. Once in the city, they searched for sources of supplies. The luxury hotels that surrounded the main plaza and connecting streets of the city were Adriana's target, as she had established connections with cooks and room managers who put aside sacks of beans, rice, potatoes, and blankets that could no longer be used for hotel guests. Often, she would pass on a portion of her latest stipend as compensation.

Juana, in turn, had tight contact with groups that worked for the same cause. One of these was known as "Las Abejas," the Bees, and they were unmatched in their success in bringing assistance from foreign donors. Working with Las Abejas, Juana soon became known for her efficiency, and she was always given supplies to transport north. But those donations, however generous and constant, were just drops in the deluge of poverty that had escalated in the camps day by day. During those months, neither Juana nor Adriana was discouraged; they worked openly, publicly, without thinking what the consequences might be for them. It was then that word of their personal relationship began to seep out. The refugees saw and understood the love Adriana and Juana shared, but unsuspected by the two women, rumors mounted, making their way to hateful ears.

On December 22, 1997, Adriana and Juana were based in Acteal. Adriana had not accompanied Juana on the trip to the city, but had stayed behind to take pictures of the refugees. She worked during the morning, making use of the early hours of sunlight before the fog rolled in. When she finished the shoot, she decided to venture out to the surrounding mountainside to take shots of the impressive panoramas. Some of the children followed her on the trek, romping and playfully posing for her. She was touched as she snapped frame after frame, seeing that hardly any of them were glum, that they had not forgotten how to play, despite their being ill and emaciated.

"¡Allí viene Juana! ¡Allí viene Juana!"

Juana had arrived, leading a convoy of two run-down vans filled with supplies. The clamor and cheering that signaled her return reached Adriana, who gathered her equipment and made her way up to the road to meet her. By the time she reached the village, Juana had already climbed out of the van and was surrounded by children and adults, who embraced her, squeezing her hand, patting her shoulders. Her arrival was always a cause for celebration because of the food and other supplies that she brought.

Adriana stood at the fringe of the crowd snapping pictures: Juana's radiant face with strands of her coarse black hair fluttering in the mountain breeze; a child holding her, his head buried between her breasts; a woman nestling her head on Juana's back.

Once the vans were unloaded and their contents distributed, most of the women and children went down to one of the shelters to pray. Juana and Adriana, with a camera still hanging around her neck, decided to go on a walk in the forest, where they found a spot covered by heavy overhanging branches. They sat there in silence for a few minutes.

Juana, nearly whispering, got very close to Adriana. "A woman came to warn that we take care. She said our enemies often speak of you and me, of our connection."

Feeling bewildered and afraid, Adriana stared at Juana, but Juana smiled.

"In lak'ech."

Adriana felt a pang of intense joy at hearing Juana utter words telling her that she was her other self. But her happiness suddenly melted away when she felt inexplicable alarm, as if a shadow standing behind her had whispered, *¡Ten cuidado!* Be careful! She was so shaken by the feeling that she looked around, expecting to find someone, but there was no one, nothing. She had imagined it. Was it nerves? She put aside her apprehension and smiled at Juana.

Suddenly, a ricocheting blast shattered the mountain tranquillity. It was a quick volley that echoed down the ravines and bounced off peaks, returning in distorted, rebounding sounds. Juana's eyes rounded as she stared at Adriana; she knew what had caused that rapid, violent noise.

Ratt-tatt-tatt!

The women got to their feet and they ran toward the firing guns. They passed a pickup truck that had been hastily parked, its doors still swinging open, its engine running.

Ratt-tatt-tatt!

Juana outran Adriana and was the first to come onto the killing scene. Adriana, rushing behind her, had a clear view of the carnage that was going on. She saw bodies piled one on top of the other, limbs entangled but struggling to escape. She heard the screaming of women and the wailing of children. She smelled the rank stench of sulfurous ammunition. She saw the backs of the shooters, men dressed in civilian clothes. In a fraction of a second, she caught a glimpse of one face. His sombrero was pulled down over his brow, his nose, mouth and chin masked by a bandanna. Then, in a nightmarish flash, she saw that all of the assassins were dressed alike.

The machine guns would not stop vomiting lead and fire, although there was no longer any movement or sound. Behind the assassins stood Juana, who had witnessed the crime. Behind her stood Adriana, whose eyes had also captured the unspeakable deed. Suddenly, one of the faces snapped in their direction; its bandanna had slipped off, revealing the shooter's identity. Adriana saw the yellow eyes of evil glaring at Juana, but she saw more; it was a face she had seen before.

Adriana recognized Palomón Cisneros, the soldier who had lied about the murdered civilians in Ocosingo. Without thinking, she lunged toward Juana, who was planted on the ground motionless, paralyzed by the horror she had just witnessed. Adriana was able to reach her but not before the vicious barrel was lifted, aimed and fired. Ratt-tatt! Two bullets hit Juana, but the weapon jammed and could not spit out more of its deadly projectiles.

"*¡Manflora! ¡Come mierda!*"

Cisneros spat out the hateful word *manflora*, lover of women. Now it was Adriana who froze. Fear seized her for a second, but Juana was still moving when Adriana finally reached her to put her arm around her waist. With a strength she did not know she possessed, she lifted Juana and dragged her toward the forest, leaving the assassin cursing his weapon for failing him.

Terrified, Adriana carried Juana, oblivious of the ruts and holes in the ground, aware only that Juana was weightless in her arms, that she was something fragile and light. Adriana ran, sensing with each moment that others were running with her, and that they were also being pursued. The shouting of the assassins became barking, snarling. Dogs were chasing after her and Juana.

Suddenly she stopped; her feet dug deep into the jungle slime as she halted abruptly, running in circles, arms rigidly outstretched. She had lost something, but she could not remember what it was that had slipped through her fingers. She dropped to her knees, groveling in the mud, digging, trying to find what it was that she had lost. Her fingers began to bleed when her nails ripped from her flesh, and her desperation grew, looming larger than even her pain, greater even than the terror of being overcome by the dogs.

The dream flashed through Adriana's mind. Her thoughts were clear as never before, and she knew now the meaning of that distant dream. Adriana saw her life clearly for the first time. She knew now that Juana was what had once slipped through her fingers and who had returned to her.

She laid her *compañera* at the foot of a tree and took her in her arms, holding and rocking her, wiping her forehead and face, which was streaked with mud and sweat. Her left side was saturated in blood. Her eyes were shut but she was still alive.

"No me dejes, Juana."

Unable to speak, Juana moved her head, letting Adriana know that she would never leave her. Then stillness overcame her, and Adriana knew that Juana had passed on to the other side of the rivers and mountain peaks, that her spirit had returned to the Lacandona Jungle.

Adriana, still swaying to and fro, pressed Juana's inert body to her breast, struggling to cope with the dry ache that had gripped her heart. Her body, convulsed by the uneven rhythm of her breathing, shivered uncontrollably, and anguished sounds from deep inside gripped her throat. Adriana wanted to cry out, to let the pain escape from where it was trapped, but she was mute; only short moans slipped through her lips.

She had no sense of how much time had passed before three villagers found her. When she first became aware of their presence, she panicked, thinking that they were the assassins, but when she recognized them, she finally began to weep, trying to describe what had happened.

"Cálmese, Adriana, sabemos lo que pasó."

They attempted to calm her, telling her they knew what had happened, and that she had no need to explain. They had come, they said, to help her with Juana. As they spoke, one of them disappeared for a while and later returned with a shovel. Taking turns, they dug a hole under the tree. Adriana, although wasted by grief and the fear of an asthma attack, insisted on helping to dig down through the rugged, rocky soil. After hours of excavating, the grave was deep enough.

Adriana wanted a part of herself to remain with Juana forever. She also desired to keep something of hers to hold for the rest of her life, so she took the woven bracelet from Juana's wrist. From her own wallet,

Adriana pulled a photograph someone had taken of the two of them. She gazed at their smiling faces and their intertwined arms, then she put it to her lips and slipped it between Juana's breasts, near her heart. On her knees, Adriana stooped down to press her cheek against Juana's, where she stayed for a time, reliving the first time they had met.

Juana's body was lowered slowly into the ground until it rested on the bottom. Adriana was aware that her companions were murmuring prayers, but she was incapable of anything except feeling grief and rage. The sound of dirt and rocks striking Juana's body crept into Adriana's ears. It was a sound that would rob her of sleep for the rest of her life.

She returned to Acteal to find it swarming with strangers and soldiers. Word had leaked out about the massacre. There was weeping and moaning everywhere because the bodies of the slaughtered had been stolen; they had now "disappeared." Hysteria prevailed, but the military police insisted that they knew nothing, had seen nothing.

Without speaking to anyone, Adriana gathered her things and began to walk the twenty miles towards San Cristóbal de las Casas. She did not stop, even when the day became night and then dawn. She kept moving, thinking only of Juana, not caring about anything, not even the fear that, in her haste, she might succumb to a breathing attack. She hiked without precaution, hoping to be killed. When she reached the city, she went to the bus station and from there she traveled until reaching Pichucalco and Chan K'in.

Time blurred for Adriana. She lost track of what day it was, how long it had taken to walk to San Cristóbal, how many days had passed before she reached Pichucalco. Her mind cleared only when she stepped off the bus and images of other visits to the village returned.

As she made her way toward Chan K'in, the aroma of maize and cooking beans reached her, reminding her that she had not eaten in days. With clarity came the awareness that she did not care about eating or anything else. All she desired was to face the only man who could decipher the enigma of her loss.

He was sitting under a *ceiba* tree, cross-legged as was his habit. He hardly glanced at Adriana, but as she stood looking down at him, he gestured that she sit down. She struggled to unbuckle her backpack and put it on the ground. After a few moments, she was facing him, sitting as she used to at the beginning of their encounters.

"*Niña,* you have found what it was that you lost in your dream."

"Yes, but as in the dream, I have lost it again."

"When you and I first spoke, you searched your memory to see if it could have been someone in your past life. At the time, you said that there was no one, not even your mother or father, yet the loss inhabited your dream. Do you remember what I said to you?"

Adriana's head was hanging, tears dripping from her chin. Her mind was churning, and she found it impossible to speak.

"I said that perhaps it could be someone whose path had crossed yours in another time, another place, and who would again come to you in the future."

"She's gone, *viejo!*"

"But not forever. We repeat ourselves. She's waiting for you in another life, where your paths will cross again."

Adriana's heart ached, wanting to believe Chan K'in, desiring with all the strength of her being that she and Juana would again meet in a repeated life. Instead, all she felt was hurt for having their present time together cut so short. She stared at the old man, hoping that his unshakable belief would penetrate her. After awhile, she lowered her eyes to look at Juana's bracelet as it clung to her wrist. She understood that it would take time, that she could do no more than wait.

"You must be patient, *niña.* In the meantime, let me give you my blessing."

Adriana shuffled closer, head bent, longing to receive Chan K'in's benediction. When she felt the weight of his gnarled hands on her head, she was impressed by their frail touch, and she prayed.

"*Viejo,* I'm leaving now. I must go home."

"Yes, but you will return."

Adriana, perplexed by the old man's words but comforted by his wisdom, got to her feet, wiped her face and went in search of her things. After emptying bags and rearranging rolls of film, note pads, two shirts and some underwear, she tucked it all into her backpack. Before leaving, she went to the center of the village to take leave of the people who had been part of her beginnings in the Lacandona Jungle. Word spread quickly from *palapa* to *palapa*. Soon, women, children and men came to wish her a happy trip, inviting her to return and reminding her that she would always have a home in Pichucalco. Adriana accepted hugs, hand clasps and small gifts. One child brought her four eggs wrapped in a handkerchief. When she turned toward the main road, she was crying again.

Chapter 31

The anguish, too, was the same.

After Pichucalco, Adriana began her journey back to Los Angeles. She still had enough money to make her way by land to Palenque, where she boarded the small craft that flew daily to Mérida, Yucatán. On arriving at that airport, she discovered that she had missed that day's only flight to Los Angeles. She was forced to stay over in the city.

It was still early, and she would need a room for the night. She asked the taxi driver to take her to a hotel. He nodded without saying a word, and after a short drive from the airport, he left her at Hotel Casa de Balám. Adriana liked the place; its Mayan decorations and its location off the main square and cathedral suited her. After checking in, a young man showed her to her room. While chatting amiably, he remarked on the weight of her backpack. She smiled, knowing that his words were a hint.

Once inside the room, Adriana gave the boy a tip and closed the door, grateful for the dark coolness of the room. She was even happier when she peeled off her shirt, bra, trousers and panties, which had become saturated with sweat during her trip. Afterward, she stood in the middle of the room, naked and barefoot for several minutes, her head buzzing with thoughts and unanswered questions. Then she went to the shower, where she let the calming spray wash over her for a long while. Splashing water on porcelain created a rhythm to which her memories swayed, thoughts dislodged and ideas surfaced.

As she abandoned her body to the chill of the water, dunking her head and face over and again, she realized that she had several hours on her hands and she could, during that time, look up a camera shop. There were rolls of undeveloped film in her pack, and she was anxious to see what she had taken.

Among those rolls were the photographs she had taken in Pichucalco years earlier, the day on which Juana had invited her to join the insurgents. Adriana remembered that afternoon so well that she could still see the women at work. She vividly remembered the young mother, the indigenous madonna with a child at her breast. Adriana even recalled her thoughts of wanting to be that child.

Then there were the last of her photographs, taken on the day of Juana's death. Those she wanted to see more than anything. Adriana yanked her head from under the spray, wiped her eyes, nose and mouth. She got out of the shower, dried herself, put on clothes, and went down to the lobby to find the address of the nearest photo lab.

"Sí, señorita. Aquí a la vuelta está un laboratorio. Pero, ¿No desea almorzar antes?"

Expressing gratefulness for the information regarding the lab, as well as for the invitation to have lunch, Adriana sped around the corner, hoping to find the shop open. It was, and the man at the counter was happy to assist her.

"Vuelva en dos horas. Estarán listas sus fotografías."

With two hours to spend before the pictures would be ready, Adriana walked to the plaza. It was not large, but it was beautiful. The cathedral took up all of the space on one side of the rectangle, and the street in front of it served as parking for horse-drawn buggies available for tourists. The square itself was bustling with vendors, shoppers, children, and stray dogs. It was market day, and the place was filled with stalls and booths. Adriana considered returning to the hotel for her camera, but decided against it. She would just take in the colors, sounds and smells with her mind's eye and preserve them in her memory.

She walked up the steps elevating the square from the street, and ambled from stall to stall, looking, touching, listening, smelling. She admired blouses, shawls, tablecloths, intricately laced doilies—all handmade, all for sale. She stopped to gaze at women sitting on their haunches in front of small heaps of peppers, lemons, seeds, bunches of herbs, tempting cooks in search of ingredients for the day's meal.

Adriana concentrated on the faces of those women: oval shapes with skin the color of cocoa beans, eyes shaped like almonds, braided hair the color of onyx. She was struck by the thought that although separated by hundreds of kilometers, these were the same people that inhabited the Lacandona Jungle, the highlands and canyons of Chiapas. She looked up beyond the tops of the trees shading the square and slowly pivoted her body, studying the architecture of the stately buildings, once mansions, now mostly banks, offices and small restaurants. When she turned to look at a child sitting on the curb, Adriana's attention was suddenly jerked away from him. Out of the corner of her eye, she saw Juana slipping behind one of the stalls. She caught only a glimpse of her rounded body, and the long black braid that twisted with the sway of her unmistakable way of walking.

Positive that it was Juana, Adriana felt her breath catch in her throat, and without thinking, she lunged toward the place where Juana had disappeared, moving so abruptly that she knocked over a small table piled high with lemons. She made an attempt to fix things but she could not waste time. Adriana sprinted over mounds of sarapes, heaps of shoes, bunches of bananas, until she reached the rear of the last stall.

Adriana turned the corner with such haste that two young women, sitting there snapping green beans, were so startled that one of them spilled the vegetables she had gathered on her lap. They stared at her face, which had the expression of having seen someone gone from this world, and they became frightened. For her part, Adriana realized at once that she had made a mistake. Although one of the women did resemble Juana, it was clearly not her.

"*¡Mil disculpas! ¡Perdónenme, por favor!*"

Adriana helped gather the vegetables as she mumbled apologies. She was embarrassed, but remained convinced that it had been Juana whom she had seen. She must have gone somewhere else. The women, once recuperated from the initial fright, smiled, saying that everything was fine.

Adriana walked away toward the opposite edge of the plaza and stood there for a while. She felt lightheaded, and her thoughts were unclear. Finally, she remembered she had not eaten for hours. Perhaps her empty stomach had caused Juana's image to appear. Adriana was not really hungry, but she understood that she needed to eat something. She bought a cone filled with fruit from a vendor and sat on the street's curb.

As she munched on chunks of mango, papaya and watermelon, Adriana began to stabilize; her mind was clearing. She was still shaken by Juana's apparition, but she was profoundly happy as well, taking pleasure in the memory of that fast-moving figure that must have been Juana. Adriana stopped chewing for a moment, closed her eyes, and prayed that she would never stop seeing her beloved *compañera,* if only for fleeting seconds at a time.

Adriana looked at her watch. She still had a few minutes to wait and so she concentrated on the structures facing her. Her eyes focused on the largest, obviously the grandest of the mansions. She scanned the carvings over the main entrance, where, chiseled deeply into the façade, she made out helmeted, armored Spanish conquistadores, lances in hand, their feet crushing the heads of indigenous men, who were depicted with stiffened tongues crying out in anguish. Behind the Spanish masters, in miniature contour, were ravenous dogs, menacing horses, other war-like figures intertwined with vines, classical sculptures, even some cherubs.

She rose to her feet, stretched, and walked to a plaque on the wall, that explained the origins of the mansion. *Casa de Montejo, primer conquistador del Yucatán.* She tried to read more description but gave up; the script was too ornate, too intricate, and too old.

She stood in front of the building, pondering why so little had changed for the people of that land. Although there were no longer conquistadores, there were mestizos. Now, instead of lances, there were machine guns, and in place of horses and dogs, there were armored vehicles. The anguish, too, was the same.

It was time. Adriana looked one last time toward the stall where she had seen Juana, then she turned her back on the Casa de Montejo and headed for the photo lab, where she found her package processed and ready. She paid the bill, made her way to the hotel, and went directly to her room. She took a few minutes to take off her clothes that had become sweaty again, and she took another shower. In a bathrobe and with her hair still dripping wet, Adriana sat down on the bed, propped herself up on a pillow against the metal headboard, and opened the large envelope. Inside she found two smaller ones.

She ripped open one and emptied the pictures onto her lap, verifying that the photos were still good, although somewhat marred because the film had aged. She looked at those pictures and saw that her camera had captured faces concentrated on weaving, on sewing. She held one showing a woman with sticky *masa* smeared on her hands and arms up to the elbows as she smiled broadly at the camera. Adriana looked at another photo showing a pregnant girl whose face was sad.

Studying the glossies carefully, Adriana realized how her work and she had matured. No longer doubtful of her skills, she compared those early pictures to her later work taken during the war and its aftermath. She was reflecting on the weaknesses of her earlier endeavors when she was forced to interrupt her train of thought by the next photo. It was of the young mother with the child at her breast. Adriana became transfixed, even elated by the image. The luminous eyes of the young woman captivated her, as did the child's mouth sucking her breast, its eyes closed, its tiny hand limp and relaxed. Adriana realized that, unlike the others, this take was not shallow. It was deep, mature; it had captured the spirit of the moment, of the woman, of the child.

Adriana, with some hesitation, next turned to the pictures in the other envelope; they were the last taken at Acteal. Children's faces looked out at her from the prints, some smiling, others bewildered. She became saddened by the certainty that they had perished in the massacre. She moved on to those of Juana's welcome to the camp on that same day, remembering how the people had converged on her, hugging and patting her back, touching her face.

Adriana felt the tears pushing at her eyes, pressing to be freed from the prison of her heart. She looked at one, two, three, four shots of Juana, some close-up, others taken at more of a distance. A few of the photos showed her profile, her face turned first to one side, then to the other, smiling, looking at her. Other shots pictured her, arms lifted, giving out blankets, a package, food. Juana became alive, eternal in the photographs taken by Adriana.

Wiping tears from her face with the palms of her hands, Adriana closed her eyes and leaned back on the pillow, where she fell into a deep sleep that lasted through the night. She awoke startled from a very real dream, but she shook it off seconds later, remembering that she needed to be at the airport by ten to make her flight. When she focused her eyes on the clock by the bed, she was relieved; she still had time.

Chapter 32

She asked me to be the lips through which their silenced voices will speak.

In flight. Merida/Los Angeles, January 2, 1998.

The execution of Orlando Flores four years ago was an act of pure hatred. He was not murdered only because he was a rebel, or because he brought Rufino Mayorga to justice, despite what they claimed. Orlando was assassinated for one reason only: He was a Lacandón, un indio *who happened to be captured, and he was put to death only because the mestizos fear and hate his kind.*

The massacre at Acteal was about hatred for women, for mujeres indias *who had proven themselves as leaders, activists and movers of their people. Those killings were committed in revenge for the embarrassment those* mujeres *brought down on the heads of the wealthy, the powerful,* los patrones, *and their lackeys in the military and politics. Acteal was nothing but payback for Comandante Insurgente Ramona, the Tzotzil woman, and the way she and a hundred other women under her command took San Cristóbal de las Casas back in 1994. And there were the other cities, also taken by women in command. Acteal was a hateful response to a woman insurgent being the one to break the army's cordon around the Lacandona Jungle in 1996. Those slayings were filled with loathing because* la gente, *the natives of that land, had dared to say* ¡Basta! Enough! *Acteal was about pure hatred.*

Juana's murder was caused by hatred, but it was even more than loathing because dangling from it, like poisonous snakes, was the repugnance and disgust for women like us. Her love for me was dis-

253

covered; word had got around and Palomón Cisneros' evil snout had picked up the scent of those rumors. She was erased because she had been strong, because she had been a leader, because she was una india, *but most of all because she had committed the forbidden act: She had been in love with another woman.*

Moved and deeply shaken by her own words, Adriana stopped writing and put the pen down beside the journal propped on the vibrating table. She leaned her head on the headrest of the seat, then she stretched to look out of the cabin window. Her eyes were inflamed and swollen from sleeplessness and crying, but she made out the cloud cover below; land was now beyond her vision. She craned her neck to look back toward the south, where Chiapas lay under its pall of hatred and fear, but all she saw was a milky void. The engines of the craft hummed now that its intended altitude had been reached. The flight was less than half-filled, so passengers settled in for the long trip to Los Angeles.

She picked up the pen to go on with her latest entry. This would be the end of her writing, now that she was leaving Mexico. She took time to read what she had written and noticed how much Spanish had taken over her thoughts and expression. It had been five years since she made her way to Mexico, a time when she had been nervous about speaking the language she had left behind with her childhood. Now she rarely spoke English. She still wrote it, but it was an English sprinkled with words and inflections from her ancestor's tongue. She thought of correcting what she had written, but decided to let it go.

December 22 was the day when those rabid dogs attacked Acteal. They were armed men, some of them barely children, dressed in civilian clothes, faces covered by bandannas so that we could see only their eyes, yellow with hatred, as they came at us. They held weapons that spit fire, and they did their evil deed knowing that the inocentes *they targeted were mostly* mujeres *and* niños *who were defenseless. And they murdered Juana Galván.*

Adriana's fingers cramped, she had been holding the pen so tightly that they ached. She loosened her grip and stared at her hand, the pen dangling between her fingers inertly. Her chest was hurting, as it did when she suffered asthma attacks, but she knew that it was the pain of trapped sorrow that was now pressing her heart against her ribs.

I felt that a limb had been torn from me. She was part of me. I felt that I couldn't breathe, that my lungs were collapsing. I had found what I had searched for only to lose it again.

After writing those words, Adriana reclined her head against the back of the seat and did not resist the tears she felt wetting her face; she did not even make an effort to dry them. She sat inertly, reliving the excruciating pain of having lost the woman she had loved with her total being, with her heart and her mind. Adriana let the tears flow, emanating from the sea of torment that was flooding her inwardly. If she did not cry and let them spill out, her heart would rupture.

It had been only ten days since that dreadful moment, and the sensations, sounds, smells were still with Adriana. She stopped writing for a while, waiting for the surge of grief to pass. She closed her eyes, hoping to get some sleep, but it was impossible. She had not truly slept since the Acteal massacre. Her eyes could not stop looking at the mangled bodies of the victims. Her vision burned with the vile face of the murderer. Her mind's eye finally settled on the forest and on Juana's body lying inertly in her arms. This parade of grim images played and replayed themselves behind her closed eyelids.

Juana and the other women were on the frontlines of the war, leading talks in the cathedral and meetings with journalists and photographers from all over the world. Those mujeres *not only inspired other women, but men as well, and this was what ate at those other* cabrones. Esas mujeres *were brave, bringing themselves together in congresses and dialogues, writing up documents that challenged all the laws that had oppressed them for centuries. They met time after time—hundreds, thousands of* mujeres—*their faces erased by masks so that their sisters might find faces of their own.*

When Major Ramona traveled to Mexico City in 1996, her body already half eaten by cancer, thousands of men and women were waiting for her; multitudes listened to her. But the snake eyes of los patrones *were watching her, Juana and all the other* mujeres *who, in the eyes of those vipers, were worse than the male insurgents simply because they were women.*

The battles for the cities and prisons ended within ten days, but the war, la guerra, *did not go away.* La gente, *uprooted and dislocated, shifted from one side of the land to the other. Roads were clogged with lost people, begging for a tortilla to give their* niñitos, *taking refuge from rain and fog anywhere they could. And* los patrones *never stopped hounding them. They unleashed their rabid dogs, the paramilitaries, to prowl the land, looting, raping, and burning* palapas *and whatever shelters could be found. And their special targets were* mujeres, *because they were the ones who recognized those dogs even after they disguised themselves like laborers, like* campesinos.

"Ladies and gentlemen, the captain has turned on the seat belt light as we begin our descent into Los Angeles. Please be sure that your tray tables are stowed and that your seat backs are in their upright positions." The flight attendant's nasalized voice sounded out, alerting the passengers of their arrival. Adriana sat up and was able to see the outskirts of the city, but she had time, so she put her journal on her lap to make her last entry.

Last night I had a dream. I dreamed that I was surrounded by mujeres *whose faces were erased by masks. One of them was Juana, who came close to me and whispered beautiful words. She reminded me of our last conversation, when she told me that I was her other self. She spoke of when we had slept in the jungle, when we had recalled our other lives among the first* patrones, *our losses, our discoveries.*

In my dream, Juana and I sat apart from the others, remembering Orlando Flores, Chan K'in, and all the other mujeres *and* hombres *who are still masked, still fighting, still dying. She told me that until she and I meet again in our next life, she will always be with me when I show my photographs, while I speak to others about* la gente *in Lacandona, about the atrocities in Acteal and in all the other places of misery. She asked me to be the lips through which their silenced voices could speak.*

Then the dream unfolded into another dream, one that had been in my memory. In it I ran, frightened and terrified because I was pursued by dogs. It was the jungle dream in which I felt that others surrounded me and I was powerless to discern their identities. This time, when I stopped and began searching for what I had lost, Juana appeared.

My dream ended when she put her arms around me and told me never to forget her or the mujeres *who have chosen to erase their faces with a mask—not out of fear, not out of shame, but inspired rather by dignity and the courage to show the way to other* mujeres.

Adriana closed the journal and tucked it into the backpack placed under her seat. She felt serene; she understood her mission. She touched Juana's bracelet as she looked out the window. This time the massive sprawl of Los Angeles met her gaze. To her left she made out the half-moon curve of Redondo Beach and, stretching her neck to look out the window across the aisle, her eyes caught the eastern regions of the city.

The craft began its descent and landed smoothly, moving until it came to a halt. When they were given clearance, the passengers stood to deplane. Adriana had her bag ready when the door was opened. She and everyone else marched through the tunnel leading to the terminal. Still pensive, still rerunning the details of her dream, she waited for immigration to clear her.

"Hmm! You've been away a long time."

"Yes."

"Doing what?"

"I'm a photographer. I've been on assignment in Mexico."

"I see. Welcome home."

"Thank you."

Adriana trudged along with the other passengers to clear customs. The wait was long. Passengers from other flights had been put on the same inspection line. While she waited, her mind returned to her dream. She wondered why her mother had not come to her with the other women. Adriana would have liked that very much. She would have told her that the rage was gone, that although she still did not understand why she had chosen to leave, Adriana wanted her to know that she realized now that she must have had a compelling reason.

Someone tapped her on the shoulder; it was her turn to approach the counter.

"Anything to declare?"

"No."

"Meat? Seeds? Food?"

"No."

"Okay! Welcome home!"

Adriana picked up her gear, placed it on her back, made her way up the ramp, down the escalator, then out the door of Tom Bradley Terminal. She blinked at the unexpected sunlight, but her vision cleared as she looked up at the new Controllers' Tower. To its side she saw the sky-high restaurant, now being remodeled. The street in front of the terminal was congested with shuttle buses and taxis. Cars streamed in and out of the parking structure, causing snarls, honking horns as they cut off and passed one another. Adriana looked around, feeling like a foreigner in her own town, a stranger among her own people. She took a deep breath, adjusted the bag on her back, and disappeared into the crowd.

Epilogue

The war was not lost by the Zapatista insurgents; rather, their struggle continued past the writing of this book. A newly elected president of Mexico returned to the table to dialogue and negotiate with the Zapatista leadership. There is hope that the fundamental rights of the indigenous people of Chiapas have been recognized and from there will come their ultimate victory.

G. L.

Books by Graciela Limón

La canción del colibrí

The Day of the Moon

El Día de la Luna

En busca de Bernabé

Erased Faces

In Search of Bernabé

Left Alive

The Memories of Ana Calderón

Song of the Hummingbird

About the Author

Graciela Limón is the critically-acclaimed and award-winning author of *Left Alive* (2005), *Erased Faces* (2001), *The Day of the Moon* (1999), *Song of the Hummingbird* (1996), *The Memories of Ana Calderón* (1994), and *In Search of Bernabé* (1993), the recipient of an American Book Award. Limón is Professor Emeritus of Loyola Marymount University in Los Angeles, where she served as a professor of U.S. Latina/o Literature.